THE MIND OF ALDOUS HUXLEY

The extraordinarily perceptive author of visionary novels here views the follies of man in the past, present, and future. As he takes the reader from the pagan city of Byblos in Greece to the Mormon Temple in the deserts of Utah, Aldous Huxley brings his brilliant insight and the vast scope of his learning to bear upon nearly every endeavor in the human experience.

"The present collection of essays has the familiar precision, clarity and allusiveness; it has also the old brightness, the perverse touches, and the old disgusts. . . . Mr. Huxley is the sole contemporary amphibian to move in the elements of science, mysticism and art, without muddying one with the others."

—V. S. PRITCHETT

The Right Copy

aldous huxley

tomorrow and tomorrow and tomorrow

and other essays

A SIGNET BOOK

Published by The New American Library

Published as a SIGNET BOOK
by arrangement with Harper & Row, Publishers, Inc.,
who have authorized this softcover edition.
A hardcover edition is available from Harper & Row,
Publishers, Inc.

First Printing, March, 1964

Acknowledgment is made to *Esquire, Encounter, Vedanta
and the West* and to *Fortnight,* as well as to the Mills
College Alumnae Quarterly for material in this book
which first appeared in those magazines.

This book is published in England
under the title of *Adonis and the Alphabet*

SIGNET TRADEMARK REG. U.S. PAT. OFF. AND FOREIGN COUNTRIES
REGISTERED TRADEMARK—MARCA REGISTRADA
HECHO EN CHICAGO, U.S.A.

SIGNET BOOKS are published by
The New American Library of World Literature, Inc.
501 Madison Avenue, New York, New York 10022

PRINTED IN THE UNITED STATES OF AMERICA

Contents

v

tomorrow
and tomorrow
and tomorrow
and other essays

The Education
of an Amphibian

Every human being is an amphibian—or, to be more accurate, every human being is five or six amphibians rolled into one. Simultaneously or alternately, we inhabit many different and even incommensurable universes. To begin with, man is an embodied spirit. As such, he finds himself infesting this particular planet, while being free at the same time to explore the whole spaceless, timeless world of universal Mind. This is bad enough; but it is only the beginning of our troubles. For, besides being an embodied spirit, each of us is also a highly self-conscious and self-centered member of a sociable species. We live in and for ourselves; but at the same time we live in and, somewhat reluctantly, for the social group surrounding us. Again, we are both the products of evolution and a race of self-made men. In other words, we are simultaneously the subjects of Nature and the citizens of a strictly human republic, which may be anything from what St. Paul called "no mean city" to the most squalid of material and moral slums.

Below the human level amphibiousness presents no difficulties. The tadpole knows precisely when to get rid of its tail and gills, and become a frog. The turtle browses under water, comes up every now and then for a breath of fresh air, crawls ashore when the mating season rolls around. And it repeats this performance with effortless punctuality for years, sometimes for centuries. With us, alas, the case is painfully different. Our human amphibiousness—the multiple double life of creatures indigenous to half a dozen incompatible worlds—is a chronic embarrassment, a source of endless errors and delinquencies, of crimes and imbecilities without number. Each field of our amphibious existence has its own peculiar problems, and to discuss them all would be an enormous task. Here I shall confine myself to one small corner of one of the fields. I shall discuss the troubles of an ape that has learned to talk—of an immortal spirit that has not yet learned to dispense with words.

The official name of our species is Homo sapiens; but there are many anthropologists who prefer to think of man as Homo faber—the smith, the maker of tools. It would be possible, I think, to reconcile these two definitions in a third. If man is a knower and an efficient doer, it is only because he is also a talker. In order to be *faber* and *sapiens*, *homo* must first be *loquax*, the loquacious one. Without language we should merely be hairless chimpanzees. Indeed, we should be something much worse. Possessed of a high IQ but no language, we should be like the Yahoos of *Gulliver's Travels*—creatures too clever to be guided by instinct, too self-centered to live in a state of animal grace, and therefore condemned to remain forever, frustrated and malignant, between contented apehood and aspiring humanity. It was language that made possible the accumulation of knowledge and the broadcasting of information. It was language that permitted the expression of religious insights, the formulation of ethical ideals, the codification of laws. It was language, in a word, that turned us into human beings and gave birth to civilization.

Every existing language is an implied theory of man and the universe, a virtual philosophy. And the virtual philosophies of many primitive peoples are at least as subtle, at least as adequate to inner and outer reality, as were the great classical languages of Europe and Asia, before they were supplemented by mathematics and the special vocabularies of science. Without exception, all languages are stupendous works of genius. But these works of genius were created by people just as stupid as we are. One is almost forced to believe in the existence, within each one of us, of something other and much more intelligent than the conscious self.

In any case, however originated and however developed, language is now one of the primary facts of every human experience. It is the medium in which we live and move and have about fifty per cent of our being. We are like icebergs, floating in the given reality of our physiology, of our intuitions and perceptions, our pains and pleasures, but projecting at the same time into the airy world of words and notions. Compared with the oceanic depths, that world is a world of light, a world in which one can see and understand. We rejoice in the verbal sunshine; we feel as free in it as birds or even angels. But, alas, this universe of ours is a place where nobody ever gets anything for nothing. Its gifts are like those so generously distributed by the makers of breakfast foods. To get them, you have to send in a box top. Take language, for example, that greatest of all our gifts. It admits us into a conceptual world of light and air. But only at a price. For this world of light and air is also a world where the winds of doctrine howl destructively; where delusive mock-suns keep popping up over the horizon; where all kinds of poison comes pouring out of the propaganda factories and the tripe mills. Living amphibiously, half in fact and half in words, half in immediate experience and half in abstract notions, we contrive most of the time to make the worst of both worlds. We use language so badly that we become the slaves of our *clichés* and are turned either into conforming Babbitts or into fanatics and doctrinaires. And we use immediate experience so badly that we become blind to the realities of our own nature and insensitive to the universe around us. The abstract knowledge which words bring us is paid for by concrete ignorance. In his classical *Remembering*, F. C. Bartlett has recorded the results of a number of experiments designed to test the influence of language upon the memories of various kinds of experience. In one of the tests, photographs of soldiers and sailors of different ranks were shown to a group of subjects, who were then asked to describe the faces and answer questions about them at intervals from half an hour to a week or more later. "A particular face often at once aroused a more or less conventional attitude appropriate to the given type. Thereupon, the attitude actively affected the detail of representation. Even in immediate memory the features of the face often tended to be made more conventional, while in subsequent recall they tended to approach yet more closely to conventional patterns." Other experiments were made with literary material. The subjects were asked to read a passage from one of Emerson's essays, and an

American Indian folk tale. When they reproduced this material immediately after reading, and again at longer intervals, all that was fresh and original in the essay and the story tended to disappear. Slaves to the *clichés* in which they habitually expressed themselves, the subjects changed what they had read into the likeness of their own familiar notions as embodied in the language of their class and culture. Summing up the results of those experiments with literary material, Bartlett concludes that, when reproduced from memory, "all the stories tend to be shorn of their individualizing features, the descriptive passages lose most of their peculiarities of style and matter . . . the arguments tend to be reduced to a bald expression of conventional opinion," or, if they express an original point of view, "tend to pass over into opposed conventional views. Where the epithets are original, they tend to become current, commonplace terms. The style gets flattened out and loses any pretensions it may have had to forcefulness and beauty." All of which merely confirms what every writer painfully discovers for himself—that full communication with a large audience is impossible, that most people read into literature the standardized notions with which they set out, that the author's laborious efforts to find an adequate verbal equivalent for experience are simply not noticed by the majority of his readers, who automatically transform what Mallarmé calls the *sens plus pur* of the artist's language into the soiled and shopworn *mots de la tribu*. Language, it is evident, has its Gresham's Law. Bad words tend to drive out good words, and words in general, the good as well as the bad, tend to drive out immediate experience and our memories of immediate experience. And yet without words, there would be precious little memory of any kind. The "wolf children" who have been brought up by animals find it impossible to remember their wordless life among the brutes. And how complete, in every one of us, is the amnesia for all the novel and immensely exciting experience of infancy—the age of the non-talker!

We ought, said St. Paul, to "serve in the newness of the spirit, and not in the oldness of the letter." For "the letter killeth, but the spirit giveth life." In other words,

Grau, theurer Freund, ist alle Theorie,
Und gruen des Lebens goldner Baum.

Gray is all theory, green life's golden tree.

And in another context Walt Whitman expresses the same idea.

When I heard the learn'd astronomer;
When the proofs, the figures, were ranged in columns before me;
When I was shown the charts and the diagrams, to add, divide, and measure them;
When I, sitting, heard the astronomer, where he lectured with much applause in the lecture-room,
How soon, unaccountable, I became tired and sick;
Till rising and gliding out, I wander'd off by myself,
In the mystical moist night-air, and from time to time
Look'd up in perfect silence at the stars.

Too much theorizing, as we all know, is fatal to the soul. Too many lectures will cause the green tree to wither, will turn its golden fruits to dust. Life flows back into us when we turn from the stale oldness of theological notions to the newness of spiritual experience; when we exchange the learn'd astronomers' proofs and figures for nocturnal silence and the stars. St. Paul and the poets are talking about some of the most obvious facts of experience. But these facts are not the only facts. Theory is gray and diagrams have no nourishment in them. And yet without scientific theories, without philosophy and theology and law, we should be nothing but Yahoos. The letter condemns us to spiritual death; but the absence of the letter condemns us to something just as bad. Whether we like it or not, we are amphibians, living simultaneously in the world of experience and the world of notions, in the world of direct apprehension of Nature, God and ourselves, and the world of abstract, verbalized knowledge about these primary facts. Our business as human beings is to make the best of both these worlds.

Unfortunately, organized education has done very little,

hitherto, to help us in this task. For organized education is predominantly verbal education. In the Middle Ages the liberal arts were seven in number. The first three—grammar, logic and rhetoric—concerned themselves with the language of common speech, philosophy and literature respectively. The fourth, arithmetic, was the art of handling the special language of numbers. Geometry was the fifth art, and included natural history; but this natural history was studied almost exclusively in encyclopedias composed by men who had studied it in other encyclopedias. The sixth of the liberal arts was astronomy; and its study entailed some observation of the non-verbal universe. In music, the seventh and last of the arts, a non-verbal aspect of the human mind was studied. (We should remember, however, that medieval educators always treated music as a science, and concerned themselves hardly at all with music as a mode of expression, a source of pleasure or of insight.)

In modern practice a course in the liberal arts is less overwhelmingly verbal than it was in the past. Words are still the medium in which teachers and pupils carry on most of their activities. But they are not the only medium. Modern education provides for numerous excursions into external fact and even into that given inner world, in which the non-verbal side of our amphibious nature has its being. Students are now required to observe non-verbal facts and make experiments with them; they are encouraged to cultivate their artistic skills, to refine their tastes and sharpen their sensibilities. All this is greatly to the good. But it is not yet enough. We must do more for the non-verbal part of our amphibious nature, we must do better, than we are doing now.

Exponents of Progressive Education probably think that they are already doing everything that can be done. Under the influence of John Dewey, they have stressed the importance of non-verbal activity as a means of learning. History, for example, is now often taught in a series of "projects." Stonehenge is reconstructed with brickbats in the back yard. Life in the Middle Ages is dramatically reproduced—minus, of course, the dirt, the violence and the theology, which were the essence of that life. Whether children learn more through these mud-pie techniques of education than they would learn by being shown pictures and reading an intelligent book, I do not profess to know. The important point, in our present context, is that the "doing," through which the children are supposed to learn, is left unanalyzed by the Progressive Educators who advocate it. So far as they are concerned, doing is doing; there is nothing to choose between one kind of doing and another. John Dewey himself knew better; but his followers have chosen to ignore his qualifications of the learning-by-doing doctrine and to plunge headlong and with unquestioning enthusiasm into their mud pies.

But before I pursue this subject any further, let me return for a moment to our amphibian. To my earlier list of man's double lives I would like to add yet another item. Every human being is a conscious self; but, below the threshold of consciousness, every human being is also a not-self—or, more precisely, he is five or six merging but clearly distinguishable not-selves. There is, first of all, the personal, home-made not-self—the not-self of habits and conditioned reflexes, the not-self of impulses repressed but still obscurely active, the not-self of buried-alive reactions to remote events and forgotten words, the not-self of fossil infancy and the festering remains of a past that refuses to die. This personal not-self is that region of the subconscious with which psychiatry mainly deals. Next comes the not-self that used to be called the vegetative soul or the entelechy. This is the not-self in charge of the body—the not-self who, when we wish to walk, actually does the walking, the not-self that controls our breathing, our heartbeat, our glandular secretions; the not-self that is prepared to digest even doughnuts; the not-self that heals wounds and brings us back to health when we have been ill. Next, there is the not-self who inhabits the world from which we derive our insights and inspirations. This is the not-self who spoke to Socrates through his daimon, who dreamed the text of *Kubla Kahn*, who dictated *King Lear* and the *Agamemnon* and the *Tibetan Book of the Dead*, the not-self who is responsible in all of us for every enhancement of wisdom, every sudden accession of vital or intellectual power. Beyond this world of inspiration lies the world of what Jung has called the Archetypes—those great shared symbols which stand for man's deepest tendencies, his perennial conflicts and ubiquitous problems. Next comes the world of visionary experience, where a mysterious not-self lives in the midst, not of shared human symbols, but of shared non-facts—facts from which the theologians of the various religions have derived their notions of the Other World, of Heaven and Hell. And finally, beyond all the rest, but immanent in every mental or material event, is that universal Not-Self, which men have called the Holy Spirit, the Atman-Brahman, the Clear Light, Suchness.

A self can affect and be affected by its associated not-selves in many different ways. Here for example is a conscious self which responds inappropriately to circumstances. In the process it is apt to fill the personal not-self with all manner of fears, greeds, hates and wrong judgments. Thus distorted, the personal not-self reacts upon the conscious self, forcing it to behave even more inappropriately than before. And so the game goes on, each party contributing to the delinquency of the other. Self and personal not-self have set up a mutual deterioration society.

For the not-self in charge of bodily functions the consequences of this are disastrous. Left to its own devices, this physiological intelligence is almost incapable of making a mistake. Interfered with by a delinquent ego and an insane personal subconscious, it loses its native infallibility, and the organism at once falls prey to psychosomatic disease. Health is a state of harmony between conscious self, personal not-self and vegetative soul.

The last three not-selves constitute the very essence of our being, and yet are so transcendently other as to be beyond our power to affect them. The ego and the personal not-self can poison one another and play havoc with the vegetative soul. They can do nothing to hurt the indwelling Spirit. What they can do, what for most people, most of the time, they actually succeed in doing, is to eclipse these inner lights. They set up a more or less completely opaque screen between our consciousness and the transcendental not-selves with which every self is associated. What is called Enlightenment is simply the removal of this eclipsing barrier.

The foregoing account of man's double life as a self associated with a group of not-selves has been, of necessity, very brief and schematic. But I hope, none the less, that it may serve to illuminate our problem: How can we educate the psycho-physical instrument, by means of which we learn and live?

The psycho-physical instrument is one and indivisible; but for practical purposes we may regard it as being made up of several distinct components. Accordingly, the curriculum of our hypothetical course in what may be called the non-verbal humanities will include the following items. Training of the kinesthetic sense. Training of the special sense. Training of memory. Training in control of the autonomic nervous system. Training for spiritual insight.

The most fundamental of our awarenesses is the kinesthetic sense. This is the sense which registers muscular tension within the body, and which tells us about the changes in muscular tension that accompany physical movement and variations in our mental state. The kinesthetic sense is the main line of communication between the conscious self and the personal subconscious on the one hand and the vegetative soul on the other. When this sense is debauched—and in our urban-industrial civilization it seems to get debauched very easily—two things happen. First, the individual develops a habit of using his psycho-physical instrument improperly. And, second, he loses his sense of what we may call muscular morality, his basic standard of physical right and wrong. Habit is second nature; and when we have gone on doing an unnatural thing long enough, it comes, by mere familiarity, to seem completely right and proper. What is needed, at this basic level of psycho-physical education, is some way of unlearning our habits of improper use, some method by which the debauched kinesthetic sense may be restored to its pristine integrity.

Such a method exists. It has been developed in more than fifty years of experimentation and teaching by Mr. F. M. Alexander, an Australian by birth who has worked for most of his long life in England and the United States.*

* For details of Alexander's educational methods the reader is referred to his four books: *Man's Supreme Inheritance, Constructive Conscious Control, The Use of the Self, The Universal Constant of Living.*

The importance of Alexander's work was early recognized by John Dewey, who contributed valuable prefaces to three of his books. Alexander's fundamental discovery (since confirmed by physiologists and zoologists working in other fields) is that there are, in Dewey's words, "certain basic, central organic habits and attitudes, which condition *every* act we perform, every use we make of ourselves." When we lose these natural good habits and impose upon ourselves improper habits of use, everything goes wrong, not merely in the body, but also (insofar as physical events condition mental events) in the mind. The degree of wrongness may be great or small; but since all bad habits tend to become worse with time, it is in the highest degree desirable that they should be corrected at the earliest opportunity. Alexander's technique, writes John Dewey, "gives the educator a standard of psycho-physical health—in which what we call morality is included. It also supplies the means whereby that standard may be progressively and endlessly achieved. It provides therefore the conditions for the central direction of all educational processes. It bears the same relation to education that education itself bears to all other human activities." These are strong words; for Dewey was convinced that man's only hope lay in education. But just as education is absolutely necessary to the world at large, so Alexander's methods of training the psycho-physical instrument are absolutely necessary to education. Schooling without proper training of the psycho-physical instrument cannot, in the very nature of things, do more than a limited amount of good and may, in the process of doing that limited amount of good, do the child a great deal of harm by systematically ingraining his habits of improper use. Learning by doing is a sound principle only if the doing is good doing. If it is bad doing (and in the vast majority of cases it *is* bad) learning by doing is hopelessly unsound.

It is a most curious fact that of the literally millions of educators who, for two generations, have so constantly appealed to Dewey's authority, only an infinitesimal handful has ever bothered to look into the method which Dewey himself regarded as absolutely fundamental to any effective system of education. The reason for this neglect is simple enough. Like everyone else, educators have a debauched kinesthetic sense; and, like everyone else, they do not know that their standards of physical right and wrong have been perverted. Long-standing habits of improper use lead them to believe that what they feel to be right and nàtural actually is right and natural. In fact, of course, it is wrong and unnatural, and feels right only because they are used to it. They cannot persuade themselves that anything is fundamentally wrong with their own psycho-physical instrument or with the psycho-physical instruments of their pupils. The disappointing results of education are attributed by them to various combinations of subsidiary and superficial causes, never to the fundamental cause of causes—improper use and loss of the natural standard of psycho-physical health.

Most of us, as Alexander is never tired of insisting, are inveterate "end-gainers." We are so anxious to achieve some particular end that we never pay attention to the psycho-physical means whereby that end is to be gained. So far as we are concerned, any old means is good enough. But the nature of the universe is such that ends can never justify means. On the contrary, the means always determine the end. Thus the end proposed by the Allies in the First World War was "to make the world safe for democracy." But the means employed was unrestricted violence, and unrestricted violence is incapable of producing world-wide democracy. Unrestricted violence produces such things as fear, hatred and social chaos. Chaos is followed by dictatorship and dictatorship combined with general fear and hatred leads once more to unrestricted violence. This is an extreme case; but the principle it illustrates is universally valid. In the field of education, for example, a child is assigned a project. The end proposed is the learning of a set of facts and the acquisition of certain skills and certain morally desirable attitudes. But among the means employed to achieve this end is the child's psycho-physical instrument. If (as is probably the case) this psycho-physical instrument has lost its standard of physical right and wrong and is a prey to bad habits, and if (as is virtually certain) nothing effective is being done to restore the standard and get rid of the bad habits, the ends proposed by well-meaning educators will not be achieved in their entirety. This failure to do anything effective about the psycho-physical instrument is surely one of the reasons why education has never justified the hopes of the idealists and reformers. Four generations ago James Mill expressed the belief that, if everybody could read and write, everything would be well, forever. Personal liberty and democratic government would be assured, wars would cease, reason would everywhere prevail. Today everybody *can* read and write, and we find ourselves living in a world where war is incessant, liberty on the decline, democracy in peril, a world moreover where most of the beneficiaries of universal education read only the tabloids, the comics and murder mysteries.

Man, as we have seen, is a self associated with not-selves. By developing bad habits, the conscious ego and the personal subconscious interfere with the normal functioning of the deeper not-selves, from which we receive the animal grace of physical health and the spiritual grace of insight. If we wish to educate the psycho-physical instrument, we must train people in the art of getting out of their own light. This truth has been discovered and rediscovered, again and again, by all the teachers of psycho-physical skills. In all the activities of life, from the most trivial to the most important, the secret of proficiency lies in an ability to combine two seemingly incompatible states—a state of maximum activity and a state of maximum relaxation. The fact that these incompatibles can actually coexist is due, of course, to the amphibious nature of the human being. That which must be relaxed is the ego and the personal subconscious, that which must be active is the vegetative soul and the not-selves which lie beyond it. The physiological and spiritual not-selves with which we are associated cannot do their work effectively until the ego and personal subconscious learn to let go.

Descartes based the whole of his philosophy on the affirmation, *Cogito ergo sum*—I think, therefore I am. This sounds good, but unfortunately it doesn't happen to be true. The truth, as von Baader pointed out, is not *Cogito ergo sum* but *Cogitor ergo sum*. My existence does not depend on the fact that I am thinking; it depends on the fact that, whether I know it or not, I am being thought—being thought by a mind much greater than the consciousness which I ordinarily identify with myself. This fact is recognized by the tennis pro as it is recognized by the mystic, by the piano teacher as by the yogin, by the vocal coach as by the Zen master and the exponent of mental prayer. If I get out of my not-selves' light, I shall be illumined. If I stop anxiously *cogito-ing*, I shall give myself a chance of being *cogitor-ed* by a committee of indwelling intelligences that can deal with my problems a great deal better than I can. We must use our conscious will—but use it for the purpose of preventing our ego from succumbing to its old bad habits or in any other way eclipsing the inner lights. This does not mean, of course, that the conscious self can ever abdicate its position as knower, reasoner and maker of moral judgments. What it does mean is that we must give up the insane illusion that a conscious self, however virtuous and however intelligent, can do its work single-handed and without assistance. Health is the harmony between self and not-selves, and proficiency in any field comes to those who have learned how to place the resources of their consciousness at the disposal of the unconscious. Genius is simultaneously inspiration and perspiration. It is no use inhaling unless we are prepared to sweat. And it is no use sweating unless we know how to inhale the life-giving airs that blow from worlds beyond our conscious selfhood.

The art of combining relaxation with activity has been invented and reinvented by the teachers of every kind of psycho-physical skill. Unfortunately these teachers have generally worked in isolation, each within the narrow field of his or her particular specialty. The activity for which they train their pupils is not the unregenerate activity for activity's sake, permitted and even encouraged by the Progressive Educationists. It is activity along the right lines, activity according to essentially sound principles. For this reason it will never do the harm which is done by unregenerate end-gaining. But though more or less harmless, it will be less beneficial than it would have been if it had been taught, not as an isolated special skill, but in conjunction with a general education of the kinesthetic sense, a total training in the use of the self, along the lines laid down by Alexander and so warmly recommended by John Dewey.

How much the indwelling not-selves can do for us, if we

give them a chance, has been set forth in two remarkable little books, published within the last few years. The first is entitled *New Pathways to Piano Technique* by the late Luigi Bonpensiere. The second, *Zen and the Art of Archery*, has as its author a German psychologist, long resident in Japan, Dr. Eugen Herrigel. Each of these books bears witness to the same fundamental truth. When the conscious will is used to inhibit indulgence in the bad habits which have come to seem natural, when the ego has been taught to refrain from "straining every nerve," from desperately trying to "do something," when the personal subconscious has been induced to release its clutching tensions, the vegetative soul and the intelligences which lie beyond the vegetative soul can be relied upon to perform miracles.

As naturalists, we are familiar with the miracles performed by the indwelling intelligence of animals—miracles all the more remarkable because of the lack of intelligence displayed on the conscious level by the creatures concerned. I am not referring, of course, to the miracles of instinct; I am speaking of what may be called the *ad hoc* intelligence which animals sometimes display in situations never previously encountered in the evolutionary history of the species. For example, when a parrot uses its noise-making apparatus to imitate the articulate sounds produced by the radically dissimilar noise-making apparatus of a human being, some indwelling not-self is performing a miraculous feat of *ad hoc* intelligence. Or consider the extraordinary performance of the shearwater that was taken in a box from Wales to Venice (far beyond the normal range of the species), was released and turned up, in due course, at its original home. Something other, something far more intelligent than the conscious bird performed the miracle of imitation for the parrot, and the still more astounding miracle of homing for the shearwater. Our business as educators is to discover how human beings can make the best of both worlds—the world of self-conscious, verbalized intelligence and the world of the unconscious intelligences immanent in the mind-body, and always ready, if we give them half a chance, to do what, for the unaided ego, is the impossible.

The kinesthetic sense tells us what is happening within our psycho-physical organism. The other senses—sight, hearing, touch, taste and smell—give us information about the outer world. Modern education does nothing to train the kinesthetic sense, and very little in regard to the other senses. Most children, it is true, receive some kind of musical education, which entails a training in auditory discrimination. But the other senses are left to educate themselves as best they may. Thus, in regard to vision—a subject in which I have been forced by circumstances to take a special and most painful interest—nothing is done to improve the acuity, speed or accuracy of perception. And what is still more surprising, next to nothing is done to prevent the onset, so distressingly frequent in our schools, of visual defects. The lighting of most schoolrooms and libraries runs the entire gamut from bad to abominable; and in these unfavorable conditions children are made to read, write and cipher without the least guidance as to the proper means whereby the proposed end should be achieved. In the circumstances it is surprising that any child should emerge from the educational ordeal with normal vision.

The preventative and remedial training of visual perception is based on the same principles as those which guide the teachers of other psycho-physical skills. To learn the art of seeing, we must learn to combine relaxation with activity—relaxation of the self and personal subconscious, activity of the vegetative soul and the deeper not-selves. The great pioneer in the field of visual education was a New York oculist, Dr. W. H. Bates, who developed his training methods during the first three decades of the present century. Bates was condemned by orthodox ophthalmologists. For orthodox ophthalmologists were and, in all too many cases, still are dedicated to the proposition that eyes are optical systems, which can be treated in isolation, without regard to the person they belong to, and without reference to the mind which interprets the messages transmitted by the eyes and which actually does the seeing. For having written a book about the theory and practice of visual education, I have been treated by professional critics as a mixture between an imbecile and a charlatan. It is therefore with a certain amusement that I now find most of Dr. Bates's and my own ideas being advocated by a group of professionals of the highest respectability. This group publishes a journal called *Psychological Optics*—

a name which implies a whole new philosophy and revolutionary methodology. Credit for the recent change in attitude towards the problem of visual education must be given, in the main, to Professor Samuel Renshaw, the eminent exponent of Gestalt psychology, who teaches at Ohio State University. Renshaw's work in the training of the special senses and of memory is of outstanding importance to all educators. He has shown that it is possible to take any group of unselected undergraduates and to train them, by suitable methods, to see with enormously increased rapidity and precision, to develop taste perception as fine as that of professional whiskey blenders, and to perform feats of memory comparable to those exhibited by so-called prodigies.

In training vision, Renshaw makes extensive use of the tachistoscope—a magic lantern fitted with a shutter that permits the projection of images for a period ranging from a tenth to a thousandth of a second or less. Most training is done with exposures of one hundredth of a second.

Tachistoscopic training is essentially a method for bypassing the bad habits acquired by the conscious self. In ordinary seeing we are hardly ever directly aware of our immediate impressions. For these immediate impressions are more or less profoundly modified by a mind that does most of its thinking in terms of words. Every perception is promptly conceptualized and generalized, so that we do not see the particular thing or event in its naked immediacy; we see only the objective illustration of some generic notion, only the concretion of an abstract word. Our ordinary habits of perception cause us to see the world as Platonists. The tachistoscope transforms us into Nominalists and Impressionists.

To our normal tendency to see the world through the refracting medium of language must be added the various aberrations occasioned by improper use of the psychophysical instrument. The tachistoscope gives us no time either to conceptualize or to bring our bad habits into play. "If you want to see, stop trying." This is a favorite aphorism of the practitioners of visual education. Indeed, it may be said that Bates's method of training was designed for the express purpose of preventing the pupil from trying and so leaving the field clear for his vegetative soul and the deeper not-selves. Similarly the tachistoscope makes it impossible for the ego to stand in its own light. You cannot *try* to see anything in a hundredth of a second. The seeing either comes to you—or it doesn't. You don't do anything about it.

The tachistoscope has also been used in the training of art students. This novel and highly successful method has been described by Professor Hoyt Sherman in an interesting little book, *Drawing Through Seeing.* Here again old bad habits of distorted and conceptualized seeing are bypassed by means of the flashing magic lantern. The student recaptures his visual innocence; for a hundredth of a second he sees only the datum, not his self-dimmed and verbalized notion of what the datum ought to be. At the beginning of Sherman's art course the data consist of abstract forms arranged in a variety of patterns. The student learns to see these forms and their relationships, and proceeds, in the half minute of darkness that follows every flash, to reproduce each successive composition, freehand, on large sheets of paper.

The tachistoscope may prove to be as valuable in general education as it has proved to be in the training of art students. In one large-scale experiment children in the first grade were given two fifteen-minute periods of tachistoscope training each week. At the end of the school year they were markedly ahead of the control group. They read better, they understood more about arithmetic and were altogether more interested in learning and consequently better behaved than comparable children brought up in the ordinary way. Moreover, the beneficial effects persisted during the next five years, despite the fact that tachistoscopic training was not continued after the first year. In the tachistoscope, it would seem, we possess a most effective instrument for the training, not only of vision, but also of that part of the mind which makes use of vision in the learning process.

From the special senses we now pass to the autonomic nervous system—that physiological not-self on which the self depends for its well-being and indeed its very life. When this physiological not-self has become delinquent, when (as happens only too frequently) our best friend has turned into our worst enemy, how can it be induced to behave itself?

Orthodox medicine makes use of a number of drugs and, in extreme cases, resorts to surgery; unorthodox medicine tries to influence the autonomic system by direct mechanical action in the form of osteopathy, chiropractic, reflex therapy and acupuncture. But, orthodox or unorthodox, medical treatment lies outside the field of education. In the present context we are concerned only with what a child or an adult can be taught to do for himself.

Let us begin with the various techniques of relaxation. By letting go of the muscles which are subject to the will, we are able, at one remove, to release some at least of the tensions in regions of the body beyond our voluntary control. Dr. Jacobson's work in this field is well known. Still more valuable are the methods developed by Mr. L. E. Eeman and described in his illuminating book, *Cooperative Healing*. Systematic relaxation is one of the means whereby the conscious ego and the personal subconscious can be induced to stop interfering with the action of the not-selves associated with them.

For those who have the desire and the necessary aptitudes, there are the much more elaborate training methods whose purpose is to establish the closest possible working partnership between conscious will and autonomic nervous system and, by so doing, to increase the range of psychophysical capacity. I myself have an Oriental friend— a doctor by profession, a dervish by avocation—who likes to say that "pain is merely an opinion," and who is ready to prove the truth of what he says by sticking skewers through his flesh and lying on beds of nails. The action of his heart is also a matter of opinion. He can slow it down, if he thinks of it beating slowly, to forty beats a minute, or speed it up, if he thinks of acceleration, to a hundred and fifty. Even his metabolism and respiration are matters of opinion; for he can go into a state of hibernation, when breathing appears to cease completely and the pulse is imperceptible, and remain in this condition for hours or even days.

The training of the dervish or the hatha-yogin is a long, laborious affair; and whether it is really worth a man's while to spend several years of his life acquiring the arts of going into catalepsy, swallowing his tongue and reversing the peristalsis of his intestine, is debatable. On the other hand, it would be extremely convenient to be able to treat neuralgia or lumbago as opinions, to calm the heart, to take the cramps out of one's viscera in moments of emotional stress, to plunge at will into profound and restorative sleep. These are accomplishments which many people can acquire without too much difficulty. For in these fields suggestion and auto-suggestion—especially when reinforced by hypnosis and the post-hypnotic suggestions which make possible the induction of auto-hypnosis—can perform the kind of wonders which, until only a few centuries ago, our ancestors unhesitatingly attributed to divine or (more probably) diabolic intervention. As an example of what can be done without the least difficulty, I will cite the case of a dentist of my acquaintance, who teaches all his child patients, and many of their elders too, to suggest themselves into local insensibility. His methods are absurdly simple and, in the great majority of cases, work like a charm.

The last and most important branch of non-verbal education is training in the art of spiritual insight. Dr. Suzuki, the great Japanese scholar to whom the West owes most of its knowledge of Zen Buddhism, has defined spiritual insight, or enlightenment, as "becoming conscious of the Unconscious." And a Roman Catholic theologian, Fr. Victor White, expresses the same idea when he writes that "it is through the sub-rational that the super-rational enters human consciousness." To know the ultimate Not-Self, which transcends the other not-selves and the ego, but which is yet closer than breathing, nearer than hands and feet—this is the consummation of human life, the end and ultimate purpose of individual existence.

The aim of the psychiatrist is to teach the (statistically) abnormal to adjust themselves to the behavior patterns of a society composed of the (statistically) normal. The aim of the educator in spiritual insight is to teach the (statistically) normal that they are in fact insane and should do something about it. The problem, as usual, is how to get out of one's own light. Our business is to free ourselves from eclipsing bad habits—bad habits not merely on the moral level but also, and more fundamentally, on the cognitive, intellectual and emotional levels. For it is these bad habits of unrealistic thinking, inappropriate feeling and debauched perception which incite the ego to behave as it does. We must, in Krishnamurti's phrase, achieve "freedom from the known"—freedom from the unanalyzed postulates in terms of which we do our second-hand experiencing, freedom from our conventional thoughts and sentiments, freedom from our stereotyped notions about inner and outer reality.

"Whatever you say about God," Eckhart declares, "is untrue." Shop-worn theological and devotional clichés are not only not the same as experience of life in its immanent and transcendent fullness; they are actually obstacles in the way of such experience. It is a case of gray theory and green reality; of the letter killing the spirit; of dogma falsifying the facts to which it is supposed to refer; of rituals and rhetoric substituting emotional thrills for the insight which is vouchsafed only to the poor in spirit, the "virgins" as Eckhart calls them.

In Zen the virgin consciousness was called *Wu-nien* or *Wuh-sin*—no-mind or no-thought. "Taking hold of the not-thought which lies in thought," says Hakuin in his *Song of Meditation*, "they [the men of insight] hear in every act they perform the voice of truth." No-thought not-thinks about the world in terms of no-things. "Seeing into no-thing-ness," says Shen-hui, "this is true seeing and eternal seeing." Words and notions are convenient, are indeed indispensable; for our humanity depends upon their use. The virgin not-thinker makes use of words and notions; but he is careful not to take them too seriously, he never permits them to re-create the world of immediate experience in their drearily human image, he is on his guard against the condemnation and the odious comparisons, the assertions of craving and aversion, which language, by its very nature, forces upon the users of language. "The perfect Way refuses to make preferences. Only when freed from love and hate does it reveal itself without disguise. To set up what you like against what you dislike, this is the disease of the mind." And so "judge not, that ye be not judged." For "God gives to everything alike," says Eckhart, "and as flowing forth from God things are all equal; angels, men and creatures proceed from God alike in their first emanation. To take things in their primal emanation" (to not-think experience with a virgin mind in non-verbal terms, as no-thingness), "is to take them all alike. . . . Any flea as it is in God is nobler than the highest of the angels in himself. Things are all the same in God; they are God Himself." Accordingly, the man "to whom God is different in one thing from another and to whom God is dearer in one thing than another, that man is a barbarian, still in the wilds, a child. He to whom God is the same in everything has come to man's estate."

The end proposed is the rediscovery within ourselves of a virgin not-mind capable of non-verbally not-thinking in response to immediate experience. But the ends we actually achieve are always determined by the means we employ. Perfect freedom will not be achieved by means of systematic limitation. Virginity of mind will not be discovered in a context of predetermined beliefs and dogmas. The unitive not-thought which experiences life in its totality will never emerge from concentrated thinking, in terms of words or visual images, about some particular aspect of life, isolated from the rest. Dr. Suzuki, in his *Zen Doctrine of No-Mind*, has translated part of a dialogue between a Zen Mawter, Shen-hui, and a member of one of the more orthodox schools of Mahayana.

"The Master asked Teng, 'What exercise do you recommend in order to see into one's self-nature?'

"Teng answered: 'First of all it is necessary to practice meditation by quietly sitting cross-legged. When this exercise is fully mastered, Prajna [intuitive understanding] grows out of it, and by virtue of this Prajna seeing into one's self-nature is attained.'

"Shen-hui inquired: 'When one is engaged in meditation, is not this a specifically contrived exercise?'

" 'Yes, it is.'

" 'If so, this specific contrivance is an act of limited consciousness, and how could it lead to the seeing of one's self-nature?' "

The answer is that it can't. For what is ordinarily called meditation is merely, in Krishnamurti's words, "the cultivation of resistance, of exclusive concentration on an idea of our choice." Yoga is the process of "building a wall of resistance" against every thought except that which you have chosen. But what makes you choose?

"Obviously the choice is based on pleasure, reward or achievement; or it is merely a reaction to one's conditioning or tradition." Then why choose?

"Instead of creating resistance, why not go into each interest as it arises and not merely concentrate on one idea, one interest?" Constant and intense self-awareness, free from preconceptions, comparisons, condemnations— this will result in what Krishnamurti calls "clarity," what Eckhart calls "virginity," what the Zen masters describe as "No-mind." "This clarity is not to be organized, for it cannot be exchanged with another. Organized group thought is merely repetitive. . . . Without understanding yourself, you have no basis for thought; without self-knowledge, what you say is not true." Truth repeated is no longer truth; it becomes truth again only when it has been realized by the speaker as an immediate experience. Organized religion has done much good; it has also done much harm. Whether the good outweighs the harm it is difficult, as one reads history, to compute. What is quite certain, however, is that those who now so eloquently assure us that mankind will be saved by a great revival of organized religion are guilty of over-simplification. Organized religion is like the Indian goddess, Kali—the Great Destroyer as well as the Great Mother and Creatrix. And the destructive side of organized religion is certain to be prominent in a world where the loudest appeals for a revival are made by men whose deepest loyalty is not to their professed Christianity or Judaism or Islam, but to Nationalism, and whose aim is to use the local faith as a weapon in the armory of power politics. But all this is by the way; for organized religion has very little to do with the subject we have been discussing—the non-verbal education of individuals for spiritual insight.

In the preceding pages I have described very briefly and very briefly discussed some of the ways in which our psycho-physical instrument might be educated to a higher pitch of efficiency. Two questions now propound themselves. First, is this kind of education in the non-verbal humanities desirable? And, second, is it practicable? Can it be made available to everyone?

To the first question my answer is an emphatic yes. The notion that one can educate young people without making any serious attempt to educate the psycho-physical instrument, by means of which they do all their learning and living, seems on the face of it radically absurd. Looking back over my own years of schooling, I can see the enormous deficiencies of a system which could do nothing better for my body than Swedish drill and compulsory football, nothing better for my character than prizes, punishments, sermons and pep talks, and nothing better for my soul than a hymn before bedtime, to the accompaniment of the harmonium. Like everyone else, I am functioning at only a fraction of my potential. How grateful I should feel if someone had taught me to be, say, thirty per cent efficient instead of fifteen or maybe twenty per cent!

To the second question—the question of practicability—I can give no answer. The problem of incorporating a decent education in the non-verbal humanities into the current curriculum is a task for professional educators and administrators. What is needed at the present stage is research—intensive, extensive and long-drawn research. Some foundation with a few scores of millions to get rid of should finance a ten or fifteen-year plan of observation and experiment. At the end of this period, we should know which are the most important items in a program of psycho-physical training, how they can best be taught in primary schools, secondary schools and colleges, and what benefits may be expected to follow such a course of training. My own expectation is that the benefits would be considerable. However, we should not forget that, though the child is father of the man, the man lives a great deal longer than the child, and that his forty or fifty years of existence in the world are incomparably more educative, for evil as well as for good, than are his ten or sixteen years in school. It is always possible that the disintegrative effects of the kind of civilization under which our technology compels us to live may completely cancel out the constructive effects of even the best and completest system of formal education. Time alone will show. Meanwhile, we can only hope for the best.

Knowledge
and Understanding

Knowledge is acquired when we succeed in fitting a new experience into the system of concepts based upon our old experiences. Understanding comes when we liberate ourselves from the old and so make possible a direct, unmediated contact with the new, the mystery, moment by moment, of our existence.

The new is the given on every level of experience—given perceptions, given emotions and thoughts, given states of unstructured awareness, given relationships with things and persons. The old is our home-made system of ideas and word patterns. It is the stock of finished articles fabricated out of the given mystery by memory and analytical reasoning, by habit and the automatic associations of accepted notions. Knowledge is primarily a knowledge of these finished articles. Understanding is primarily direct awareness of the raw material.

Knowledge is always in terms of concepts and can be passed on by means of words or other symbols. Understanding is not conceptual, and therefore cannot be passed on. It is an immediate experience, and immediate experience can only be talked about (very inadequately), never shared. Nobody can actually feel another's pain or grief, another's love or joy or hunger. And similarly nobody can experience another's understanding of a given event or situation. There can, of course, be knowledge of such an understanding, and this knowledge may be passed on in speech or writing, or by means of other symbols. Such communicable knowledge is useful as a reminder that there have been specific understandings in the past, and that understanding is at all times possible. But we must always remember that knowledge of understanding is not the same thing as the understanding, which is the raw material of that knowledge. It is as different from understanding as the doctor's prescription for penicillin is different from penicillin.

Understanding is not inherited, nor can it be laboriously acquired. It is something which, when circumstances are favorable, comes to us, so to say, of its own accord. All of us are knowers, all the time; it is only occasionally and in spite of ourselves that we directly understand the mystery of given reality. Consequently we are very seldom tempted to equate understanding with knowledge. Of the exceptional men and women, who have understanding in every situation, most are intelligent enough to see that understanding is different from knowledge and that conceptual systems based upon past experience are as necessary to the conduct of life as are spontaneous insights into new experiences. For these reasons the mistake of identifying understanding with knowledge is rarely perpetrated and therefore poses no serious problem.

How different is the case with the opposite mistake, the mistake of supposing that knowledge is the same as understanding and interchangeable with it! All adults possess vast stocks of knowledge. Some of it is correct knowledge, some of it is incorrect knowledge, and some of it only looks like knowledge and is neither correct nor incorrect; it is merely meaningless. That which gives meaning to a proposition is not (to use the words of an eminent contemporary philosopher, Rudolf Carnap) "the attendant images or thoughts, but the possibility of deducing from it perceptive propositions, in other words the possibility of verification. To give sense to a proposition, the presence of images is not sufficient, it is not even necessary. We have no image of the electromagnetic field, nor even, I should say, of the gravitational field; nevertheless the proposition which physicists assert about these fields have a perfect sense, because perceptive propositions are deducible from them." Metaphysical doctrines are propositions which cannot be operationally verified, at least on the level of ordinary experience. They may be expressive of a state of mind, in the way that lyrical poetry is expressive; but they have no assignable meaning. The information they convey is only pseudo-knowledge. But the formulators of metaphysical doctrines and the believers in such doctrines have always mistaken this pseudo-knowledge for knowledge and have proceeded to modify their behavior accordingly. Meaningless pseudo-knowledge has at all times been one of the principal motivators of individual and collective action. And that is one of the reasons why the course of human history has been so tragic and at the same time so strangely grotesque. Action based upon meaningless pseudo-knowledge is always inappropriate, always beside the point, and consequently always results in the kind of mess mankind has always lived in—the kind of mess that makes the angels weep and the satirists laugh aloud.

Correct or incorrect, relevant or meaningless, knowledge and pseudo-knowledge are as common as dirt and are therefore taken for granted. Understanding, on the contrary, is as rare, very nearly, as emeralds, and so is highly prized. The knowers would dearly love to be understanders; but either their stock of knowledge does not include the knowledge of what to do in order to be understanders; or else they know theoretically what they ought to do, but go on doing the opposite all the same. In either case they cherish the comforting delusion that knowledge and, above all, pseudo-knowledge *are* understanding. Along with the closely related errors of over-abstraction, over-generalization and over-simplification, this is the commonest of all intellectual sins and the most dangerous.

Of the vast sum of human misery about one third, I would guess, is unavoidable misery. This is the price we must pay for being embodied, and for inheriting genes which are subject to deleterious mutations. This is the rent extorted by Nature for the privilege of living on the surface of a planet, whose soil is mostly poor, whose climates are capricious and inclement, and whose inhabitants include a countless number of micro-organisms capable of causing in man himself, in his domestic animals and cultivated plants, an immense variety of deadly or debilitating diseases. To these miseries of cosmic origin must be added the much larger group of those avoidable disasters we bring upon ourselves. For at least two thirds of our miseries spring from human stupidity, human malice and those great motivators and justifiers of malice and stupidity, idealism, dogmatism and proselytizing zeal on behalf of religious or political idols. But zeal, dogmatism and idealism exist only because we are forever committing intellectual sins. We sin by attributing concrete significance to meaningless pseudo-knowledge; we sin in being too lazy to think in terms of multiple causation and indulging instead in over-simplification, over-generalization and over-abstraction; and we sin by cherishing the false but agreeable notion that conceptual knowledge and, above all, conceptual pseudo-knowledge are the same as understanding.

Consider a few obvious examples. The atrocities of organized religion (and organized religion, let us never forget, has done about as much harm as it has done good) are all due, in the last analysis, to "mistaking the pointing finger for the moon"—in other words to mistaking the verbalized notion for the given mystery to which it refers or, more often, only seems to refer. This, as I have said, is one of the original sins of the intellect, and it is a sin in which, with a rationalistic bumptiousness as grotesque as it is distasteful, theologians have systematically wallowed. From indulgence in this kind of delinquency there has arisen, in most of the great religious traditions of the world, a fantastic over-valuation of words. Over-valuation of words leads all too frequently to the fabrication and idolatrous worship of dogmas, to the insistence on uniformity of belief, the demand for assent by all and sundry to a set of propositions which, though meaningless, are to be regarded as sacred. Those who do not consent to this idolatrous worship of words are to be "converted" and, if that should prove impossible, either persecuted or, if the dogmatizers lack political power, ostracized and denounced. Immediate experience of reality unites men. Conceptualized beliefs, including even the belief in a God of love and righteousness, divide them and, as the dismal record of religious history bears witness, set them for centuries on end at each other's throats.

Over-simplification, over-generalization and over-abstraction are three other sins closely related to the sin of imagining that knowledge and pseudo-knowledge are the same as understanding. The over-generalizing over-simplifier is the man who asserts, without producing evidence, that "All X's are Y," or, "All A's have a single cause, which is B." The over-abstractor is the one who cannot be bothered to deal with Jones and Smith, with Jane and Mary, as individuals, but enjoys being eloquent on the subject of Humanity, of Progress, of God and History and the Future. This brand of intellectual delinquency is indulged in by every demagogue, every crusader. In the Middle Ages the favorite over-generalization was "All infidels are damned." (For the Moslems, "all infidels" meant "all Christians"; for the Christians, "all Moslems.") Almost as popular was the nonsensical proposition, "All heretics are inspired by the devil" and "All eccentric old women are witches." In the sixteenth and seventeenth centuries the wars and persecutions were justified by the luminously clear and simple belief that "All Roman Catholics (or, if you happened to be on the Pope's side, all Lutherans, Calvinists and Anglicans) are God's enemies." In our own day Hitler proclaimed that all the ills of the world had one cause, namely Jews, and that all Jews were sub-human enemies of mankind. For the Communists, all the ills of the world have one cause, namely capitalists, and all capitalists and their middle-class supporters are subhuman enemies of mankind. It is perfectly obvious, on the face of it, that none of these over-generalized statements can possibly be true. But the urge to intellectual sin is fearfully strong. All are subject to temptation and few are able to resist.

There are in the lives of human beings very many situations in which only knowledge, conceptualized, accumulated and passed on by means of words, is of any practical use. For example, if I want to manufacture sulphuric acid or to keep accounts for a banker, I do not start at the beginnings of chemistry or economics; I start at what is now the end of these sciences. In other words, I go to a school where the relevant knowledge is taught, I read books in which the accumulations of past experience in these particular fields are set forth. I can learn the functions of an accountant or a chemical engineer on the basis of knowledge alone. For this particular purpose it is not necessary for me to have much understanding of concrete situations as they arise, moment by moment, from the depths of the given mystery of our existence. What is important for me as a professional man is that I should be familiar with all the conceptual knowledge in my field. Ours is an industrial civilization, in which no society can prosper unless it possesses an elite of highly trained scientists and a considerable army of engineers and technicians. The possession and wide dissemination of a great deal of correct, specialized knowledge has become a prime condition of national survival. In the United States, during the last twenty or thirty years, this fact seems to have been forgotten. Professional educationists have taken John Dewey's theories of "learning through doing" and of "education as life-adjustment," and have applied them in such a way that, in many American schools, there is now doing without learning, along with courses in adjustment to everything except the basic twentieth-century fact that we live in a world where ignorance of science and its methods is the surest, shortest road to national disaster. During the past half century every other nation has made great efforts to impart more knowledge to more young people. In the United States professional educationists have chosen the opposite course. At the turn of the century fifty-six per cent of the pupils in American high schools studied algebra; today less than a quarter of them are so much as introduced to the subject. In 1955 eleven per cent of American boys and girls were studying geometry; fifty years ago the figure was twenty-seven per cent. Four per cent of them now take physics, as against nineteen per cent in 1900. Fifty per cent of American high schools offer no courses in chemistry, fifty-three per cent no courses in physics. This headlong decline in knowledge has not been accompanied by any increase in understanding; for it goes without saying that high school courses in life adjustment do not teach understanding. They teach only conformity to current conventions of personal and collective behavior. There is no substitute for correct knowledge, and in the process of acquiring correct knowledge there is no substitute for concentration and prolonged practice. Except for the unusually gifted, learning, by whatever method, must always be hard work. Unfortunately there are many professional educationists who seem to think that children should never be required to work hard. Wherever educational methods are based on this assumption, children will not in fact acquire much knowledge; and if the methods are followed for a generation or two, the society which tolerates them will find itself in full decline.

In theory, deficiencies in knowledge can be made good

simply by changing the curriculum. In practice, a change in the curriculum will do little good, unless there is a corresponding change in the point of view of professional educationists. For the trouble with American educationists, writes a distinguished member of their profession, Dr. H. L. Dodge, is that they "regard any subject from personal grooming to philosophy as equally important or interchangeable in furthering the process of self-realization. This anarchy of values had led to the displacement of the established disciplines of science and the humanities by these new subjects." Whether professional educationists can be induced to change their current attitudes is uncertain. Should it prove impossible, we must fall back on the comforting thought that time never stands still and that nobody is immortal. What persuasion and the threat of national decline fail to accomplish, retirement, high blood pressure and death will bring to pass, more slowly, it is true, but much more surely.

The dissemination of correct knowledge is one of the essential functions of education, and we neglect it at our peril. But, obviously, education should be more than a device for passing on correct knowledge. It should also teach what Dewey called life adjustment and self-realization. But precisely how should self-realization and life adjustment be promoted? To this question modern educators have given many answers. Most of these answers belong to one or other of two main educational families, the Progressive and the Classical. Answers of the Progressive type find expression in the provision of courses in such subject as "family living, consumer economics, job information, physical and mental health, training for world citizenship and statesmanship and last, and we are afraid least" (I quote again the words of Dr. Dodge) "training in fundamentals." Where answers of the Classical type are preferred, educators provide courses in Latin, Greek and modern European literature, in world history and in philosophy— exclusively, for some odd reason, of the Western brand. Shakespeare and Chaucer, Virgil and Homer—how far away they seem, how irrevocably dead! Why, then, should we bother to teach the classics? The reasons have been stated a thousand times, but seldom with more force and lucidity than by Albert Jay Nock in his *Memoirs of a Super-*

fluous Man. "The literatures of Greece and Rome provide the longest, the most complete and most nearly continuous record we have of what the strange creature Homo sapiens has been busy about in virtually every department of spiritual, intellectual and social activity. Hence the mind that has canvassed this record is much more than a disciplined mind; it is an experienced mind. It has come, as Emerson says, into a feeling of immense longevity, and it instinctively views contemporary man and his doings in the perspective set by this profound and weighty experience. Our studies were properly called formative, because, beyond all others, their effect was powerfully maturing. Cicero told the unvarnished truth in saying that those who have no knowledge of what has gone before them must for ever remain children. And if one wished to characterize the collective mind of this period, or indeed of any period, the use it makes of its powers of observation, reflection, logical inference, one would best do it by the word 'immaturity.' "

The Progressive and the Classical approaches to education are not incompatible. It is perfectly possible to combine a schooling in the local cultural tradition with a training, half vocational, half psychological, in adaptation to the current conventions of social life, and then to combine this combination with training in the sciences, in other words with the inculcation of correct knowledge. But is this enough? Can such an education result in the self-realization which is its aim? The question deserves our closest scrutiny. Nobody, of course, can doubt the importance of accumulated experience as a guide for individual and social conduct. We are human because, at a very early stage in the history of the species, our ancestors discovered a way of preserving and disseminating the results of experience. They learned to speak and were thus enabled to translate what they had perceived, what they had inferred from given fact and home-grown phantasy, into a set of concepts, which could be added to by each generation and bequeathed, a treasure of mingled sense and nonsense, to posterity. In Mr. Nock's words "the mind that has canvassed this record is an experienced mind." The only trouble, so far as *we* are concerned, is that the vicarious experience derived from a study of the classics is, in certain respects, completely irrelevant to twentieth-century facts. In many ways, of course, the modern world resembles the world inhabited by the men of antiquity. In many other ways, however, it is radically different. For example, in *their* world the rate of change was exceedingly slow; in *ours* advancing technology produces a state of chronic revolution. *They* took infanticide for granted (Thebes was the only Greek city which forbade the exposure of babies) and regarded slavery as not only necessary to the Greek way of life, but as intrinsically natural and right; *we* are the heirs of eighteenth- and nineteenth-century humanitarianism and must solve *our* economic and demographic problems by methods less dreadfully reminiscent of recent totalitarian practice. Because all the dirty work was done by slaves, *they* regarded every form of manual activity as essentially unworthy of a gentleman and in consequence never subjected their over-abstract, over-rational theories to the test of experiment; *we* have learned, or at least are learning, to think operationally. *They* despised "barbarians," never bothered to learn a foreign language and could therefore naively regard the rules of Greek grammar and syntax as the Laws of Thought; *we* have begun to understand the nature of language, the danger of taking words too seriously, the ever-present need for linguistic analysis. *They* knew nothing about the past and therefore, in Cicero's words, were like children. (Thucydides, the greatest historian of antiquity, prefaces his account of the Peloponnesian War by airily asserting that nothing of great importance had happened before his own time.) *We*, in the course of the last five generations, have acquired a knowledge of man's past extending back to more than half a million years and covering the activities of tribes and nations in every continent. *They* developed political institutions which, in the case of Greece, were hopelessly unstable and, in the case of Rome, were only too firmly fixed in a pattern of aggressiveness and brutality; but what *we* need is a few hints on the art of creating an entirely new kind of society, durable but adventurous, strong but humane, highly organized but liberty-loving, elastic and adaptable. In this matter Greece and Rome can teach us only negatively—by demonstrating, in their divergent ways, what *not* to do.

From all this it is clear that a classical education in the humanities of two thousand years ago requires to be supplemented by some kind of training in the humanities of today and tomorrow. The Progressives profess to give such a training; but surely we need something a little more informative, a little more useful in this vertiginously changing world of ours, than courses in present-day consumer economics and current job information. But even if a completely adequate schooling in the humanities of the past, the present and the foreseeable future could be devised and made available to all, would the aims of education, as distinct from factual and theoretical instruction, be thereby achieved? Would the recipients of such an education be any nearer to the goal of self-realization? The answer, I am afraid, is, No. For at this point we find ourselves confronted by one of those paradoxes which are of the very essence of our strange existence as amphibians inhabiting, without being completely at home in, half a dozen almost incommensurable worlds—the world of concepts and the world of data, the objective world and the subjective, the small, bright world of personal consciousness and the vast, mysterious world of the unconscious. Where education is concerned, the paradox may be expressed in the statement that the medium of education, which is language, is absolutely necessary, but also fatal; that the subject matter of education, which is the conceptualized accumulation of past experiences, is indispensable, but also an obstacle to be circumvented. "Existence is prior to essence." Unlike most metaphysical propositions, this slogan of the existentialists can actually be verified. "Wolf children," adopted by animal mothers and brought up in animal surroundings, have the form of human beings, but are not human. The essence of humanity, it is evident, is not something we are born with; it is something we make or grow into. We learn to speak, we accumulate conceptualized knowledge and pseudo-knowledge, we imitate our elders, we build up fixed patterns of thought and feeling and behavior, and in the process we become human, we turn into persons. But the things which make us human are precisely the things which interfere with self-realization and prevent understanding. We are humanized by imitating others, by learning their speech and by acquiring the accumulated knowledge which language makes available. But we understand only when, by liberating ourselves from the tyranny of words, conditioned reflexes and social conventions, we establish direct, unmediated contact with experience. The greatest paradox of our existence consists in this: that, in order to understand, we must first encumber ourselves with all the intellectual and emotional baggage which is an impediment to understanding. Except in a dim, pre-conscious way, animals do not understand a situation, even though, by inherited instinct or by an *ad hoc* act of intelligence, they may be reacting to it with complete appropriateness, *as though* they understood it. Conscious understanding is the privilege of men and women, and it is a privilege which they have earned, strangely enough, by acquiring the useful or delinquent habits, the stereotypes of perception, thought and feeling, the rituals of behavior, the stock of second-hand knowledge and pseudo-knowledge, whose possession is the greatest obstacle to understanding. "Learning," says Lao-tsu, "consists in adding to one's stock day by day. The practice of the Tao consists in subtracting." This does not mean, of course, that we can live by subtraction alone. Learning is as necessary as unlearning. Wherever technical proficiency is needed, learning is indispensable. From youth to old age, from generation to generation, we must go on adding to our stock of useful and relevant knowledge. Only in this way can we hope to deal effectively with the physical environment, and with the abstract ideas which make it possible for men to find their way through the complexities of civilization and technology. But this is not the right way to deal with our personal reactions to ourselves or to other human beings. In such situations there must be an unlearning of accumulated concepts; we must respond to each new challenge not with our old conditioning, not in the light of conceptual knowledge based on the memory of past and different events, not by consulting the law of averages, but with a consciousness stripped naked and as though newborn. Once more we are confronted by the great paradox of human life. It is our conditioning which develops our consciousness; but in order to make full use of this developed consciousness, we must start by getting rid of the conditioning which developed it. By adding conceptual knowledge to conceptual knowledge, we make conscious understanding possible; but this potential understanding can be actualized only when we have subtracted all that we have added.

It is because we have memories that we are convinced of our self-identity as persons and as members of a given society.

> The child is father of the Man;
> And I could wish my days to be
> Bound each to each by natural piety.

What Wordsworth called "natural piety" a teacher of understanding would describe as indulgence in emotionally charged memories, associated with childhood and youth. Factual memory—the memory, for example, of the best way of making sulphuric acid or of casting up accounts— is an unmixed blessing. But psychological memory (to use Krishnamurti's term), memory carrying an emotional charge, whether positive or negative, is a source at the worst of neurosis and insanity (psychiatry is largely the art of ridding patients of the incubus of their negatively charged memories), at the best of distractions from the task of understanding—distractions which, though socially useful, are none the less obstacles to be climbed over or avoided. Emotionally charged memories cement the ties of family life (or sometimes make family life impossible!) and serve, when conceptualized and taught as a cultural tradition, to hold communities together. On the level of understanding, on the level of charity and on the level, to some extent, of artistic expression, an individual has it in his power to transcend his social tradition, to overstep the bounds of the culture in which he has been brought up. On the level of knowledge, manners and custom, he can never get very far away from the *persona* created for him by his family and his society. The culture within which he lives is a prison—but a prison which makes it possible for any prisoner who so desires to achieve freedom, a prison to which, for this and a host of other reasons, its inmates owe an enormous debt of gratitude and loyalty. But though it is our duty to "honour our father and our mother," it is also our duty "to hate our father and our mother, our

brethren and our sisters, yea and our own life"—that
socially conditioned life we take for granted. Though it
is necessary for us to add to our cultural stock day by day,
it is also necessary to substract and subtract. There is, to
quote the title of Simone Weil's posthumous essay, a great
"Need for Roots"; but there is an equally urgent need, on
occasion, for total rootlessness.

In our present context this book by Simone Weil and the
preface which Mr. T. S. Eliot contributes to the English
edition are particularly instructive. Simone Weil was a
woman of great ability, heroic virtue and boundless spiritual aspiration. But unfortunately for herself, as well as
for her readers, she was weighed down by a burden of knowledge and pseudo-knowledge, which her own almost mani-
acal over-valuation of words and notions rendered intoler-
ably heavy. A clerical friend reports of her that he did not
"ever remember Simone Weil, in spite of her virtuous desire
for objectivity, give way in the course of a discussion."
She was so deeply rooted in her culture that she came to
believe that words were supremely important. Hence her
love of argument and the obstinacy with which she clung
to her opinions. Hence too her strange inability, on so many
occasions, to distinguish the pointing finger from the indicated moon. "But why do you prate of God?" Meister Eckhart asked; and out of the depth of his understanding of
given reality, he added "Whatever you say of Him is untrue." Necessarily so; for "the saving truth was never
preached by the Buddha," or by anyone else.

Truth can be defined in many ways. But if you define it
as understanding (and this is how all the masters of the
spiritual life have defined it), then it is clear that "truth
must be lived and there is nothing to argue about in this
teaching; any arguing is sure to go against the intent of
it." This was something which Emerson knew and consistently
acted upon. To the almost frenzied exasperation of that
pugnacious manipulator of religious notions, the elder
Henry James, he refused to argue about anything. And
the same was true of William Law. "Away, then, with
the fictions and workings of discursive reason, either for or
against Christianity! They are only the wanton spirit of
the mind, whilst ignorant of God and insensible of its own
nature and condition. . . . For neither God, nor heaven,

nor hell, nor the devil, nor the flesh, can be any other way knowable in you or by you, but by their own existence and manifestation in you. And any pretended knowledge of any of those things, beyond and without this self-evident sensibility of their birth within you, is only such knowledge of them as the blind man hath of the light that has never entered into him." This does not mean, of course, that discursive reason and argument are without value. Where knowledge is concerned, they are not only valuable; they are indispensable. But knowledge is not the same thing as understanding. If we want to understand, we must uproot ourselves from our culture, by-pass language, get rid of emotionally charged memories, hate our fathers and mothers, subtract and subtract from our stock of notions. "Needs must it be a virgin," writes Meister Eckhart, "by whom Jesus is received. Virgin, in other words, is a person, void of alien images, free as he was when he existed not."

Simone Weil must have known, theoretically, about this need for cultural virginity, of total rootlessness. But, alas, she was too deeply embedded in her own and other people's ideas, too superstitious a believer in the magic of the words she handled with so much skill, to be able to act upon this knowledge. "The food," she wrote, "that a collectivity supplies to those who form part of it has no equivalent in the universe." (Thank God! we may add, after sniffing the spiritual nourishment provided by many of the vanished collectivities of the past.) Furthermore, the food provided by a collectivity is food "not only for the souls of the living, but also for souls yet unborn." Finally, "the collectivity constitutes the sole agency for preserving the spiritual treasures accumulated by the dead, the sole transmitting agency by means of which the dead can speak to the living. And the sole earthly reality which is connected with the eternal destiny of man is the irradiating light of those who have managed to become fully conscious of this destiny, transmitted from generation to generation." This last sentence could only have been penned by one who systematically mistook knowledge for understanding, home-made concepts for given reality. It is, of course, desirable that there should be knowledge of what men now dead have said about their understanding of reality. But to maintain that a knowledge of other people's understanding is the same, for us, as understanding, or can even directly lead us to understanding, is a mistake against which all the masters of the spiritual life have always warned us. The letter in St. Paul's phrase, is full of "oldness." It has therefore no relevance to the ever novel reality, which can be understood only in the "newness of the spirit." As for the dead, let them bury their dead. For even the most exalted of past seers and avatars "never taught the saving truth." We should not, it goes without saying, neglect the records of dead men's understandings. On the contrary, we ought to know all about them. But we must know all about them without taking them too seriously. We must know all about them, while remaining acutely aware that such knowledge is not the same as understanding and that understanding will come to us only when we have subtracted what we know and made ourselves void and virgin, free as we were when we were not.

Turning from the body of the book to the preface, we find an even more striking example of that literally preposterous over-valuation of words and notions to which the cultured and the learned are so fatally prone. "I do not know," Mr. Eliot writes, "whether she [Simone Weil] could read the Upanishads in Sanskrit—or, if so, how great was her mastery of what is not only a highly developed language, but a way of thought, the difficulties of which become more formidable to a European student the more diligently he applies himself to it." But like all the other great works of Oriental philosophy, the Upanishads are not systems of pure speculation, in which the niceties of language are all important. They were written by Transcendental Pragmatists, as we may call them, whose concern was to teach a doctrine which could be made to "work," a metaphysical theory which could be operationally tested, not through perception only, but by a direct experience of the whole man on every level of his being. To understand the meaning of *tat tvam asi*, "thou art That," it is not necessary to be a profound Sanskrit scholar. (Similarly, it is not necessary to be a profound Hebrew scholar in order to understand the meaning of "thou shalt not kill.") Understanding of the doctrine (as opposed to conceptualized knowledge about the doctrine) will come only to those who choose to perform the operations that permit *tat tvam asi* to become a given fact of direct, un-mediated experience, or in Law's words "a self-evident sensibility of its birth within them." Did Simone Weil know Sanskrit, or didn't she? The question is entirely beside the point—is just a particularly smelly cultural red herring dragged across the trail that leads from selfhood to more-than-selfhood, from notionally conditioned ego to un-conditioned spirit. In relation to the Upanishads or any other work of Hindu or Buddhist philosophy, only one question deserves to be taken with complete seriousness. It is this. How can a form of words, *tat tvam asi,* a meta-physical proposition such as *Nirvana and samsara are one,* be converted into the direct, unmediated experience of a given fact? How can language and the learned foolery of scholars (for, in this vital context, that is all it is) be cir-cumvented, so that the individual soul may finally under-stand the *That* which, in spite of all its efforts to deny the primordial fact, is identical with the *thou*? Specifically, what methods should we follow? Those inculcated by Patanjali, or those of the Hinayana monks? Those of the Tantriks of northern India and Tibet, those of the Far East Taoists, of the followers of Zen? Those de-scribed by St. John of the Cross and the author of *The Cloud of Unknowing*? If the European student wishes to remain shut up in the prison created by his private cravings and the thought patterns inherited from his predecessors, then by all means let him plunge, through Sanskrit, or Pali, or Chinese, or Tibetan, into the verbal study of "a way of thought, the difficulties of which become more formid-able the more diligently he applies himself to it." If, on the other hand, he wishes to transcend himself by actually understanding the primordial fact described or hinted at in the Upanishads and the other scriptures of what, for lack of a better phrase, we will call "spiritual religion," then he must ignore the problems of language and specu-lative philosophy, or at least relegate them to a secondary position, and concentrate his attention on the practical means whereby the advance from knowledge to understanding may best be made.

From the positively charged collective memories, which are organized into a cultural or religious tradition, let us now return to the positively charged private memories, which individuals organize into a system of "natural piety." We have no more right to wallow in natural piety— that is to say, in emotionally charged memories of past happiness and vanished loves—than to bemoan earlier miseries and torment ourselves with remorse for old offenses. And we have no more right to waste the present instant in relishing future and entirely hypothetical pleasures than to waste it in the apprehension of possible disasters to come. "There is no greater pain," says Dante, "than, in misery, to remember happy times." "Then stop remembering happy times and accept the fact of your present misery," would be the seemingly unsympathetic answer of all those who have had understanding. The emptying of memory is classed by St. John of the Cross as a good second only to the state of union with God, and an indispensable condition of such union.

The word *Buddha* may be translated as "awakened." Those who merely know about things, or only think they know, live in a state of self-conditioned and culturally conditioned somnambulism. Those who understand given reality as it presents itself, moment by moment, are wide awake. Memory charged with pleasant emotions is a soporific or, more accurately, an inducer of trance. This was discovered empirically by an American hypnotist, Dr. W. B. Fahnestock, whose book *Statuvolismor, or Artificial Somnambulism,* was published in 1871. "When persons are desirous of entering into this state [of artificial somnambulism] I place them in a chair, where they may be at perfect ease. They are next instructed to throw their minds to some familiar place it matters not where, so that they have been there before and seem desirous of going there again, even in thought. When they have thrown the mind to the place, or upon the desired object, I endeavour by speaking to them frequently to keep their mind upon it. . . . This must be persisted in for some time." In the end, "clairvoyancy will be induced." Anyone who has experimented with hypnosis, or who has watched an experienced operator inducing trance in a difficult subject, knows how effective Fahnestock's method can be. Incidentally, the relaxing power of positively charged memory was rediscovered, in another medical context, by an oculist, Dr. W. H. Bates, who used to make his patients cover their eyes and revisit in memory the scenes of their happiest experiences. By this means muscular and mental tensions were reduced and it became possible for the patients to use their eyes and minds in a relaxed and therefore efficient way. From all this it is clear that, while positively charged memories can and should be used for specific therapeutic purposes, there must be no indiscriminate indulgence in "natural piety"; for such indulgence may result in a condition akin to trance—a condition at the opposite pole from the wakefulness that is understanding. Those who live with unpleasant memories become somnambulistic; sufficient unto the day is the evil thereof—*and* the good thereof.

The Muses, in Greek mythology, were the daughters of Memory, and every writer is embarked, like Marcel Proust, on a hopeless search for time lost. But a good writer is one who knows how to *"donner un sens plus pur aux mots de la tribu."* Thanks to this purer sense, his readers will react to his words with a degree of understanding much greater than they would have had, if they had reacted, in their ordinary self-conditioned or culture-conditioned way, to the events to which the words refer. A great poet must do too much remembering to be more than a sporadic understander; but he knows how to express himself in words which cause other people to understand. Time lost can never be regained; but in his search for it, he may reveal to his readers glimpses of timeless reality.

Unlike the poet, the mystic is "a son of time present." "Past and present veil God from our sight," says Jalal-ud din Rumi, who was a Sufi first and only secondarily a great poet. "Burn up both of them with fire. How long will you let yourself be partitioned by these segments like a reed? So long as it remains partitioned, a reed is not privy to secrets, neither is it vocal in response to lips or breathing." Along with its mirror image in anticipation, emotionally charged memory is a barrier that shuts us out from understanding.

Natural piety can very easily be transformed into artificial piety; for some emotionally charged memories are common to all the members of a given society and lend themselves to being organized into religious, political or cultural traditions. These traditions are systematically drummed into the young of each successive generation and play an important part in the long drama of their conditioning for citizenship. Since the memories common to one group are different from the memories shared by other groups, the social solidarity created by tradition is always partial and exclusive. There is natural and artificial piety in relation to everything belonging to *us*, coupled with suspicion, dislike and contempt in relation to everything belonging to *them*.

Artificial piety may be fabricated, organized and fostered in two ways—by the repetition of verbal formulas of belief and worship, and by the performance of symbolic acts and rituals. As might be expected, the second is the more effective method. What is the easiest way for a skeptic to achieve faith? The question was answered three hundred years ago by Pascal. The unbeliever must act "as though he believed, take holy water, have masses said etc. This will naturally cause you to believe and will besot you." *(Cela vous abêtira—* literally, will make you stupid.) We have to be made stupid, insists Professor Jacques Chevalier, defending his hero against the critics who have been shocked by Pascal's blunt language; we have to stultify our intelligence, because "intellectual pride deprives us of God and debases us to the level of animals." Which is, of course, perfectly true. But it does not follow from this truth that we ought to besot ourselves in the manner prescribed by Pascal and all the propagandists of all the religions. Intellectual pride can be cured only by devaluating pretentious words, only by getting rid of conceptualized pseudo-knowledge and opening ourselves to reality. Artificial piety based on conditioned reflexes merely transfers intellectual pride from the bumptious individual to his even more bumptious Church. At one remove, the pride remains intact. For the convinced believer, understanding or direct contact with reality is exceedingly difficult. Moreover, the mere fact of having a strong reverential feeling about some hallowed thing, person or proposition is no guarantee of the existence of the thing, the infallibility of the person or the truth of the proposition. In this context, how instructive is the account of an experiment undertaken by that most imaginative and versatile of the Eminent Victorians, Sir Francis Galton! The aim of the experiment, he writes in his *Autobiography,* was to "gain an insight into the abject feelings of barbarians and others concerning the power of images which they know to be of human handiwork. I wanted if possible to enter into these feelings. . . . It was difficult to find a suitable object for trial, because it ought to be in itself quite unfitted to arouse devout feelings. I fixed on a comic picture, it was that of Punch, and made believe in its possession of divine attributes. I addressed it with much quasi-reverence as possessing a mighty power to reward or punish the behaviour of men towards it, and found little difficulty in ignoring the impossibilities of what I professed. The experiment succeeded. I began to feel and long retained for the picture a large share of the feelings that a barbarian entertains towards his idols, and learned to appreciate the enormous potency they might have over him."

The nature of a conditioned reflex is such that, when the bell rings, the dog salivates, when the much worshiped image is seen, or the much repeated credo, litany or mantram is pronounced, the heart of the believer is filled with reverence and his mind with faith. And this happens regardless of the content of the phrase repeated, the nature of the image to which obeisance has been made. He is not responding spontaneously to given reality; he is responding to some thing, or word, or gesture, which automatically brings into play a previously installed post-hypnotic suggestion. Meister Eckhart, that acutest of religious psychologists, clearly recognized this fact. "He who fondly imagines to get more of God in thoughts, prayers, pious offices and so forth than by the fireside or in the stall in sooth he does but take God, as it were, and swaddle His head in a cloak and hide Him under the table. For he who seeks God in settled forms lays hold of the form, while missing the God concealed in it. But he who seeks God in no special guise lays hold of him as He is in Himself, and such an one lives with the Son and is the life itself."

"If you look for the Buddha, you will not see the Buddha." "If you deliberately try to become a Buddha, your Buddha is samsara." "If a person seeks the Tao, that person loses the Tao." "By intending to bring yourself into accord with Suchness, you instantly deviate." "Whosoever will save his life shall lose it." There is a Law of Reversed Effort. The harder we try with the conscious will to do something, the less we shall succeed. Proficiency and the results of proficiency come only to those who have learned the paradoxical art of simultaneously doing and not doing, of combining relaxation with activity, of letting go as a person in order that the immanent and transcendent Unknown Quantity may take hold. We cannot make ourselves understand; the most we can do is to foster a state of mind, in which understanding may come to us. What is this state? Clearly it is not any state of limited consciousness. Reality as it is given moment by moment cannot be understood by a mind acting in obedience to post-hypnotic suggestion, or so conditioned by its emotionally charged memories that it responds to the living *now* as though it were the dead *then*. Nor is the mind that has been trained in concentration any better equipped to understand reality. For concentration is merely systematic exclusion, the shutting away from consciousness of all but one thought, one ideal, one image, or one negation of all thoughts, ideals and images. But however true, however lofty, however holy, no thought or ideal or image can contain reality or lead to the understanding of reality. Nor can the negation of awareness result in that completer awareness necessary to understanding. At the best these things can lead only to a state of ecstatic dissociation, in which one particular aspect of reality, the so-called "spiritual" aspect, may be apprehended. If reality is to be understood in its fullness, as it is given moment by moment, there must be an awareness which is not limited, either deliberately by piety or concentration, or involuntarily by mere thoughtlessness and the force of habit. Understanding comes when we are totally aware—aware to the limits of our mental and physical potentialities. This, of course, is a very ancient doctrine. "Know thyself" is a piece of advice which is as old as civilization, and probably a great deal older. To follow that advice, a man must do more than indulge in introspection. If I would know myself, I must know my environment; for as a body, I am part of the environment, a natural object among other natural objects, and, as a mind, I consist to a great extent of my immediate reactions to the environment and of my secondary reactions to those primary reactions. In practice "know thyself" is a call to total awareness. To those who practice it, what does total awareness reveal? It reveals, first of all, the limitations of the thing which each of us calls "I," and the enormity, the utter absurdity of its pretensions. "I am the master of my fate," poor Henley wrote at the end of a celebrated morsel of rhetoric, "I am the captain of my soul." Nothing could be further from the truth. My fate cannot be mastered; it can only be collaborated with and thereby, to some extent, directed. Nor am I the captain of my soul; I am only its noisiest passenger—a passenger who is not sufficiently important to sit at the captain's table and does not know, even by report, what the soul-ship looks like, how it works or where it is going. Total awareness starts, in a word, with the realization of my ignorance and my impotence. How do electro-chemical events in my brain turn into the perception of a quartet by Haydn or a thought, let us say, of Joan of Arc? I haven't the faintest idea—nor has anyone else. Or consider a seemingly much simpler problem. Can I lift my right hand? The answer is, No, I can't. I can only give the order; the actual lifting is done by somebody else. Who? I don't know. How? I don't know. And when I have eaten, who digests the bread and cheese? When I have cut myself, who heals the wound? While I am sleeping, who restores the tired body to strength, the neurotic mind to sanity? All I can say is that "I" cannot do any of these things. The catalogue of what I do not know and am incapable of achieving could be lengthened almost indefinitely. Even my claim to think is only partially justified by the observable facts. Descartes's primal certainty, "I think, therefore I am," turns out, on closer examination, to be a most dubious proposition. In actual fact is it *I* who do the thinking? Would it not be truer to say, "Thoughts come into existence, and sometimes I am aware of them"? Language, that treasure house of fossil observations and latent philosophy, suggests that this is in fact what happens. Whenever I find myself thinking more than ordinarily well, I am apt to say, "An idea has occurred to me," or, "It came into my head," or, "I see it clearly." In each case the phrase implies that thoughts have their origin "out there," in something analogous, on the mental level, to the external world. Total awareness confirms the hints of idiomatic speech. In relation to the subjective "I," most of the mind is out there. My thoughts are a set of mental, but still external facts. I do not invent my best thoughts; I find them.

Total awareness, then, reveals the following facts: that I am profoundly ignorant, that I am impotent to the point of helplessness and that the most valuable elements in my personality are unknown quantities existing "out there," as mental objects more or less completely independent of my control. This discovery may seem at first rather humiliating and even depressing. But if I wholeheartedly accept them, the facts become a source of peace, a reason for serenity and cheerfulness. I am ignorant and impotent and yet, somehow or other, here I am, unhappy, no doubt, profoundly dissatisfied, but alive and kicking. In spite of everything, I survive, I get by, sometimes I even get on. From these two sets of facts—my survival on the one hand and my ignorance and impotence on the other—I can only infer that the not-I, which looks after my body and gives me my best ideas, must be amazingly intelligent, knowledgeable and strong. As a self-centered ego, I do my best to interfere with the beneficent workings of this not-I. But in spite of my likes and dislikes, in spite of my malice, my infatuations, my gnawing anxieties, in spite of all my overvaluation of words, in spite of my self-stultifying insistence on living, not in present reality, but in memory and anticipation, this not-I, with whom I am associated, sustains me, preserves me, gives me a long succession of second chances. We know very little and can achieve very little; but we are at liberty, if we so choose, to co-operate with a greater power and a completer knowledge, an unknown quantity at once immanent and transcendent, at once physical and mental, at once subjective and objective. If we co-operate, we shall be all right, even if the worst should happen. If we refuse to co-operate, we shall be all wrong even in the most propitious of circumstances.

These conclusions are only the first-fruits of total awareness. Yet richer harvests are to follow. In my ignorance I am sure that I am eternally I. This conviction is rooted in emotionally charged memory. Only when, in the words of St. John of the Cross, the memory has been emptied, can I escape from the sense of my watertight separateness and so prepare myself for the understanding, moment by moment, of reality on all its levels. But the memory cannot be emptied by an act of will, or by systematic discipline or by concentration—even by concentration on the idea of emptiness. It can be emptied only by total awareness. Thus, if I am aware of my distractions—which are mostly emotionally charged memories or phantasies based upon such memories—the mental whirligig will automatically come to a stop and the memory will be emptied, at least for a moment or two. Again, if I become totally aware of my resentment, my uncharitableness, these feelings will be replaced, during the time of my awareness, by a more realistic reaction to the events taking place around me. My awareness, of course, must be uncontaminated by approval of condemnation. Value judgments are conditioned, verbalized reactions to primary reactions. Total awareness is a primary, choiceless, impartial response to the present situation as a whole. There are in it no limiting conditioned reactions to the primary reaction, to the pure cognitive apprehension of the situation. If memories of verbal formulas of praise or blame should make their appearance in consciousness, they are to be examined impartially as any other present datum is examined. Professional moralists have confidence in the surface will, believe in punishments and rewards and are adrenalin addicts who like nothing better than a good orgy of righteous indignation. The masters of the spiritual life have little faith in the surface will or the utility, for their particular purposes, of rewards or punishments, and do not indulge in righteous indignation. Experience has taught them that the highest good can never, in the very nature of things, be achieved by moralizing. "Judge not that ye be not judged" is their watchword and total awareness is their method.

Two or three thousand years behind the times, a few contemporary psychiatrists have now discovered this method. "Socrates," writes Professor Carl Rogers, "developed novel ideas, which have proven to be socially constructive." Why? Because he was "notably non-defensive and open to experience. The reasoning behind this is based primarily upon the discovery in psychotherapy that if we can add to the sensory and visceral experiencing, characteristic of the whole animal kingdom, the gift of a free undirected awareness, of which only the human animal seems fully capable, we have an organism which is as aware of the demands of the culture as it is of its own physiological demands for food and sex, which is just as aware of its desire for friendly relationships as it is aware of its desire to aggrandize itself; which is just as aware of its delicate and sensitive tenderness towards others as it is of its hostilities towards others. When man is less than fully man, when he denies to awareness various aspects of his experience, then indeed we have all too often reason to fear him and his behaviour, as the present world situation testifies. But when he is most fully man, when he is his complete organism, when awareness of experience, that peculiarly human attribute, is fully operating, then his behaviour is to be trusted." Better late than never! It is comforting to find the immemorial commonplaces of mystical wisdom turning up as a brand-new discovery in psychotherapy. *Gnosce teipsum*—know yourself. Know yourself in relation to your overt intentions and your hidden motives, in relation to your thinking, your physical functioning and to those greater not-selves, who see to it that, despite all the ego's attempts at sabotage, the thinking shall be tolerably relevant and the functioning not too abnormal. Be totally aware of what you do and think and of the persons with whom you are in relationship, the events which prompt you at every moment of your existence. Be aware impartially, realistically, without judging, without reacting in terms of remembered words to your present cognitive reactions. If you do this, the memory will be emptied, knowledge and pseudo-knowledge will be relegated to their proper place, and you will have understanding—in other words, you will be in direct contact with reality at every instant. Better still, you will discover what Carl Rogers calls your "delicate and sensitive tenderness towards others." And not only *your* tenderness, the cosmic tenderness, the fundamental all-rightness of the universe—in spite of death, in spite of suffering. "Though He slay me, yet will I trust Him." This is the utterance of someone who is totally aware. And another such utterance is, "God is love." From the standpoint of common sense, the first is the raving of a lunatic, the second flies in the face of all experience and is obviously untrue. But common sense is not based on total awareness; it is a product of convention, of organized memories of other people's words, of personal experiences limited by passion and value judgments, of hallowed notions and naked self-interest. Total awareness opens the way to understanding, and when any given situation is understood, the nature of all reality is made manifest, and the nonsensical utterances of the mystics are seen to be true, or at least as nearly true as it is possible for a verbal expression of the ineffable to be. One in all and all in One; samsara and nirvana are the same; multiplicity is unity, and unity is not so much one as not-two; all things are void, and yet all things are the Dharma-Body of the Buddha—and so on. So far as conceptual knowledge is concerned, such phrases are completely meaningless. It is only when there is understanding that they make sense. For when there is understanding, there is an experienced fusion of the End with the Means, of the Wisdom which is the timeless realization of Suchness with the Compassion which is Wisdom in action. Of all the worn, smudged, dog's-eared words in our vocabulary, "love" is surely the grubbiest, smelliest, slimiest. Bawled from a million pulpits, lasciviously crooned through hundreds of millions of loud-speakers, it has become an outrage to good taste and decent feeling, an obscenity which one hesitates to pronounce. And yet it has to be pronounced, for, after all, Love is the last word.

The Desert

Boundlessness and emptiness—these are the two most expressive symbols of that attributeless Godhead, of whom all that can be said is St. Bernard's *Nescio nescio* or the Vedantist's "not this, not this." The Godhead, says Meister Eckhart, must be loved "as not-God, not-Spirit, not-person, not-image, must be loved as He is, a sheer pure absolute One, sundered from all twoness, and in whom we must eternally sink from nothingness to nothingness." In the scriptures of Northern and Far Eastern Buddhism the spatial metaphors recur again and again. At the moment of death, writes the author of the *Bardo Thodol*, "all things are like the cloudless sky; and the naked immaculate Intellect is like unto a translucent void without circumference or centre." "The great Way," in Sosan's words, "is perfect, like unto vast space, with nothing wanting, nothing superfluous." "Mind," says Hui-neng (and he is speaking of that universal ground of consciousness, from which all beings, the unenlightened no less than the enlightened, take their source), "mind is like emptiness of space. . . . Space contains sun, moon, stars, the great earth, with its mountains and rivers. . . . Good men and bad men, good things and bad things, heaven and hell—they are all in empty space. The emptiness of Self-nature is in all people just like this." The theologians argue, the dogmatists declaim their credos; but their propositions "stand in no intrinsic relation to my inner light. This Inner Light" (I quote from Yoka Dashi's "Song of Enlightenment") "can be likened to space; it knows no boundaries; yet it is always here, is always with us, always retains its serenity and fullness. . . . You cannot take hold of it, and you cannot get rid of it; it goes on its own way. You speak and it is silent; you remain silent, and it speaks."

Silence is the cloudless heaven perceived by another sense. Like space and emptiness, it is a natural symbol of the divine. In the Mithraic mysteries, the candidate for initiation was told to lay a finger to his lips and whisper: "Silence! Silence! Silence—symbol of the living imperishable God!" And long before the coming of Christianity to the Thebaid, there had been Egyptian mystery religions, for whose followers God was a well of life, "closed to him who speaks, but open to the silent." The Hebrew scriptures are eloquent almost to excess; but even here, among the splendid rumblings of prophetic praise and impetation and anathema, there are occasional references to the spiritual meaning and the therapeutic virtues of silence. "Be still, and know that I am God." "The Lord is in his holy temple; let all the world keep silence before him." "Keep thou silence at the presence of the Lord God." The desert, after all, began within a few miles of the gates of Jerusalem.

The facts of silence and emptiness are traditionally the symbols of divine immanence—but not, of course, for everyone, and not in all circumstances. "Until one has crossed a barren desert, without food or water, under a burning

tropical sun, at three miles an hour, one can form no conception of what misery is." These are the words of a gold-
seeker, who took the southern route to California in 1849.
Even when one is crossing it at seventy miles an hour on a
four-lane highway, the desert can seem formidable enough.
To the forty-niners it was unmitigated hell. Men and women
who are at her mercy find it hard to see in Nature and her
works any symbols but those of brute power at the best and,
at the worst, of an obscure and mindless malice. The
desert's emptiness and the desert's silence reveal what we
may call their spiritual meanings only to those who enjoy
some measure of physiological security. The security may
amount to no more than St. Anthony's hut and daily ration
of bread and vegetables, no more than Milarepa's cave
and barley meal and boiled nettles—less than what any
sane economist would regard as the indispensable minimum,
but still security, still a guarantee of organic life and,
along with life, of the possibility of spiritual liberty and
transcendental happiness.

But even for those who enjoy security against the assaults
of the environment, the desert does not always or inevitably
reveal its spiritual meanings. The early Christian hermits
retired to the Thebaid because its air was purer, because
there were fewer distractions, because God seemed nearer
there than in the world of men. But, alas, dry places are
notoriously the abode of unclean spirits, seeking rest and
finding it not. If the immanence of God was sometimes more
easily discoverable in the desert, so also, and all too frequently, was the immanence of the devil. St. Anthony's
temptations have become a legend, and Cassian speaks
of "the tempests of imagination" through which every new-
comer to the eremitic life had to pass. Solitude, he writes,
makes men feel "the many-winged folly of their souls . . . ;
they find the perpetual silence intolerable, and those whom
no labour on the land could weary, are vanquished by
doing nothing and worn out by the long duration of their
peace." *Be still, and know that I am God;* be still, and
know that *you* are the delinquent imbecile who snarls and
gibbers in the basement of every human mind. The desert
can drive men mad, but it can also help them to become
supremely sane.

The enormous draughts of emptiness and silence prescribed by the eremites are safe medicine only for a few exceptional souls. By the majority the desert should be taken either dilute or, if at full strength, in small doses. Used in this way, it acts as a spiritual restorative, as an anti-hallucinant, as a de-tensioner and alternative.

In his book, *The Next Million Years,* Sir Charles Darwin looks forward to thirty thousand generations of ever more humans pressing over more heavily on ever dwindling resources and being killed off in ever increasing numbers by famine, pestilence and war. He may be right. Alternatively, human ingenuity may somehow falsify his predictions. But even human ingenuity will find it hard to circumvent arithmetic. On a planet of limited area, the more people there are, the less vacant space there is bound to be. Over and above the material and sociological problems of increasing population, there is a serious psychological problem. In a completely home-made environment, such as is provided by any great metropolis, it is as hard to remain sane as it is in a completely natural environment such as the desert or the forest. O Solitude, where are thy charms? But, O Multitude, where are *thine*? The most wonderful thing about America is that, even in these middle years of the twentieth century, there are so few Americans. By taking a certain amount of trouble you might still be able to get yourself eaten by a bear in the state of New York. And without any trouble at all you can get bitten by a rattler in the Hollywood hills, or die of thirst, while wandering through an uninhabited desert, within a hundred and fifty miles of Los Angeles. A short generation ago you might have wandered and died within only a hundred miles of Los Angeles. Today the mounting tide of humanity has oozed through the intervening canyons and spilled out into the wide Mojave. Solitude is receding at the rate of four and a half kilometers per annum.

And yet, in spite of it all, the silence persists. For this silence of the desert is such that casual sounds, and even the systematic noise of civilization, cannot abolish it. They coexist with it—as small irrelevances of right angles to an enormous meaning, as veins of something analogous to darkness within an enduring transparency. From the irrigated land come the dark gross sounds of lowing cattle, and above them the plovers trail their vanishing threads of shrillness. Suddenly, startlingly, out of the sleeping sagebrush there bursts the shrieking of coyotes—Trio for Ghoul and Two Damned Souls. On the trunks of cottonwood trees, on the wooden walls of barns and houses, the woodpeckers rattle away like pneumatic drills. Picking one's way between the cactuses and the creosote bushes one hears, like some tiny shirring clockwork, the soliloquies of invisible wrens, the calling, at dusk, of the nightjays and even occasionally the voice of Homo sapiens—six of the species in a parked Chevrolet, listening to the broadcast of a prize fight, or else in pairs necking to the delicious accompaniment of Crosby. But the light forgives, the distances forget, and this great crystal of silence, whose base is as large as Europe and whose height, for all practical purposes, is infinite, can coexist with things of a far higher order of discrepancy than canned sentiment or vicarious sport. Jet planes, for example—the stillness is so massive that it can absorb even jet planes. The screaming crash mounts to its intolerable climax and fades again, mounts as another of the monsters rips through the air, and once more diminishes and is gone. But even at the height of the outrage the mind can still remain aware of that which surrounds it, that which preceded and will outlast it.

Progress, however, is on the march. Jet planes are already as characteristic of the desert as are Joshua trees or burrowing owls; they will soon be almost as numerous. The wilderness has entered the armament race, and will be in it to the end. In its multi-million-acred emptiness there is room enough to explode atomic bombs and experiment with guided missiles. The weather, so far as flying is concerned, is uniformly excellent, and in the plains lie the flat beds of many lakes, dry since the last Ice Age, and manifestly intended by Providence for hot-rod racing and jets. Huge airfields have already been constructed. Factories are going up. Oases are turning into industrial towns. In brand-new Reservations, surrounded by barbed wire and the FBI, not Indians but tribes of physicists, chemists, metallurgists, communication engineers and mechanics are working with the co-ordinated frenzy of termites. From their air-conditioned laboratories and machine shops there flows a steady stream of marvels, each one more expensive and each more fiendish than the last. The desert silence is still there; but so, ever more noisily, are the scientific irrelevances. Give the boys in the reservations a few more years and another hundred billion dollars, and they will succeed (for with technology all things are possible) in abolishing the silence, in transforming what are now irrelevancies into the desert's fundamental meaning. Meanwhile, and luckily for us, it is noise which is exceptional; the rule is still this crystalline symbol of universal Mind.

The bulldozers roar, the concrete is mixed and poured, the jet planes go crashing through the air, the rockets soar aloft with their cargoes of white mice and electronic instruments. And yet for all this, "nature is never spent; there lives the dearest freshness deep down things."

And not merely the dearest, but the strangest, the most wonderfully unlikely. I remember, for example, a recent visit to one of the new Reservations. It was in the spring of 1952 and, after seven years of drought, the rains of the preceding winter had been copious. From end to end the Mojave was carpeted with flowers—sunflowers, and the dwarf phlox, chicory and coreopsis, wild hollyhock and all the tribe of garlics and lilies. And then, as we neared the Reservation, the flower carpet began to move. We stopped the car, we walked into the desert to take a closer look. On the bare ground, on every plant and bush innumerable caterpillars were crawling. They were of two kinds—one smooth, with green and white markings, and a horn, like that of a miniature rhinoceros, growing out of its hinder end. The caterpillar, evidently, of one of the hawk moths. Mingled with these, in millions no less uncountable, were the brown hairy offspring of (I think) the Painted Lady butterfly. They were everywhere—over hundreds of square miles of the desert. And yet, a year before, when the eggs from which these larvae had emerged were laid, California had been as dry as a bone. On what, then, had the parent insects lived? And what had been the food of their innumerable offspring? In the days when I collected butterflies and kept their young in glass jars on the window sill of my cubicle at school, no self-respecting caterpillar would feed on anything but the leaves to which its species had been predestined. Puss moths laid their eggs on poplars, spurge hawks on spurges; mulleins were frequented by the gaily piebald caterpillars of one rather rare and rigidly fastidious moth. Offered an alternative diet, my caterpillars would turn away in horror. They were like orthodox Jews confronted by pork or lobsters; they were like Brahmins at a feast of beef prepared by Untouchables. Eat? Never. They would rather die. And if the right food were not forthcoming, die they did. But these caterpillars of the desert were apparently different. Crawling into irrigated regions, they had devoured the young leaves of entire vineyards and vegetable gardens. They had broken with tradition, they had flouted the immemorial taboos. Here, near the Reservation, there was no cultivated land. These hawk moth and Painted Lady caterpillars, which were all full grown, must have fed on indigenous growths—but which, I could never discover; for when I saw them the creatures were all crawling at random, in search either of something juicier to eat or else of some place to spin their cocoons. Entering the Reservation, we found them all over the parking lot and even on the steps of the enormous building which housed the laboratories and the administrative offices. The men on guard only laughed or swore. But could they be *absolutely* sure? Biology has always been the Russians' strongest point. These innumerable crawlers— perhaps they were Soviet agents? Parachuted from the stratosphere, impenetrably disguised, and so thoroughly indoctrinated, so completely conditioned by means of post-hypnotic suggestions that even under torture it would be impossible for them to confess, even under DDT. . . .

Our party showed its pass and entered. The strangeness was no longer Nature's; it was strictly human. Nine and a half acres of floor space, nine and a half acres of the most extravagant improbability. Sagebrush and wild flowers beyond the windows; but here, within, machine tools capable of turning out anything from a tank to an electron microscope; million-volt X-ray cameras; electric furnaces; wind tunnels; refrigerated vacuum tanks; and on either side of endless passages closed doors bearing inscriptions which had obviously been taken from last year's science fiction magazines. (This year's space ships, of course, have harnessed gravitation and magnetism.) ROCKET DEPARTMENT, we read on door after door. ROCKET AND EXPLOSIVES DEPARTMENT, ROCKET PERSONNEL

DEPARTMENT. And what lay behind the unmarked doors? Rockets and Canned Tularemia? Rockets and Nuclear Fission? Rockets and Space Cadets? Rockets and Elementary Courses in Martian Language and Literature?

It was a relief to get back to the caterpillars. Ninety-nine point nine recurring per cent of the poor things were going to die—but not for an ideology, not while doing their best to bring death to other caterpillars, not to the accompaniment of *Te Deums,* of *Dulce et decorums,* of "We shall not sheathe the sword, which we have not lightly drawn, until . . ." Until what? The only completely unconditional surrender will come when everybody—but *everybody* —is a corpse.

For modern man, the really blessed thing about Nature is its otherness. In their anxiety to find a cosmic basis for human values, our ancestors invented an emblematic botany, a natural history composed of allegories and fables, an astronomy that told fortunes and illustrated the dogmas of revealed religion. "In the Middle Ages," writes Emile Mâle, "the idea of a thing which a man formed for himself, was always more real than the thing itself. . . . The study of things for their own sake held no meaning for the thoughtful man. . . . The task for the student of nature was to discover the eternal truth which God would have each thing express." These eternal truths expressed by things were not the laws of physical and organic being— laws discoverable only by patient observation and the sacrifice of preconceived ideas and autistic urges; they were the notions and fantasies engendered in the minds of logicians, whose major premises, for the most part, were other fantasies and notions bequeathed to them by earlier writers. Against the belief that such purely verbal constructions were eternal truths, only the mystics protested; and the mystics were concerned only with that "obscure knowledge," as it was called, which comes when a man "sees all in all." But between the real but obscure knowledge of the mystic and the clear but unreal knowledge of the verbalist, lies the clearish and realish knowledge of the naturalist and the man of science. It was knowledge of a kind which most of our ancestors found completely uninteresting.

Reading the older descriptions of God's creatures, the

older speculations about the ways and workings of Nature, we start by being amused. But the amusement soon turns to the most intense boredom and a kind of mental suffocation. We find ourselves gasping for breath in a world where all the windows are shut and everything "wears man's smudge and shares man's smell." Words are the greatest, the most momentous of all our inventions, and the specifically human realm is the realm of language. In the stifling universe of medieval thought, the given facts of Nature were treated as the symbols of familiar notions. Words did not stand for things; things stood for pre-existent words. This is a pitfall which, in the natural sciences, we have learned to avoid. But in other contexts than the scientific— in the context, for example, of politics—we continue to take our verbal symbols with the same disastrous seriousness as was displayed by our crusading and persecuting ancestors. For both parties, the people on the other side of the Iron Curtain are not human beings, but merely the embodiments of the pejorative phrases coined by propagandists.

Nature is blessedly non-human; and insofar as we belong to the natural order, we too are blessedly non-human. The otherness of caterpillars, as of our own bodies, is an otherness underlain by a principal identity. The non-humanity of wild flowers, as of the deepest levels of our own minds, exists within a system which includes and transcends the human. In the given realm of the inner and outer not-self, we are all one. In the home-made realm of symbols we are separate and mutually hostile partisans. Thanks to words, we have been able to rise above the brutes; and thanks to words, we have often sunk to the level of the demons. Our statesmen have tried to come to an international agreement on the use of atomic power. They have not been successful. And even if they had, what then? No agreement on atomic power can do any lasting good, unless it be preceded by an agreement on language. If we make a wrong use of nuclear fission, it will be because we have made a wrong use of the symbols, in terms of which we think about ourselves and other people. Individually and collectively, men have always been the victims of their own words; but, except in the emotionally neutral field of science, they have never been willing to admit their linguistic ineptitude, and correct their mistakes. Taken too seriously, symbols have motivated and justified all the horrors of recorded history. On every level from the personal to the international, the letter kills. Theoretically we know this very well. In practice, nevertheless, we continue to commit the suicidal blunders to which we have become accustomed.

The caterpillars were still on the march when we left the Reservation, and it was half an hour or more, at a mile a minute, before we were clear of them. Among the phloxes and the sunflowers, millions in the midst of hundreds of millions, they proclaimed (along with the dangers of overpopulation) the strength, the fecundity, the endless resourcefulness of life. We were in the desert, and the desert was blossoming, the desert was crawling. I had not seen anything like it since that spring day, in 1948, when we had been walking at the other end of the Mojave, near the great earthquake fault, down which the highway descends to San Bernardino and the orange groves. The elevation here is around four thousand feet and the desert is dotted with dark clumps of juniper. Suddenly, as we moved through the enormous emptiness, we became aware of an entirely unfamiliar interruption to the silence. Before, behind, to right and to left, the sound seemed to come from all directions. It was a small sharp crackling, like the ubiquitous frying of bacon, like the first flames in the kindling of innumerable bonfires. There seemed to be no explanation. And then, as we looked more closely, the riddle gave up its answer. Anchored to a stem of sagebrush, we saw the horny pupa of a cicada. It had begun to split and the full-grown insect was in process of pushing its way out. Each time it struggled, its case of amber-colored chitin opened a little more widely. The continuous crackling that we heard was caused by the simultaneous emergence of thousands upon thousands of individuals. How long they had spent underground I could never discover. Dr. Edmund Jaeger, who knows as much about the fauna and flora of the Western deserts as anyone now living, tells me that the habits of this particular cicada have never been closely studied. He himself had never witnessed the mass resurrection upon which we had had the good fortune to stumble. All one can be sure of is that these creatures had spent anything from two to seventeen years in the soil, and that they had all chosen this particular May morning to climb out of the grave, burst their coffins, dry their moist wings and embark upon their life of sex and song.

Three weeks later we heard and saw another detachment of the buried army coming out into the sun among the pines and the flowering fremontias of the San Gabriel Mountains. The chill of two thousand additional feet of elevation had postponed the resurrection; but when it came, it conformed exactly to the pattern set by the insects of the desert: the risen pupa, the crackle of splitting horn, the helpless imago waiting for the sun to bake it into perfection, and then the flight, the tireless singing, so unremitting that it becomes a part of the silence. The boys in the Reservations are doing their best; and perhaps, if they are given the necessary time and money, they may really succeed in making the planet uninhabitable. Applied Science is a conjuror, whose bottomless hat yields impartially the softest of Angora rabbits and the most petrifying of Medusas. But I am still optimist enough to credit life with invincibility, I am still ready to bet that the non-human otherness at the root of man's being will ultimately triumph over the all too human selves who frame the ideologies and engineer the collective suicides. For our survival, if we do survive, we shall be less beholden to our common sense (the name we give to what happens when we try to think of the world in terms of the unanalyzed symbols supplied by language and the local customs) than to our caterpillar- and cicada-sense, to intelligence, in other words, as it operates on the organic level. That intelligence is at once a will to persistence and an inherited knowledge of the physiological and psychological means by which, despite all the follies of the loquacious self, persistence can be achieved. And beyond survival is transfiguration; beyond and including animal grace is the grace of that other not-self, of which the desert silence and the desert emptiness are the most expressive symbols.

Ozymandias,
the Utopia That Failed

In this part of the desert Ozymandias* consists of an abandoned silo and the ruins of a cow byre. "The hands that mocked"—mocked themselves in the very act of so laboriously creating these poor things—were the hands of a thousand idealists; "the heart that fed" belonged to a Marxist lawyer, with a Gladstone collar and the face of a revivalist or a Shakespearean actor. Job Harriman was his name; and if the McNamara brothers had not unexpectedly confessed to the dynamiting of the *Times* building, he would in all probability have become the first Socialist mayor of Los Angeles. But with that confession, his passionately defended clients ceased to be proletarian martyrs and became the avowed killers of twenty-six unfortunate printers and newspapermen. Job Harriman's chance of winning the election abruptly declined to zero. Another man would have admitted defeat. Not Harriman. If Los Angeles would not have him as its mayor, he would go out into the wilderness and there create a new, better city of his own. On May Day, 1914, the Llano del Rio Cooperative Colony (incorporated first in California and later under the more easy-going laws of Nevada) received its first contingent of settlers.

Three years later, in the *Llano View Book*, an anonymous enthusiast wrote of the event with a mixture of biblical and patriotic solemnity. "May first, 1914, a hardy little band of pioneers, likened unto those who courageously founded the Plymouth Colony in Massachusetts so many years ago, went forth into the Antelope Valley to found another Colony, destined through the years to be quite as historical and quite as significant of the founding of a New

* Located approximately 75 miles from Los Angeles in the Antelope Valley.

68

Civilization." And this May Day promise had already been fulfilled. "The success of complete cooperation has now been demonstrated convincingly. The demonstration is the most thorough that can be asked for." The colony is now "too firmly established to be affected by anything except a concerted and organized effort backed by Capital. Its future is clear." These words were penned and printed, at the Llano publishing house, in the summer of 1917. Before the year was out, that clear future was a thing of the past. The company was bankrupt, the colonists had dispersed. Within twenty-four hours of their departure playful iconoclasts had smashed five hundred dollars' worth of windows; within a week, a large frame hotel and several scores of houses and workshops had been demolished and carried off piecemeal by the homesteaders who precariously represented capitalism in the wilderness. Only the silo and the foundations of the cow byre remained; they were made of concrete and could not be hauled away.

> Round the decay
> Of that colossal wreck, boundless and bare,
> The lone and level sands stretch far away.

A more squeamish artist than Shelley would have avoided the reduplication of those alliterative epithets. "Boundless and bare," "lone and level"—one is reminded of a passage in Lewis Carroll's versified essay on poetic diction: "The wild man went his weary way to a strange and lonely pump." But the general effect, albeit a little cheap, is dramatically good and even sufficiently true, despite the fact that the sands hereabouts are neither bare nor indefinitely level. A few miles south of Ozymandias the desert tilts upwards to a range of wooded and, in winter, snow-covered mountains. To the north stretches a plain; but its levels are dotted with isolated buttes and rimmed, in the far distance, by other ranges of mountains. And over all the ground spreads the thin carpet of those astonishingly numerous plants and bushes which have learned to adapt themselves to a land where it rains eight or nine inches during the winter and not at all from May to November.

To the brute facts of meteorology in arid country Job Harriman was resolutely indifferent. When he thought of human affairs, he thought of them only as a Socialist, never as a naturalist. Thus, with a population of only three hundred thousand, Los Angeles was already becoming uncomfortably dry. But because its water would enrich the real-estate operators, Job Harriman opposed the construction of the Owens Valley Aqueduct. Worse, he rationalized his opposition by the obviously absurd statement that the city could grow indefinitely on its local resources. The same ill-informed optimism made nonsense of his plan for Llano. In a good year (and every other year is bad) water from the Big Rock Creek makes possible the raising, at Llano, of crops and cattle worth perhaps a hundred thousand dollars. The Colony owned rights to part of this water. On its irrigated acres fifty or, at the most, a hundred persons might have eked out a precarious living. But by the beginning of 1917 Harriman had accepted the applications of almost a thousand eager co-operators. Every applicant had to buy two thousand shares of the company's stock, for which he was to pay five hundred, or preferably a thousand, dollars in cash, and the balance in labor. In a year or two, it was assumed, the Colony would be self-sufficient; until then, it would have to live on the cash invested by its members.

For as long as the cash lasted, times were good, enthusiasm high and achievement correspondingly great. A wagon road was driven through the foothills, up into the timberland of the San Gabriel Mountains. Trees were felled and laboriously brought down to the sawmill in the plain, below. A quarry was opened, a lime kiln constructed. The tents of the first colonists gave place to shacks, the shacks to houses. Next a hotel was built, to accommodate the interested visitors from the infernal regions of capitalism. Schools and workshops appeared as though by magic. Irrigation ditches were dug and lined. Eighty horses and a steam tractor cleared, leveled, plowed and harvested. Fruit trees were planted, pears canned, alfalfa cut and stored, cows milked and "the West's most modern rabbitry" established. Nor were the spiritual needs of the colonists neglected. From the print shop issued two weekly newspapers and a stream of pamphlets. Among the amenities were a woman's exchange, a Socialist local, several quartets, two orchestras, a brass band and a mandolin club.

One of the old-timers has often talked to me nostalgically of that brass band, those mandolins and barber-shop ensembles. What pleasure, on a mild night in May or June, to sit out of doors under one's privately owned cottonwood tree and listen, across a mile of intervening sagebrush, to the music of Socialists! The moon is full, the last snow still glitters on the summit of Mount Baden Powell and, to the accompaniment of the steady croaking of frogs along the irrigation ditch and the occasional frantic shrieks of the coyotes, the strains of Sousa and "Sweet Adeline" and the Unfinished Symphony transcribed for mandolins and saxophone, come stealing with extraordinary distinctness upon the ear. Only Edward Lear can do full justice to such an occasion. It must have been, in the very highest degree, "meloobious and genteel." But, alas, every magical night is succeeded by yet another busy morning. The *al fresco* concert was delightful; but that did not make it any easier to collect, next day, from the communal treasury. As well as the mandolins, my old-timer friend recalls his efforts to get paid for services rendered. After long haggling he would think himself lucky if he came away with two dollars in silver and the rest in hay or pumpkins.

For most of the co-operators, the morning after a concert was less disillusioning. I have met three or four ex-colonists—older, sadder, possibly wiser—and all of them bore witness to the happiness of those first months at Llano. Housing, to be sure, was inadequate; food monotonous, and work extremely hard. But there was a sense of shared high purpose, a sustaining conviction that one had broken out of an age-old prison and was marching, shoulder to shoulder with loyal comrades, towards a promised land. "Bliss was it in that dawn to be alive." And this applies to all dawns without distinction—the dawn of a war and the dawn of a peace, the dawn of revolution and the dawn of reaction, the dawn of passion and in due course the blessed coolness of the dawn of indifference, the dawn of marriage and then, at Reno, the long awaited dawn of divorce. In co-operative communities dawns are peculiarly rosy. For this very reason, midday is apt to be peculiarly stifling, and the afternoons intolerable and interminable. To the ordinary hazards of community life Llano added the insurmountable obstacles of too many people, too little water and, after three years, no money.

As the situation grew worse, the propagandists became more lyrical. "Llano offers hope and inspiration for the masses. . . . Its purpose is to solve unemployment, to assure safety and comfort for the future and old age." And the words were accompanied by a detailed plan of the city which was just about to be built. "It will be different in design from any other in the world. Its houses will be comfortable, sanitary, handsome, home-like, modern and harmonious with their surroundings, and will insure greater privacy than any other houses ever constructed. They are unique and designed especially for Llano." The publicity worked. Applications and, more important, checks kept steadily coming in. With each arrival of an idealist's life savings, there was a respite. But a respite at a price. For with those life-savings came another member and his family. The Colony had acquired three days' supply of food, but it had also acquired five extra mouths. Each successive windfall went a little less far. And meanwhile our old friend, Human Nature, was busily at work.

In his office and in court Harriman was a successful attorney. Outside he was an idealist and theorizer, whose knowledge was not of men and women but of sociological abstractions and the more or less useful fictions of economics.

In a preface which he contributed in 1924 to Ernest Wooster's *Communities Past and Present* Harriman writes, (how touchingly!) about his self-imposed ignorance and subsequent enlightenment. "Believing that life arose out of chemical action and that form was determined by the impinging environment, I naturally believed that all would react more or less alike to the same environment." But in fact they didn't. Against all the rules, "we found more well-to-do-men among the unselfish than there were among the selfish." Worse still, "we found to our surprise that there were more selfish men among the poor in proportion to their number, than there were among the well-to-do. . . ." Worst and most unexpected was the fact that the selfish "persisted in their course with a persistence that was amazing." From amazement the poor man passed to downright "confusion" at the discovery that there are "those who are extremely active (in the work of the Colony) and yet who are also extremely selfish. If their behavior is closely observed, they will invariably be found to be working for self-glory or for power." These discoveries of the immemorially obvious led him to two conclusions, whose extremely unoriginal character is the guarantee of their soundness. First, "theories and intellectual concepts play a very small part in our reactions." And, second, "economic determination seems to play no part in separating the sheep from the goats." In the process of reaching these conclusions, Job Harriman had to pass through ten years of an excruciatingly educative purgatory.

No effort had been made to exclude from Llano the sort of people whose presence is fatal to any close-knit community, and there was no system of rules by which, having been admitted, such persons might be controlled. From the first Harriman found himself confronted by a cantankerous minority of trouble-makers. There were the idealistic purists, who complained that he was making too many compromises with the devils of capitalism; there were the malingerers who criticized but refused to work; there were the greedy, with their clamor for special privileges; there were the power lovers who envied him and were ambitious to take his place. Meeting secretly in the desert, the "brush gang," as these malcontents were called, plotted his overthrow. It came at last at the hands of a trusted lieutenant who, in Harriman's absence, disposed of the Llano property to private owners—including, in a big way, himself. But, long before this final catastrophe, there had been nothing to eat, and the majority of the colonists had returned, without their savings, to the world of free competition. A few, under Harriman's leadership, migrated in a special train to Louisiana, where they had collectively bought an abandoned lumber camp and several thousand denuded acres. There was another blissful dawn, followed by a prolonged struggle with a hundred ferocious Texans, who had been invited to join the community, but had not, apparently, been told that it was a co-operative. When these extremely rugged individualists had gone, taking with them most of the Colony's livestock and machinery, the survivors settled down to the dismal realities of life on an inadequate economic foundation. Work was hard, and for diversion there were only the weekly dances, the intrigues of several rival brush gangs and the spectacle of the struggle for power between the ailing Harriman and an ex-insurance salesman of boundless energy, called George T. Pickett. By 1924, Harriman was out—for good.

The new manager was one of those "born leaders," who have no patience with democratic methods and are seriously convinced that they always know best. "I'd rather work with a bunch of morons than with a lot of over-educated kickers." But the colonists—or at least some of them—refused to accept his benevolent dictatorship. Brush gangs bored from within; heretics and seceders campaigned from without. From the neighboring town of Leesville two dissident and mutually hostile groups bombarded the loyalists with anonymous letters and denounced the management and, of course, one another in any left-wing paper that would print their articles.

And all the time New Llano was as far as ever from self-sufficiency. The Colony could boast of no less than thirty-eight industrial and agricultural departments. But all of them, unfortunately, were running at a loss. The only solid asset was Pickett's incomparable salesmanship; the only steady source of income, his far-ranging drives for funds. Through the years a trickle of money flowed in— never quite enough to buy the colonists new shoes, but sufficient at least to prevent actual starvation. In the thirties wildcatters persuaded the management that there was oil on the Colony's property. A number of idealists were talked into a speculative investment, and three wells were drilled. Needless to say, all of them were dry.

Then came the Revolution. While Pickett was away, soliciting Federal funds at Washington, his enemies called a meeting of the entire membership. By a majority vote of the minority who attended, Pickett was deposed. For the dominant brush gang and its supporters, what a blissful dawn! For the rest, it looked like the midnight of all hope.

The author of a rare little book, *The Crisis in Llano Colony, An Epic Story*, belonged to the second group. To express his feelings about Pickett, mere prose seemed inadequate. The history of the conspiracy culminates in a lyric.

> He came from out the Land of Graft
> 　To lend a hand to Llano,
> Its industry and handicraft,
> 　And added to its cargo.
>
> He quit the struggle in the bog,
> 　Where devil take the hindmost,
> He left the realm where dog eat dog,
> 　With Equity his guide-post.
>
> A better life the world to show,
> 　A work he tires of never,
> While men may come and men may go,
> 　Will he go on forever.

"Forever" was perhaps a little too optimistic. But the fact remains that, in due course, George T. Pickett did come back to Llano. In his *Can We Co-operate?* Bob Brown prints a letter from one of the surviving colonists, dated November, 1937. "Things in hell of a shape here. No food for the past week but sweet potatoes, and darn small ones at that. . . . No electricity for two months, and I buy plenty kerosene. . . . Very little money coming in, and what little there is Pickett takes it for his own use. Seems to think everything belongs to him. . . . Lots of people pretty mad here since Pickett took over again. . . . I expect few people on the outside would believe the truth about this place. Just try and tell some of those old friends, who sent money in through *The Colonist*, that one works 365 days a year in this Socialist paradise, then supplies one's own clothes, most of one's own food, light, etc., and they might say one was a liar."

Two years later it was finished. All the Colony property had been sold up, and the colonists (most of them old people who had invested their savings and their work in Llano for the sake of security in their declining years) were on relief. All that remained, after twenty-five years of idealistic struggle, was a small brick hotel and a recreation hall.

> And on the pedestal these words appear:
> "My name is Ozymandias, king of kings:
> Look on my work, ye Mighty, and despair!"

But *despair* is only the penultimate word, never the last. The last word is *realism*—the acceptance of facts as they present themselves, the facts of nature and of human nature, and the primordial fact of that spirit which transcends them both and yet is in all things. The original Ozymandias was no realist; nor was poor Mr. Harriman. In the conditions prevailing at Llano and, later, at New Llano, integral co-operation was as fatally condemned to self-destruction as are, in any circumstances, the ambitions of a king of kings. Fortunately, unrealistic co-operation does no harm except to the co-operators. Unrealistic imperialism, on the other hand, cannot commit suicide without inflicting misery and death upon innumerable victims.

The economic problems of community living can be solved by any group possessed of common sense and capital. The psychological problems are much more difficult and demand, for their solution, something rarer than either cash or shrewdness.

Life in a community is life in a crowd—the same old crowd, day in, day out. At Llano the colonists divided mankind into two groups—themselves and people "on the outside." The same distinction, in the same words, is made by convicts. "On the inside" we are; "on the outside" lies the whole wide world. Of those nineteenth-century American communities which survived long enough to rear a second generation of co-operators, few were able to resist the impact of the bicycle. Mounted on a pair of wheels, the young people were able to explore that unredeemed but fascinating world "on the outside." After each expedition, it was with mounting reluctance that they returned to the all too familiar crowd. In the end reluctance hardened into refusal. They went out one day and never came back.

The attraction of life "on the outside" can be counteracted in several ways. Shared religious faith is helpful, but not, of itself, enough. One can believe as the others believe, and yet detest the sight of them. "*Ave Virgo!*—Gr-rr—you swine!" Browning's fictional soliloquist is echoed, more decorously, by such real and historical figures as the saintly Dame Gertrude More. "Living in religion (as I can speak by experience), if one is not in a right course of prayer and other exercises between God and our soul, one's nature groweth much worse than it would have been if one had lived in the world." It grows worse because there is no escape from the objects of one's unreasoned abhorrence. "On the outside," we are constantly imitating the conduct of the Old Man in the limerick, "who purchased a steed, which he rode at full speed, to escape from the people of Basing." "On the inside," be it of Alcatraz, of Llano, of a cloister, there are no steeds; and unless they can learn the difficult art of being charitable, the inmates of such penal, socialistic or religious colonies will find themselves condemned to a life sentence of boredom, distaste and loathing. Vows, rules and a hierarchy can forcibly constrain a man to remain in his community. Only "a course of prayer, by which the soul turneth towards God and learneth from Him the lesson of truly humbling itself," can soften his heart to the point where it becomes susceptible of loving even his exasperating brothers.

At Llano shared religious faith was replaced, less effectively, by a vague Pickwickian belief that, thanks to Socialism, everything would be much better in the twenty-second century. "You've got to get up on some private hill to view the future. I've been on this job ten years, and there has been some real progress. But when I'm overwhelmed by the ugliness, the seemingly useless struggle of it all, I just climb up my hill and see the whole place as it should be."

More effective, as a binding force, than religious or Utopian belief, is the presence among the faithful of some dominant and fascinating personality. These are the human magnets, in relation to whom ordinary men and women behave like iron filings. Their attractive power is hard to analyze and explain. Impressiveness of appearance and high intelligence are sometimes present, but not invariably. A glittering eye, a mysterious manner, a disconcerting fluctuation between remoteness and concern—these are never amiss. A gift of the gab is useful, and becomes quite invaluable when combined with the right kind of voice—the kind of voice which seems to act directly on the autonomic nervous system and the subconscious mind. Finally, indispensably, there is the will of iron, there is the unswerving tenacity of purpose, the boundless self-confidence—all the qualities which are so conspicuously absent in the common run of anxious, bewildered and vacillating humanity. A community having capital, sound management and a leader possessed of magnetic qualities can hardly fail to survive.

Unfortunately (or rather, thank God!) the magnetic leader is not immortal. When his current is turned off, the iron filings fly apart, and yet another experiment in integral co-operation is at an end.

Is there any reason, someone may ask, why it should ever have been begun? For the Marxist, a religious community is anathema and a secular co-operative colony represents no more than "a working-class form of escape, corresponding to the white-collar boy's flight to Montparnasse." For the capitalist, any kind of integral co-operation is a gratuitous absurdity which might, if it worked too well, become dangerously subversive. But for anyone who is interested in human beings and their so largely unrealized potentialities, even the silliest experiment has value, if only as demonstrating what ought not to be done. And many of the recorded experiments were far from silly. Well planned and carried out with skill and intelligence, some of them have contributed significantly to our knowledge of that most difficult and most important of all the arts—the art of living together in harmony and with benefit for all concerned. Thus, the Shakers cultivated the sense of togetherness by means of the sacramental dance, through collective "speaking with tongues" and in spiritualistic séances, at which mediumship was free to all. The Perfectionists practiced mutual criticism—a drastic form of group therapy which often worked wonders, not only for neurotics, but even for the physically sick. Sex is "the lion of the tribe of human passions"; to tame the lion, John Humphrey Noyes devised, and for thirty years his community at Oneida put into effect, a system of "Complex Marriage," based upon "Male Continence." Separated, by means of a carefully inculcated technique, from propagation, the "amative function" was refined, taught good manners, reconciled with Protestant Christianity and made to serve the purpose of religious self-transcendence. "Amativeness," Noyes could truthfully write, "is conquered and civilized among us."* A similar conquest had been achieved, in India, by those Tantrik prophets, in whom the world-affirming spirit of the Vedas had come to terms, through sacramentalism, with the world-denying spirit of Jainism, Yoga and early Buddhism. In the West, however, Noyes's experiment stands alone not indeed in its intention (for many before him had tried to do the same thing), but in the realistic and therefore successful way it was carried out. The members of the Oneida Community seem to have been happier, healthier, better behaved and more genuinely religious than most of their contemporaries "on the outside." That they should have been forced, under the threat of ecclesiastical persecution, to abandon their experiment is a real misfortune. The course of Freudian and post-Freudian psychology would have run a good deal more smoothly, if there had been a place, like Oneida, where theorists might have tested their frequently preposterous notions against the realities of a co-operating group, in which the lion no longer raged and a reconciliation between sex, religion and society was an accomplished fact.

Except in a purely negative way, the history of Llano is sadly uninstructive. All that it teaches is a series of don'ts. Don't pin your faith on a water supply which, for half the time, isn't there. Don't settle a thousand people on territory which cannot possibly support more than a hundred. Don't admit to your fellowship every Tom, Dick and Harry who may present himself. Don't imagine that a miscellaneous group can live together, in closest physical proximity, without rules, without shared beliefs, without private and public "spiritual exercises" and, without a magnetic leader. At Llano everything that ought not to have been done was systematically done. A pathetic little Ozymandias is all that remains to tell the tale.

From where I used to live, on the fringes of what had been the colony's land, this Ozymandias was the only visible trace of human handiwork. Gleaming in the morning

* See Appendix.

light or black against the enormous desert sunsets, that silo was like a Norman keep rising, against all the probabilities, from the sagebrush. *The splendour falls on castle walls. Childe Roland to the dark tower came*—came, and looking through the opening in the dark tower's wall, saw within a heap of tin cans, some waste paper and half a dozen empty bottles of Pepsi-Cola. The ruin stands very close to the highway and there are still a few motorists prepared, at a pinch, to walk a quarter of a mile.

But Ozymandias is not the only relic of the co-operative past. Two or three miles to the southeast, on the almost obliterated wagon road over which the colonists once hauled their timber from the mountains, is the Socialist cemetery.

It lies astride of the four-thousand-foot contour line, that ecological frontier where the creosote bushes abruptly give place to junipers, the Joshua trees to common yuccas. One ancient and gigantic Joshua—the last outpost of the great army of Joshuas encamped on the side plains below the foothills—stands like a sentinel on guard over the dead. In a little tumbledown enclosure of wooden palings and chicken wire three or four anonymous mounds have returned completely to the desert.

On what was once bare and weeded ground, the sage and the buckwheat have taken root again and are flourishing as though they had never been disturbed. Nearby a concrete headstone commemorates someone who, to judge by his name, must have been of Scandinavian origin. His epitaph is purely quantitative, and all the inscription tells us is that he lived sixty-eight years, seven months, four days and eleven hours. The most pretentious of the tombs is a mausoleum in the form of a hollow cube of cement. Entering through the broken door one finds a slab, headstone and an incredible quantity of the desiccated droppings of small rodents. The dance goes on. A human pattern, made up of the patterns of patterns, is resolved into the simpler forms that are its elements. Another vortex catches and draws them into itself. Patterns are built up into patterns of a higher order, and for a few months a little pattern of these patterns of patterns hurries, squeaking, along the rat roads.

Outside, the Joshua tree stands guard in the empty sunlight, in the almost supernatural silence. A monstrous yucca at the limit of its natural habitat? A symbol within the cosmic symbol? The eye travels out across the plain. The buttes are like kneeling elephants and beyond them, far away, are the blue ghosts of mountains. There is a coolness against the cheek, and from overhead comes the scaly rattling of the wind in the dead dry leaves of the Joshua tree. And suddenly the symbol is essentially the same as what it symbolizes; the monstrous yucca in the desert is at once a botanical specimen and the essential Suchness. What we shall all know, according to the *Barbo Thodol*, at the moment of Death may also be known by casual flashes, transfiguringly, while we inhabit this particular pattern of patterns. There is a consciousness of the Pure Truth, like a light "moving across the landscape in springtime in one continuous stream of vibration." Be not afraid. For this "is the radiance of your own true nature. Recognize it." And from out of this light comes "the natural sound of Reality reverberating like a thousand thunders." But, again, be not afraid. For this is the natural sound of your own real self—a thousand thunders which have their source in silence and in some inexpressible way are identical with silence.

Liberty,
Quality, Machinery

John Ruskin deplored the railway engine. It might be useful; but why, why did it have to *look* like a railway engine? Why couldn't it be dressed up as a fiery dragon, breathing flames as it rushed along, and flapping iron wings? Machines, Ruskin thought, and all their productions are intrinsically hideous. If we must have them, let it be with Gothic trimmings.

To William Morris, power-driven contraptions were odious, even in fancy dress, even when disguised as wiverns or basilisks. He objected to them on aesthetic grounds, and, as a sociologist, he loathed them. In the process of creating ugliness and multiplying monotony, machines had destroyed the old order and were turning the men and women who tended them into brutes and automata. Morris's ideal was the Middle Ages. Not, it goes without saying, the real Middle Ages, but an improved Victorian version of Merrie England—clean, kindly and sensible, free from bad smells and religious dogmas, from bubonic plague and papal indulgences and periodic famines. A snug little world of healthy, virtuous craftsmen, craftswomen and craftschildren, producing not for somebody else's profit but for their own use and for the greater glory of God, and having, in the process, a really wonderful time.

Today we like to think of applied science as a kind of domesticated djinn, indentured to the service of the no-longer-toiling masses. Half a century ago Tolstoy saw in applied science the greatest threat to liberty, the most powerful instrument of oppression in the hands of tyrants. "If the arrangement of society is bad (as ours is) and if a small number of people have power over the majority and oppress them, every victory over Nature will inevitably serve to increase that power and that oppression. This is what is actually happening." It was for this reason (among others) that Tolstoy advocated a return to handicraft production within village communities, which were to be, as nearly as possible, self-sufficient. His greatest disciple, Mahatma Gandhi, preached the same doctrine—and lived long enough to see the nation, whose independence he had won, adopt a policy of all-out industrialization.

It is easy enough to detect the flaws in these classical arguments against machinery and in favor of a return to handicraft production. All of them fail to take into account the most important single fact of modern history—the rapid, the almost explosive increase in human numbers. Within the combined life spans of Tolstoy and Gandhi the population of the planet was more than trebled. Let us consider a few of the aesthetic, psychological and political consequences of this unprecedented event in human history.

By no means all the ugliness of which Ruskin and Morris

complained was due to the substitution of machine production for handicrafts. Much of it was simply the result of there being, every year, more and more people. Beyond a certain point, human beings cannot multiply without producing an environment which, at the best, is predominantly dreary, soul-stultifying and hideous, at the worst foul and squalid into the bargain. There have been beautiful cities of as many as two or three hundred thousand inhabitants. There has never been a beautiful city of a million or over. The old, unindustrialized parts of Cairo or Bombay are worse than fully industrialized London, or New York, or the Ruhr. Man cannot live satisfactorily by bricks and mortar alone. This would be true even if the bricks and mortar were put together in decent houses. In actual practice a little good architecture has always been surrounded, in the world's great capitals, by vast expanses of mean and dreary squalor. In the small cities of earlier centuries, filth and ugliness surrounded the splendid churches and palaces; but these slums were to be measured in acres, not in square miles. Small quantities of man-made squalor can be taken with impunity, particularly when associated with the woods and fields which surrounded the small city on every side, endowing it, as an urban unit, with a kind of over-all beauty of its own. This kind of over-all urban beauty has never existed in a great metropolis, most of which must always seem, by the mere fact that it goes on and on, unutterably dull, hideous and soul-destroying. What Ruskin and William Morris were really objecting to was the consequence, not of machinery, but of Victorian fertility combined with improved sanitation and cheap food from the New World. Families were large and, for the first time in history, most of their members survived infancy and grew up to produce large families of their own—and, in the process, to create hundreds of monster cities, tens of thousands of square miles of squalor and ugliness.

Thanks to the advanced technology of which Tolstoy and Gandhi so passionately disapproved, one third, more or less, of the earth's twenty-five hundred million inhabitants enjoy unprecedented prosperity and longevity, and the remaining two thirds contrive, however miserably, to remain alive, on the average, for thirty years or so. A return to handicraft production would entail the outright liquidation, within a few years, of at least a billion men, women and children. Moreover, if, while returning to handicraft production, we were to maintain our present standards of cleanliness and public health, numbers would tend once more to increase, and within half a century the liquidated billion would be back again, and ripe for new famines and another liquidation. Where Nature kills the majority of human beings in childhood, the practice of contraception is suicidal. But where human beings understand the principles of sanitation and where, consequently, most of the members of large families survive to become parents in their turn, it is unrestricted fertility that threatens to destroy not merely happiness and liberty, but, as numbers outrun resources, life itself. Generalized death control imposes the duty of generalized birth control. Gandhi was aware of the population problem and hoped (he can hardly have believed) that it could be solved by the inculcation of sexual continence among young married couples. In actual fact it is unlikely to be solved until such time as the physiologists and pharmacologists can provide the Asiatic and African masses with a contraceptive pill that can be swallowed, every few weeks, like an aspirin tablet. Within a generation of the discovery of such a pill, world population may be stabilized—somewhere, let us hope, on this side of five thousand millions. After which it may be possible to raise the standard of Far Eastern, Middle Eastern, Near Eastern, African and Caribbean living to levels somewhat less subhuman than those now prevailing—a feat which will require all man's good will, all his best intelligence and (far from a return to handicraft production) a yet more advanced technology.

But the fact that man cannot now survive without advanced technology does not mean that Tolstoy was entirely wrong. Every victory over Nature does unquestionably strengthen the position of the ruling minority. Modern oligarchs are incomparably better equipped than were their predecessors. Thanks to fingerprinting, punched cards and IBM machines, they know practically everything about practically everyone. Thanks to radios, planes, automobiles and the whole huge armory of modern weapons, they can apply force wherever it is called for, almost instantaneously. Thanks to the media of mass communication, they can browbeat, persuade, hypnotize, tell lies and suppress truth on a national, even a global scale. Thanks to hidden microphones and the arts of wire tapping, their spies are omnipresent. Thanks to their control of production and distribution, they can reward the faithful with jobs and sustenance, punish malcontents with unemployment and starvation. Reading the history, for example, of the French Revolution and Napoleon's dictatorship, one is constantly amazed at the easygoing ineptitude of earlier governmental procedures. Until very recent times such liberties as existed were assured, not by constitutional guarantees, but by the backwardness of technology and the blessed inefficiency of the ruling minority.

In the West our hard-won guarantees of personal liberty have not, so far, been offset by the political consequences of advancing technology. Applied science has put more power into the hands of the ruling few; but the many have been protected by law and, to make assurance doubly sure, have created (in the form of trade unions, cooperatives, political machines and lobbies) great systems of power to counterbalance the power systems of the industrialists, government officials and soldiers, who own or can command the resources of modern technology. Where, as in Russia or in Nazi Germany, the masses have not been protected by law and have been unable to create or maintain their own defensive power systems, Tolstoy's predictions have been fulfilled to the letter. Every victory over Nature has been at the same time a victory of the few over the many. And all the while the machinery of mass production is growing larger, more elaborate, increasingly expensive. In consequence its possession is coming to be confined more and more exclusively to the wielders of financial power and the wielders of political power—to big business, in a word, and big government. Never was there a greater need for the old Eternal Vigilance than exists today.

But here let us note a development entirely unforeseen by Ruskin and Morris, by Tolstoy, Gandhi and most even of the more recent philosophers and sociologists who have viewed with alarm man's increasing dependence on the machine as producer of necessities and luxuries, the dispenser of entertainment and distractions, the fabricator of synthetic works of art, of tin or plastic surrogates for the immemorial products of manual skill. While big machines have been growing spectacularly bigger, new races of dwarf machines have quietly come into existence and, at least in America, are now proliferating like rabbits. These little machines are for private individuals, not for the great organizations directed by the wielders of financial and political power. They are produced by big business; but their purpose, paradoxically enough, is to restore to the individual consumer some, at least, of that independence of big business which was his in that not-too-distant past, when there was no big business to depend on. Small power tools, in conjunction with new gadgets of every variety, new synthetic raw materials, new paints and putties, new solders and adhesives, have called into existence (and at the same time have been called into existence by) a new breed of artisans. These new artisans pass their working hours in a factory that turns out mass-produced goods, in an office that arranges for their distribution, in a store that sells them, a truck or train that delivers them to their destination. But in their spare time—and a forty-hour week leaves a good deal of spare time—they become craftsmen, using the tools and materials supplied by the mass producers, but working for themselves, either for the sheer fun of it, or because they cannot afford to pay someone else to do the job, or else (deriving pleasure from what they are forced to do by economic necessity) for both reasons at once.

The "do-it-yourself" movement has its comic aspects. But then so does almost everything else in this strange vale of tears and guffaws, which is the scene of our earthly pilgrimages. The important fact is not that amateur plumbing is a fruitful subject for the cartoonist, but that something is actually being done to solve, at least partially, some of the problems created by a technology rapidly advancing, in industry after industry, towards complete automation. Millions of persons have grown tired of being merely spectators or listeners, and have decided to fill their leisure with some kind of constructive activity. Most of this activity is utilitarian in character; but there are also many cases in which these new handicraft workers of the machine age supplement their utilitarian hobbies with the practice of one of the fine arts. There is a countless host, not only of amateur plumbers, but also of amateur sculptors, painters, ceramists. Never before has there been so general an interest in art (you can buy books on Picasso and Modigliani at the five-and-ten), and never before have there been so many wielders of paintbrushes and modelers of clay. Are we then (in spite of all that Ruskin and Morris and their followers said about machinery) on the threshold of a new Golden Age of creative achievement? I wonder. . . .

Art is not one thing, but many. Metaphysically speaking, it is a device for making sense of the chaos of experience, for imposing order, meaning and a measure of permanence on the incomprehensible flux of our perpetual perishing. The nature of the order imposed, of the significance discovered and expressed, depends upon the native endowments and the social heredity of the person who does the imposing, discovering and expressing. And this brings us to art as communication, art as the means whereby exceptionally gifted individuals convey to others their reactions to events, their insights into the nature of man and the universe, their visions of ideal order. All of us have such visions and insights; but whereas ours are commonplace, *theirs* are unique and enlightening. Art-as-communication is pretty pointless, unless the things communicated are worth communicating. But even in cases where they are not worth communicating, art is still valuable—if not to the persons who look at it, at least to those who produce it. For art is also a method of self-discovery and self-expression; an untier of knots, an unscrambler of confusions; a safety valve for blowing off emotional steam; a cathartic (the medical metaphor is as old as Aristotle) for purging the system of the products of the ego's constant auto-intoxication. Art-as-therapy is good for everybody—for children and the aged, for imbeciles and alcoholics, for neurotic adolescents and tired businessmen, for prime ministers on week ends and monarchs on the sly (Queen Victoria, for example, took drawing lessons from Edward Lear, the author of *The Book of Nonsense*). Art-as-therapy is even good for great artists.

> To me alone there came a thought of grief;
> A timely utterance gave that thought relief,
> And I again am strong.

Besides being a masterpiece of art-as-communication, Wordsworth's great Ode was also a (to him) most salutary dose of art-as-therapy. Involving, as they do, the highest manual skill, sculpture, painting and ceramics are more effective as therapy than is poetry, at any rate Western poetry. In China writing is a branch of painting— or perhaps it would be truer to say that painting is a branch of the fine art of writing. In the West the writing even of the noblest poem is a purely mechanical act and so can never afford psychological relief comparable to that which we obtain from an art involving manual skill.

The spread of amateur housebuilding, of amateur painting and sculpture, will soothe many tempers and prevent the onset of a host of neuroses, but it will not add appreciably to the sum of architectural, pictorial and plastic masterpieces. At every period of history the number of good artists has been very small, the number of bad and indifferent artists very great. Because immense numbers of people now practice art as therapy, it does not follow that there will be any noticeable increase in the output of masterpieces. Because I feel better for having expressed my feelings in a daub, it does not follow that you will feel better for looking at my daub. On the contrary, you may feel considerably worse. So let us practice art-as-therapy, but never exhibit the stuff as though it were art-as-communication.

We should not even expect to see an increase in the amount of good craftsmanship. In the past good craftsmanship has been contingent on two factors—intense and prolonged specialization in a single field, and ignorance of every style but that which happens to be locally dominant. Before the invention of foolproof machines nobody became an acknowledged master of his craft without going through a long apprenticeship. Moreover, the Jack of All Trades was, proverbially and almost by definition, the master of none. If you wanted to have your house thatched, you went to the thatcher; if you needed a table, you applied to the joiner. And so on. Specialization in the crafts and arts goes back to remotest antiquity. Archaeologists assure us that the great paleolithic cave paintings were executed, in all probability, by teams of traveling artists, whose native skill had been increased by constant practice. As for flint arrowheads, these were manufactured in places where the raw material was plentiful and distributed to consumers over enormous areas.

Our new artisans, with their power tools and amazingly diversified raw materials, are essentially Jacks of All Trades, and their work consequently is never likely to exhibit the kind of excellence which distinguishes the work of highly trained specialists in a single craft. Moreover, the older craftsmen took for granted the style in which they had been brought up and reproduced the old models with only the slightest modification. When they departed from the traditional style, their work was apt to be eccentric or even downright bad. Today we know too much to be willing to follow any single style. Scholarship and photography have placed the whole of human culture within our reach. The modern amateur craftsman or amateur artist finds himself solicited by a thousand different and incompatible models. Shall he imitate Pheidias or the Melanesians? Miró or Van Eyck? Being under no cultural compulsion to adopt any particular line, he selects, combines and blends. The result, in terms of art-as-significant-communication, is either negligible or monstrous, either an insipid hash or the most horrifying kind of raspberry, sardine and chocolate sundae. Never mind! As a piece of occupational therapy, as a guarantee against boredom and an antidote to TV and the other forms of passive entertainment, the thing is altogether admirable.

Censorship
and Spoken Literature

Peacefully coexisting, two forms of censorship are at work in the world today. In the totalitarian countries there is political censorship, deliberately enforced by the ruling oligarchy and its executive agencies. In the democratic countries there is no political censorship, except in regard to military secrets. Instead, we have economic censorship, which is being enforced, unintentionally and blindly, by the steady rise in the cost of producing books, plays and films.

Under totalitarianism, purposeful censorship goes hand in hand with purposeful, one-directional propaganda. Facts, ideas and attitudes, agreeable to the ruling oligarchy, are constantly harped upon and inculcated. Attitudes, ideas and facts of which the ruling oligarchy disapproves are either condemned or, more often, ignored, as though they did not exist. In the molding of public opinion sustained, systematic silence is at least as effective as systematically reiterated speech.

Where the government is democratic, speech and silence, propaganda and censorship are not prescribed by any single will. They simply happen under the influence of economic pressures and as a diversity of conflicting wills and interests may decide. These conflicting wills and interests are of several kinds—philosophical, religious, political and, above all, commercial. For every thousand words of printed or spoken commercial propaganda, we are treated to, possibly, one word of philosophical, ten of religious and fifty to a hundred words of political propaganda. And not only does money speak; it also imposes silence. Philosophers have no power of direct censorship, and politicians not much, except in the military field. Clergymen, it is true, have been able to compel the manufacturers of mass entertainment (but, fortunately, not the producers of books and plays) to conform to a curious little code of religious respectability and sexual make-believe. But the great silencer, the muffler attached to every channel of intellectual and artistic expression, is money. No evil director has willed this censorship. It has come about automatically and by accident. But, though unintentional, it is nonetheless effective and nonetheless harmful. What is the nature of this economic censorship and what can we do about it?

Twenty years ago a sale of two thousand copies was enough to recoup an American publisher for the costs of producing a book. Above that point, he was making a profit. In the countries of Western Europe the break-even point was still lower, and publishers found themselves earning money after a sale of only fifteen or even twelve hundred copies. Today an American publisher cannot break even on a sale of less than about seven thousand copies. In Western Europe the critical figure is slightly lower, but still at least three times what it used to be before the Second World War. The price of books has, of course, been considerably increased in recent years. Whether it can be increased much further seems doubtful. People will cheerfully pay four or five times as much as they used to pay for a dinner at their favorite restaurant; but they will not pay more than about twice, or two and a half times, as much as they used to pay for a good book by their favorite author. Sales resistance begins at two hundred per cent of prewar prices, but production costs stand at three hundred per cent. Profit can be made only when sales are substantial. Books are therefore subjected to an even more rigorous ordeal of economic selection. It is becoming increasingly difficult for any work which lacks the obvious earmarks of popularity to get published.

An analogous situation exists in the theater and the motion-picture industry. To stage the most modest play on Broadway costs about seventy thousand dollars, and from ten to twenty times that amount is needed for the production of a not very spectacular movie. Prices of admission have not risen proportionately to costs of production. If a profit is to be made, there must be longer runs and larger audiences than in the past. Whatever its intrinsic merit, the worst seller has no chance of being staged or screened, at any rate on Broadway or in Hollywood. In Western Europe the situation is somewhat better—but still bad enough to justify the gravest misgivings for the future.

The new economic censorship is directed, as we have seen, against any book unlikely to sell seven thousand copies or more, any play unlikely to fill a theater for at least three or four months, any movie unlikely to "pack them in" to the tune of several millions.

The exponents of Communism and Moral Rearmament are agreed on one point—the primary importance of the theater as an instrument of propaganda. Behind the Iron Curtain ideologically correct plays are used as weapons in the Cold War, while, for *their* campaigns, the Moral Rearmers have a whole arsenal of Christian *Oklahomas* and ethical *Cats on Hot Tin Roofs*. Whether the drama is really as effective in molding opinion as Dr. Buchman and the Russians believe, it is hard indeed to say. Personally I doubt it. People go to the theater in order to have their emotions excited and, when the excitement has lasted long enough, cathartically appeased. The excitement and the appeasement make up a single self-contained experience, having little or no relevance to the non-emotional aspects of the spectator's life. Voltaire, for example, was the author of a number of tragedies, highly esteemed in their day; but it was by his pamphlets, his metaphysical treatises, his articles in the Encyclopedia that he left his mark on the world. Whether deliberate or unintentional, censorship is always undesirable. There are, however, certain fields in which it does less damage than in others. As a medium for conveying important information and expounding significant ideas, the drama is not so effective as the essay, the treatise or even the fictional narrative with digressions. Consequently the prevailing economic censorship of plays, movies and television shows is not so serious a matter as the corresponding censorship of books and periodicals.

Economic censorship can be circumvented in a number of ways. The simplest and most obvious method is the granting of a subsidy. The subsidy may be provided by the author—if he is rich enough. Or by the publishers—if they care sufficiently for worst-selling artistic merit or unpopular notions, and if they have had enough bad luck with the book clubs, or possess a large enough captive audience for their textbooks, to be able to implement their good intentions. Alternatively the subsidy may come from some foundation, whose directors regard it as part of their duty to encourage literary experimentation and the dissemination of unpopular ideas. Finally the money may, conceivably, be put up by a commercial sponsor, who is ready to take the risk of having his advertisements associated with an obscure, unorthodox and worst-selling piece of literature. As a general rule, of course, commercial sponsorship is forthcoming only for the work which has the least need of it. To those who have popularity shall be given the princely largess of the advertising agencies. From those who have it not shall be taken away all hope of ever getting published.

At the present time most of the serious monthlies and quarterlies of the democratic West are subsidized. The censorship imposed by rising costs is so effective that, if there were no "angels," there would be no worst-selling literature to leaven the enormous lump of intellectual and artistic conformity. But angelic intervention on the part of rich individuals or foundations offers only a partial and not entirely satisfactory solution to the problem of economic censorship. It would be far better for all concerned if the business of publishing could be made self-supporting, or at least as nearly self-supporting as it used to be in the not-too-distant past. The problem here is primarily a technical one. How can books be produced so cheaply as to warrant the publication of a worst seller?

Typesetting, even in its most highly mechanized form, is a slow and very costly procedure. Someday, it may be, a much cheaper photographic alternative to typesetting may be developed. At present the available alternatives are almost as expensive as typesetting and their general adoption would help hardly at all to solve the problems of economic censorship.

But if publishers can no longer afford to manufacture and distribute worst sellers, why shouldn't the job be done by the authors? In the Middle Ages an author had no choice in the matter; he *had* to be his own publisher. Petrarch and Boccaccio, for example, made manuscript copies of their own writings and even had time, between books, to make copies of works by classical authors. Thanks to the type-writer and the duplicating machine, a writer can now quite easily make hundreds of copies of his book. From carpentry, plumbing and electronics, the "do it yourself" movement is bound to pass, as the economic censorship becomes more and more rigorous, to book production and publishing. School magazines and the journals of small, impecunious scientific associations are already being published in this "do it yourself" way. Within a few years we may expect to see co-operative societies of unpopular authors, mimeographing their works and selling them by mail to the select few who take an interest in artistic experimentation and are not afraid of "dangerous thoughts."

Modern technology has resuscitated the author-scribe. Carrying us a stage further back in the history of culture, it is now in process of rescuing from oblivion the Homeric author-bard and the wandering minstrel of the Middle Ages. Members of these now-extinct species were to be met with, in the English countryside, as late as the seventeenth century. "When I was a boy," writes John Aubrey, who was born in 1625, "every Gentleman almost kept a Harper in his house." Harpers made a certain amount of music; but their main function was to intone from memory those interminable ballads in which the most striking events of remote and recent history had been recorded, sometimes by the harpers themselves—for "some of them," Aubrey tells us, "could versify." In Catholic monasteries there were no harpers; but at every meal one of the brethren read aloud to the assembled community something edifying from the Lives of the Saints or the works of the Church Fathers.

The modern hostess would do well to take a tip from St. Benedict. How pleasant even the most drearily uncongenial dinner party would be if we could cut out the small talk and listen to a reading from some intelligent book! And this, precisely, is what modern technology has made physically possible and what its further advance will make economically feasible to an ever-increasing extent. For the blind, there exists already a whole library of talking books, which can be played on a phonograph. These talking books are not available to members of the general public, who must be content with the score or two of readings listed, at exorbitantly high prices, in the record catalogues. If the Homeric bard is to be called back to life, if the minstrel and the monastic lector are to be restored to the position they should never have lost, we must find a way of selling the spoken word at a cheaper rate. Technically the problem can be solved without the slightest difficulty. It is merely a matter of reducing the speed at which records are made to revolve. At least one company manufactures phonographs with turntables which can be run at half the speed of the conventional record player. And this is not the lowest speed at which the speaking voice can be adequately reproduced. With a good needle one can get satisfactory speech recording at eight or even six revolutions a minute. At this rate it would be possible to make a pressing of a fair-sized book on two twelve-inch records.

In time, no doubt, tape recorders and the actual tapes themselves will be drastically cheapened. For the moment, however, it looks as though we must depend on the vinylite record and the slow-speed phonograph for any large-scale revival of spoken literature.

But why, it may be asked, should we wish to revive spoken literature? There are a number of sound reasons. First of all, it may soon come to be actually cheaper to publish a book on a slow-playing record than to publish it in a printed volume. The cost of making the matrices from which two slow-playing records can be pressed is far lower than the cost of setting up a sixty-thousand-word book and making the plates from which it will be printed. When the technicians have done the job required of them, worst-selling authors will have a way of defying the economic censorship on their works.

And this is not the only, nor even perhaps the most important, reason for desiring a revival of spoken literature. In this universally educated population vast numbers never read, or read only the most rudimentary kinds of sub-literature and Neanderthal journalism. Many of these illiterates are the victims of a theory of education, which has carried a praiseworthy concern with synthesis and wholeness to the grotesque point, where it is regarded as improper to teach a child how to analyze a word into its constituent letters. The result, as Mr. Rudolph Flesch has pointed out in his lively book *Why Johnny Can't Read*, is that thousands upon thousands of boys and girls spend ten years at school without fully mastering an art which, under the old analytical methods of teaching, was in most cases perfectly well understood by the age of five or six. To the hosts of non-readers and poor readers must be added all the radio and television addicts who have never acquired the habit of reading and whose reaction to a book in a hard cover is one of mistrust and a kind of fear. Seeing it, they *know*, without further investigation, that it is not for them—that if they tried to read it, they would understand nothing and be bored to death. But it can be shown experimentally that, if you can get these non-readers, poor readers or reluctant readers to listen to someone else reading aloud from a book which they themselves would never dream of opening, many of them will not only understand what is being read, but will become passionately interested in it.

Ours is a world in which knowledge accumulates and wisdom decays. Inevitably so; for advancing science and technology require the services of specialists, to each of whom is assigned the job (and it is a whole-time, a more than whole-time job) of mastering the intricacies of his particular field and keeping up with the changes in theory and practice brought about by scientific discovery and technical invention. That such specialists may and often do become highly trained barbarians has been, for some years past, the growing concern of educators. To civilize our future physicists and chemists and engineers, our doctors to be, our lawyers and actuaries and managers in the bud, the heads of most universities and technical schools have insisted that specialist training be accompanied and preceded by a course in the humanities. The intentions here are excellent; but what are the results? Not, I would guess from casual observation, entirely satisfactory. And the reason, it seems to me, is that the humanities, in so far as they are genuinely humane, do not lend themselves to being taught with an eye to future examinations and the accumulation of credits. If specialists are to be civilized— and it is imperative that they should be civilized, and civilized, what is more, on every level of the hierarchy, from garage mechanic up to atomic physicist—something less formal, less formidable and, above all, less silly than credit-gaining courses in insight, evaluation and life wisdom should be offered. If marks are to be given, a great deal of time will have to be wasted on the question, so dear to pedants, but so totally beside the point: Who influenced whom to say what when? Whereas the only question that really matters, the only question whose correct answer can exert a civilizing influence on the future specialist, is the question asked by Buddha and Jesus, by Lao-tsu and Socrates, by Job and Aeschylus, and Chaucer and Shakespeare and Dostoevsky, by every philosopher, every mystic, every great artist: Who am I and what, if anything, can I do about it? Implicitly, this question is asked and answered (needless to say, incorrectly) by those anonymous writers of advertising copy, whose words are read and listened to more frequently and by greater numbers of people than the words of any saint or sage, any sacred book or divine revelation. The problem which confronts the educator can be summed up in a few sentences. Shall we allow the advertisers in the democratic countries and the ruling oligarchies under totalitarianism to enjoy a monopoly in formulating the popular philosophy of life? Shall we, in the higher ranks of the specialists' hierarchy, allow the unrealistic "Nothing-But" philosophies, now fashionable in scientific circles, to pass unquestioned? And, if the answer is, No, is there any better way of imparting the immemorial wisdom of mankind than the current method of offering credit-gaining courses in the humanities? To this last and most practical question, my own answer would be that there is such a way. Let there be lectures of orientation within the field of the humanities; but rely for your civilizing influence on a constant and informal exposure of the pupil to the actual utterances of those men and women of the past who have had the greatest insight and the greatest power of expressing that insight. This constant and informal exposure to wisdom is most effective when the words of wisdom are spoken, not read. Except by very few, very recent writers, poetry has always been composed in order to be recited or read aloud. And the same is true of what we may call the literature of wisdom. Most of the saints and sages have taught by word of mouth; and even when they committed them to paper, their words (as anyone can discover for himself) are more effective, have a greater degree of penetrative force, when they are heard than when they are seen on the printed page. And this is true, I believe, not only of sacred and devotional writings, but also of secular wisdom. Listen to the reading aloud of an essay by Bacon or Emerson, by Hume or Bagehot or Russell or Santayana; you will find yourself getting more out of it than you got when you read it to yourself—particularly if you were compelled to read it under the threat of not getting a credit. Printed, the Hundred Great Books are apt to remain unopened on the library shelves. Recorded (in part—for heaven forbid that anyone should waste his voice on recording them all, or recording each one in its entirety), they can be listened to painlessly—at meals, while washing up, as a substitute for the evening paper, in bed on a Sunday morning—and with a degree of understanding, of sympathy and acceptance rarely evoked in the average reader by the printed page. To any foundation in any way interested in the problems which beset an urban-industrial society in a state of technological, intellectual and ethical flux, I would make the following recommendations. Make the best of mankind's literature of wisdom available on cheap, slow-playing records. Do the same, in each of the principal languages, for the best poetry written in that language. Also, perhaps, for a few of the best novels, plays, biographies and memoirs. Encourage manufacturers to turn out phonographs equipped to play these recordings and at the same time arrange for distribution at cost of the simple planetary gears, by means of which conventional turntables can be used for slow-playing disks. Five or ten millions spent in this way would I am convinced, do incomparably more good than hundreds of millions spent on endowing new universities or enlarging those that already exist.

Canned Fish

An enormous new building had been added to the cannery. From now on, in straight-line and continuous production, six hundred women would daily convert three hundred and fifty tons of frozen carcasses into seven hundred thousand tins of tuna. Today the new facilities were being dedicated.

It was a solemn occasion. A rostrum had been erected on the wharf outside the factory. Bunting flapped in the fishy breeze. Mayors, senators, vice-governors were on hand to say a few well-chosen words. The new cannery, it appeared, was a triumph not only of technology, but also and above all of Private Enterprise, of the American Way of Life. It represented, we were told, two million dollars' worth of faith in the Future, of fidelity to the Past, of belief in Progress, of trust in . . . But listening to eloquence is something I have never been very good at. I looked at my companion, and my companion looked at me. Without a word we rose and tiptoed away.

A friendly engineer offered to show us round the factory. We began with the thawing tanks, into which the ocean-going trawlers discharge their refrigerated cargo. Next came the butchering tables, where the great fish are cleaned, and from which their heads, guts and tails are spirited away across the street, to a processing plant that transforms them (not without an overpowering stench) into fish meal for poultry. From the butchering tables we moved to the huge pressure cookers, the cooling shelves, the long conveyor belts of stainless steel, the machines for filling the cans, the machines for sealing and sterilizing the cans, the machines for labeling the cans, the machines for packing the cans in cartons.

So far as tunas were concerned, this was a holiday. The factory was empty; our voices reverberated in a cathedral silence. But next door, in the mackerel department, the work of canning was in full swing. Standing at an immensely long workbench, a line of overalled women receded into the dim distance. Beyond the bench was a trough full of rapidly flowing water, and beyond the trough were the conveyor belt and, above it, on a shelf, an inexhaustible reservoir of empty cans. From an upper story, where, invisible to us, the butchering was evidently going on, a wide-mouthed pipe descended perpendicularly. About once every minute a plug was pulled and a cataract came rushing down the pipe. Floating in the water were thousands of cross sections of mackerel. At breakneck speed they were whirled along the trough. As they passed, each woman reached out a gloved hand and dragged ashore as much as she needed for the five or six cans that she would fill before the next discharge. The cross sections were rammed into place—a big chunk, a smaller chunk, a tiny chunk, whatever piece would fit into the three-dimensional jigsaw—and the tightly packed can was placed on the conveyor belt, along which it moved, unhurrying, toward the weighers, the sealers, the sterilizers, labelers and craters. I clocked the performance and found that it took from ten to fifteen seconds to fill a can. Three hundred, on an average, every hour; two thousand four hundred in the course of a working day; twelve thousand a week.

Outside, in the hazy sunshine, a dignitary of some sort was still talking. "Liberty," he declaimed, and a second, distant loud-speaker repeated the overlapping syllables: "Liberty—berty."

Once more the plug was pulled. Another Niagara of water and sliced fish came rushing down the flume.

"Oppor—opportunity," bawled the loud-speakers. "Way of life—of life."

Buried in every language are nodules of petrified poetry, rich and unsuspected veins of fossil wisdom. Consider, for example, the French word *travail*. It is derived from Late Latin *trepalium*, the name of a kind of rack used for punishing criminals or persuading reluctant witnesses. Etymologically, work is the equivalent of torture. In English we preserve the word's original sense in relation to obstetrics (a woman "in travail") and have endowed it with the secondary meaning, not of work, but of wayfaring. Journeys in the Middle Ages were exhausting and dangerous. "Travel" is *trepalium*—torment for tourists.

The word "work" is emotionally neutral; but "toil" and the now obsolete "swink" carry unpleasant overtones. It was the same in the languages of classical antiquity. *Ponos* in Greek and *labor* in Latin signify both "work" and "suffering." "And Rachel travailed," we read in the Book of Genesis, "and she had hard labor." Two words for work, two words for pain. Moreover, when Modern English "labor" carries its primary meaning, it generally stands for work of the most disagreeable kind—compulsory work, as in the case of penal "hard labor," or the heavy, unskilled work which is performed by "laborers."

Backward-looking sentimentalists are never tired of telling us that in the Middle Ages, work was all joy and spontaneous creativity. Then what, one may ask, could have induced our ancestors to equate labor with anguish? And why, when they wanted a name for work, did they borrow it from the torture chamber?

> Who first invented work, and bound the free
> And holiday-rejoicing spirit down
> To the ever-haunting importunity
> Of business in the green fields, and the town—
> To plow, loom, anvil, spade—and, oh! most sad,
> To that dry drudgery of the desk's dry wood?
> Who but the Being unblest, alien from good,
> Sabbathless Satan, he who his unglad
> Task ever plies 'mid rotatory burnings,
> That round and round incalculably reel—
> For wrath divine hath made him like a wheel—
> In that red realm from which are no returnings,
> Where toiling and turmoiling ever and aye,
> He and his thoughts keep pensive working-day.

Lamb was quite right. In every civilization work, for all but a favored few, has always been a thing of hideous dreariness, an infernal monotony of boredom at the best and, at the worst, of discomfort or even sheer anguish. One remembers the description, in *The Golden Ass,* of the animals and humans who worked, while the owner's wife amused herself with magic and adultery, at the flour mill.

Men and asses, mules and boys—they were all in travail, all on the *trepalium*, bruised, galled, strained beyond the limits of organic endurance. And the life of laborers in a medieval village, the life of journeymen and apprentices in the workshop of a master craftsman in the town, was hardly less dismal than that of their pre-Christian ancestors. In its beginnings industrialization merely aggravated an already intolerable state of affairs. The physical tortures imposed in the dark satanic mills of Georgian and Early Victorian England were worse, because more systematic, better organized, than the travail of earlier centuries. Thanks to automatic machines and labor laws, thanks to trade unions and the internal-combustion engine, thanks to hoists and belts and humanitarianism, there are now few tasks which actually hurt. The rack has been abolished. But the boredom, the frightful punctuality of wheels returning again and again to the same old position—these remain. Remain under free enterprise, remain under Socialism, remain under Communism.

Under the present technological dispensations the opportunity to escape from the tyranny of repetition comes only to a very small minority. But with the multiplication of fully automatic machines, fully automatic factories, even fully automatic industries, the case will be altered. Some of those now condemned to the task of keeping time with wheels will become the highly skilled doctors and nurses of the new, all-but-human gadgets. The rest will do—what? It remains to be seen. Only one thing seems tolerably certain. Owing to the deplorable lack of quantitative and qualitative uniformity displayed by living organisms, the fish-canning industry will be one of the last to become fully automatic. The technical procedures current today will probably be current, with only trifling modifications, a generation from now. Should we rejoice over this island of stability in a flux of change? Or should we lament? In another twenty-five or thirty years we may be in a position to answer.

And meanwhile what will have happened to the raw material of our industry? What, in a word, will the fish be up to? A generation ago the biologist and the commercial fisherman would have answered, without hesitation: "If they aren't overfished, they will be doing exactly what they are doing now." Times have changed, and today the answer to our question would probably be: "Goodness only knows." For in recent years fishes have been behaving in the most eccentric and indecorous manner. Consider, for example, the European tuna. Forty years ago individual specimens of *Thunnus thynnus* were caught, at certain seasons, in the English Channel and the North Sea; but there was no tuna-packing industry north of Portugal, and the main supply of tinned or salted tunny came from the Mediterranean islands of Sardinia and Sicily. Today there is a flourishing tunny industry in Norway.

And the tuna's is by no means an isolated or exceptional case. Fishes which, not long ago, were thought of as being exclusively tropical, are now caught off the New England coast, and fishes once regarded as natives of the temperate zone have moved into the Arctic. The North Sea has ceased to be the great fishing ground of Western Europe. Today ocean-going trawlers, equipped with freezing units, make long voyages to the coasts of Iceland and northernmost Scandinavia. The Eskimos of Greenland have given up their traditional occupation, the hunting of seals, and have taken instead to fishing for cod. What were once regarded as immutable behavior patterns have changed, almost over-night. The world of fishes is in a state of revolution. Within the next twenty or thirty years the strangest things may happen in that world—with incalculable results for all concerned in the catching and processing of sea food.

This revolution in the watery world of the fish is a consequence of a larger revolution in the earth's atmosphere— a revolution which is changing the climate of the northern hemisphere and is likely to affect profoundly the course of human history during the next few generations or even centuries. The causes of this climatic revolution are obscure, but its effects are manifest. The glaciers are everywhere melting. The snow pack on the mountains has diminished to such an extent that the Jungfrau is now thirty feet lower than it used to be when I was a boy. The Spizbergen Archipelago, which used to be open for shipping for about four months out of the twelve, is now open for eight or nine. Russian icebreakers and cargo ships sail the once impassable seas that wash the northern coasts of the Soviet empire. In Canada and Siberia agriculture is moving steadily into higher and higher latitudes. Plants, birds and mammals, hitherto unknown in those regions, have now made their entrance and may soon take the place of the cold-loving species which are beginning to find their environment uncomfortably balmy.

This sort of thing, we should remember, has happened before, not merely in the remote geological past, but in quite recent historical times. In the early Middle Ages, Europe (and presumably the rest of the northern hemisphere) enjoyed two or three centuries of most unusual weather. There was enough sunshine in southern England to ripen grapes, and for four or five generations it was possible to drink British wine. Then, about the time of Chaucer, the climate changed again, and for a couple of centuries Europe experienced the rigors of what has been called the Little Ice Age. In Denmark and northern Germany many villages had to be abandoned. In Iceland the cultivation of cereals became impossible, and the fields, in many cases, were covered by the encroaching glaciers. Today the glaciers are in full retreat, and there is every reason to believe that in a few years rye and barley will once more be grown, to the further enrichment of a country which has already profited by the migration to its shores of innumerable fishes fleeing from the increasing warmth of the North Sea.

But if the high latitudes of the northern hemisphere become pleasantly warmer, does it not follow that the low latitudes will grow most *un*pleasantly hotter? There are some indications that this may be actually happening. In Africa, north of the equator, forests are giving place to savannas, and savannas are drying up into deserts. And what of the long, hardly intermitted drought, from which large areas of the American Southwest have recently been suffering? Is this the usual kind of cyclical dry spell, or does it presage a relatively permanent worsening of an arid or semiarid climate? Time alone will show. Meanwhile, if I had a few millions to invest for the benefit of my grandchildren, I would put them all into Canada rather than Texas. "Westward the course of empire takes its way." So wrote the good Bishop Berkeley two centuries ago. Reincarnated today, the philosopher-poet would probably turn his prophetic eyes ninety degrees to the right. Westward no longer, but northward, northward moves the course of empire. The tunas, the pilchards, the sharks and codfish— these forward-looking pioneers have already made the move, or at least are swimming in the right direction. In ever-increasing numbers, men will soon be following their example.

Tomorrow
and Tomorrow and Tomorrow

Between 1800 and 1900 the doctrine of Pie in the Sky gave place, in a majority of Western minds, to the doctrine of Pie on the Earth. The motivating and compensatory Future came to be regarded, not as a state of disembodied happiness, to be enjoyed by me and my friends after death, but as a condition of terrestrial well-being for my children or (if that seemed a bit too optimistic) my grandchildren, or maybe my great-grandchildren. The believers in Pie in the Sky consoled themselves for all their present miseries by the thought of posthumous bliss, and whenever they felt inclined to make other people more miserable than themselves (which was most of the time), they justified their crusades and persecutions by proclaiming, in St. Augustine's delicious phrase, that they were practicing a "benignant asperity," which would ensure the eternal welfare of souls through the destruction or torture of mere bodies in the inferior dimensions of space and time. In our days, the revolutionary believers in Pie on the Earth console themselves for *their* miseries by thinking of the wonderful time people will be having a hundred years from now, and then go on to justify wholesale liquidations and enslavements by pointing to the nobler, humaner world which these atrocities will somehow or other call into existence.

Not all the believers in Pie on the Earth are revolutionaries, just as not all believers in Pie in the Sky were persecutors. Those who think mainly of other people's future life tend to become proselytisers, crusaders and heresy hunters. Those who think mainly of their own future life become resigned. The preaching of Wesley and his followers had the effect of reconciling the first generations of industrial workers to their intolerable lot and helped to preserve England from the horrors of a full-blown political revolution.

Today the thought of their great-grandchildren's happiness in the twenty-first century consoles the disillusioned beneficiaries of progress and immunizes them against Communist propaganda. The writers of advertising copy are doing for this generation what the Methodists did for the victims of the first Industrial Revolution.

The literature of the Future and of that equivalent of the Future, the Remote, is enormous. By now the bibliography of Utopia must run into thousands of items. Moralists and political reformers, satirists and science fictioneers —all have contributed their quota to the stock of imaginary worlds. Less picturesque, but more enlightening, than these products of phantasy and idealistic zeal are the forecasts made by sober and well-informed men of science. Three very important prophetic works of this kind have appeared within the last two or three years—*The Challenge of Man's Future* by Harrison Brown, *The Foreseeable Future* by Sir George Thomson, and *The Next Million Years* by Sir Charles Darwin. Sir George and Sir Charles are physicists and Mr. Brown is a distinguished chemist. Still more important, each of the three is something more and better than a specialist.

Let us begin with the longest look into the future—*The Next Million Years.* Paradoxically enough, it is easier, in some ways, to guess what is going to happen in the course of ten thousand centuries than to guess what is going to happen in the course of one century. Why is it that no fortune tellers are millionaires and that no insurance companies go bankrupt? Their business is the same—foreseeing the future. But whereas the members of one group succeed all the time, the members of the other group succeed, if at all, only occasionally. The reason is simple. Insurance companies deal with statistical averages. Fortune tellers are concerned with particular cases. One can predict with a high degree of precision what is going to happen in regard to very large numbers of things or people. To predict what is going to happen to any particular thing or person is for most of us quite impossible and even for the specially gifted minority, exceedingly difficult. The history of the next century involves very large numbers; consequently it is possible to make certain predictions about it with a fairly high degree of certainty. But though we can pretty confidently say that there will be revolutions, battles, massacres, hurricanes, droughts, floods, bumper crops and bad harvests, we cannot specify the dates of these events nor the exact locations, nor their immediate, short-range consequences. But when we take the longer view and consider the much greater numbers involved in the history of the next ten thousand centuries, we find that these ups and downs of human and natural happenings tend to cancel out, so that it becomes possible to plot a curve representing the average of future history, the mean between ages of creativity and ages of decadence, between propitious and unpropitious circumstances, between fluctuating triumph and disaster. This is the actuarial approach to prophecy—sound on the large scale and reliable on the average. It is the kind of approach which permits the prophet to say that there will be dark handsome men in the lives of x per cent of women, but not which particular woman will succumb.

A domesticated animal is an animal which has a master who is in a position to teach it tricks, to sterilize it or compel it to breed as he sees fit. Human beings have no masters. Even in his most highly civilized state, Man is a wild species, breeding at random and always propagating his kind to the limit of available food supplies. The amount of available food may be increased by the opening up of new land, by the sudden disappearance, owing to famine, disease or war, of a considerable fraction of the population, or by improvements in agriculture. At any given period of history there is a practical limit to the food supply currently available. Moreover, natural processes and the size of the planet being what they are, there is an absolute limit, which can never be passed. Being a wild species, Man will always tend to breed up to the limits of the moment. Consequently very many members of the species must always live on the verge of starvation. This has happened in the past, is happening at the present time, when about sixteen hundred millions of men, women and children are more or less seriously undernourished, and will go on happening for the next million years—by which time we may expect that the species Homo sapiens will have turned into some other species, unpredictably unlike ourselves but still, of course, subject to the laws governing the lives of wild animals.

We may not appreciate the fact; but a fact nevertheless it remains: we are living in a Golden Age, the most gilded Golden Age of human history—not only of past history, but of future history. For, as Sir Charles Darwin and many others before him have pointed out, we are living like drunken sailors, like the irresponsible heirs of a millionaire uncle. At an ever accelerating rate we are now squandering the capital of metallic ores and fossil fuels accumulated in the earth's crust during hundreds of millions of years. How long can this spending spree go on? Estimates vary. But all are agreed that within a few centuries or at most a few millennia, Man will have run through his capital and will be compelled to live, for the remaining nine thousand nine hundred and seventy or eighty centuries of his career as Homo sapiens, strictly on income. Sir Charles is of the opinion that Man will successfully make the transition from rich ores to poor ores and even sea water, from coal, oil, uranium and thorium to solar energy and alcohol derived from plants. About as much energy as is now available can be derived from the new sources—but with a far greater expense in man hours, a much larger capital investment in machinery. And the same holds true of the raw materials on which industrial civilization depends. By doing a great deal more work than they are doing now, men will contrive to extract the diluted dregs of the planet's metallic wealth or will fabricate non-metallic substitutes for the elements they have completely used up. In such an event, some human beings will still live fairly well, but not in the style to which we, the squanderers of planetary capital, are accustomed.

Mr. Harrison Brown has his doubts about the ability of the human race to make the transition to new and less concentrated sources of energy and raw materials. As he

sees it, there are three possibilities. "The first and by far
the most likely pattern is a return to agrarian existence."
This return, says Mr. Brown, will almost certainly take
place unless Man is able not only to make the technological transition to new energy sources and new raw materials, but also to abolish war and at the same time
stabilize his population. Sir Charles, incidentally, is convinced that Man will never succeed in stabilizing his population. Birth control may be practiced here and there for
brief periods. But any nation which limits its population
will ultimately be crowded out by nations which have not
limited theirs. Moreover, by reducing cut-throat competition within the society which practices it, birth control re-
stricts the action of natural selection. But wherever natural
selection is not allowed free play, biological degeneration
rapidly sets in. And then there are the short-range, practical difficulties. The rulers of sovereign states have never
been able to agree on a common policy in relation to
economics, to disarmament, to civil liberties. Is it likely,
is it even conceivable, that they will agree on a common
policy in relation to the much more ticklish matter of birth
control? The answer would seem to be in the negative.
And if, by a miracle, they should agree, or if a world government should someday come into existence, how could a
policy of birth control be enforced? Answer: only by totalitarian methods and, even so, pretty ineffectively.

Let us return to Mr. Brown and the second of his alternative futures. "There is a possibility," he writes, "that sta-
bilization of population can be achieved, that war can
be avoided, and that the resource transition can be successfully negotiated. In that event mankind will be confronted
with a pattern which looms on the horizon of events as the
second most likely possibility—the completely controlled,
collectivized industrial society." (Such a future society was
described in my own fictional essay in Utopianism, *Brave
New World*.)

"The third possibility confronting mankind is that of a
world-wide free industrial society, in which human beings
can live in reasonable harmony with their environment."
This is a cheering prospect; but Mr. Brown quickly chills our
optimism by adding that "it is unlikely that such a pattern
can exist for long. It certainly will be difficult to achieve,

and it clearly will be difficult to maintain once it is established."

From these rather dismal speculations about the remoter future it is a relief to turn to Sir George Thomson's prophetic view of what remains of the present Golden Age. So far as easily available power and raw materials are concerned, Western man never had it so good as he has it now and, unless he should choose in the interval to wipe himself out, as he will go on having it for the next three, or five, or perhaps even ten generations. Between the present and the year 2050, when the population of the planet will be at least five billions and perhaps as much as eight billions, atomic power will be added to the power derived from coal, oil and falling water, and Man will dispose of more mechanical slaves than ever before. He will fly at three times the speed of sound, he will travel at seventy knots in submarine liners, he will solve hitherto insoluble problems by means of electronic thinking machines. High-grade metallic ores will still be plentiful, and research in physics and chemistry will teach men how to use them more effectively and will provide at the same time a host of new synthetic materials. Meanwhile the biologists will not be idle. Various algae, bacteria and fungi will be domesticated, selectively bred and set to work to produce various kinds of food and to perform feats of chemical synthesis, which would otherwise be prohibitively expensive. More picturesquely (for Sir George is a man of imagination), new breeds of monkeys will be developed, capable of performing the more troublesome kinds of agricultural work, such as picking fruit, cotton and coffee. Electron beams will be directed onto particular areas of plant and animal chromosomes and, in this way, it may become possible to produce controlled mutations. In the field of medicine, cancer may finally be prevented, while senility ("the whole business of old age is odd and little understood") may be postponed, perhaps almost indefinitely. "Success," adds Sir George, "will come, when it does, from some quite unexpected directions; some discovery in physiology will alter present ideas as to how and why cells grow and divide in the healthy body, and with the right fundamental knowledge, enlightenment will come. It is only the rather easy superficial problems that can be solved by working on them directly; others depend on still undiscovered fundamental knowledge and are hopeless till this has been acquired."

All in all, the prospects for the industrialized minority of mankind are, in the short run, remarkably bright. Provided we refrain from the suicide of war, we can look forward to very good times indeed. That we shall be discontented with our good time goes without saying. Every gain made by individuals or societies is almost instantly taken for granted. The luminous ceiling towards which we raise our longing eyes becomes, when we have climbed to the next floor, a stretch of disregarded linoleum beneath our feet. But the right to disillusionment is as fundamental as any other in the catalogue. (Actually the right to the pursuit of happiness is nothing else than the right to disillusionment phrased in another way.)

Turning now from the industrialized minority to that vast majority inhabiting the underdeveloped countries, the immediate prospects are much less reassuring. Population in these countries is increasing by more than twenty millions a year and in Asia at least, according to the best recent estimates, the production of food per head is now ten per cent less than it used to be in 1938. In India the average diet provides about two thousand calories a day—far below the optimum figure. If the country's food production could be raised by forty per cent—and the experts believe that, given much effort and a very large capital investment, it could be increased to this extent within fifteen or twenty years—the available food would provide the present population with twenty-eight hundred calories a day, a figure still below the optimum level. But twenty years from now the population of India will have increased by something like one hundred millions, and the additional food, produced with so much effort and at such great expense, will add little more than a hundred calories to the present woefully inadequate diet. And meanwhile it is not at all probable that a forty per cent increase in food production will in fact be achieved within the next twenty years.

The task of industrializing the underdeveloped countries, and of making them capable of producing enough food for their peoples, is difficult in the extreme. The industrialization of the West was made possible by a series of historical accidents. The inventions which launched the Industrial Revolution were made at precisely the right moment. Huge areas of empty land in America and Australasia were being opened up by European colonists or their descendants. A great surplus of cheap food became available, and it was upon this surplus that the peasants and farm laborers, who migrated to the towns and became factory hands, were enabled to live and multiply their kind. Today there are no empty lands—at any rate none that lend themselves to easy cultivation—and the over-all surplus of food is small in relation to present populations. If a million Asiatic peasants are taken off the land and set to work in factories, who will produce the food which their labor once provided? The obvious answer is: machines. But how can the million new factory workers make the necessary machines if, in the meanwhile, they are not fed? Until they make the machines, they cannot be fed from the land they once cultivated; and there are no surpluses of cheap food from other, emptier countries to support them in the interval.

And then there is the question of capital. "Science," you often hear it said, "will solve all our problems." Perhaps it will, perhaps it won't. But before science can start solving any practical problems, it must be applied in the form of usable technology. But to apply science on any large scale is extremely expensive. An underdeveloped country cannot be industrialized, or given an efficient agriculture, except by the investment of a very large amount of capital. But what is capital? It is what is left over when the primary needs of a society have been satisfied. In most of Asia the primary needs of most of the population are never satisfied; consequently almost nothing is left over. Indians can save about one hundredth of their per capita income. Americans can save between one tenth and one sixth of what they make. Since the income of Americans is much higher than that of Indians, the amount of available capital in the United States is about seventy times as great as the amount of available capital in India. To those who have shall be given and from those who have not shall be taken away even that which they have. If the underdeveloped countries are to be industrialized, even partially, and made self-supporting in the matter of food, it will be necessary to establish a vast international Marshall Plan providing subsidies in grain, money, machinery, and trained manpower. But all these will be of no avail, if the population in the various underdeveloped areas is permitted to increase at anything like the present rate. Unless the population of Asia can be stabilized, all attempts at industrialization will be doomed to failure and the last state of all concerned will be far worse than the first—for there will be many more people for famine and pestilence to destroy, together with much more political discontent, bloodier revolutions and more abominable tyrannies.

Hyperion to a Satyr

A few months before the outbreak of the Second World War I took a walk with Thomas Mann on a beach some fifteen or twenty miles southwest of Los Angeles. Between the breakers and the highway stretched a broad belt of sand, smooth, gently sloping and (blissful surprise!) void of all life but that of the pelicans and godwits. Gone was the congestion of Santa Monica and Venice. Hardly a house was to be seen; there were no children, no promenading loincloths and brassières, not a single sun-bather was practicing his strange obsessive cult. Miraculously, we were alone. Talking of Shakespeare and the musical glasses, the great man and I strolled ahead. The ladies followed. It was they, more observant than their all too literary spouses, who first remarked the truly astounding phenomenon. "Wait," they called, "wait!" And when they had come up with us, they silently pointed. At our feet, and as far as the eye could reach in all directions, the sand was covered with small whitish objects, like dead caterpillars. Recognition dawned. The dead caterpillars were made of rub-

ber and had once been contraceptives of the kind so eloquently characterized by Mantegazza as *"una tela di
ragno contro l'infezione, una corazza contro il piacere."*

> Continuous as the stars that shine
> And twinkle in the milky way,
> They stretched in never-ending line
> Along the margin of a bay:
> Ten thousand saw I at a glance ...

Ten thousand? But we were in California, not the Lake
District. The scale was American, the figures astronomi-
cal. Ten million saw I at a glance. Ten million emblems
and mementoes of Modern Love.

> O bitter barren woman! what's the name,
> The name, the name, the new name thou hast won?

And the old name, the name of the bitter fertile woman—
what was that? These are questions that can only be
asked and talked about, never answered in any but the
most broadly misleading way. Generalizing about Woman is like indicting a Nation—an amusing pastime,
but very unlikely to be productive either of truth or utility.

Meanwhile, there was another, a simpler and more concrete question: How on earth had these objects got here,
and why in such orgiastic profusion? Still speculating, we
resumed our walk. A moment later our noses gave us the
unpleasant answer. Offshore from this noble beach was
the outfall through which Los Angeles discharged, raw and
untreated, the contents of its sewers. The emblems of modern
love and the other things had come in with the spring tide.
Hence that miraculous solitude. We turned and made
all speed towards the parked car.

Since that memorable walk was taken, fifteen years
have passed. Inland from the beach, three or four large
cities have leapt into existence. The bean fields and Japanese truck gardens of those ancient days are now covered
with houses, drugstores, supermarkets, drive-in theaters,
junior colleges, jet-plane factories, laundromats, six-lane
highways. But instead of being, as one would expect,

even more thickly constellated with Malthusian flotsam and unspeakable jetsam, the sands are now clean, the quarantine has been lifted. Children dig, well-basted sunbathers slowly brown, there is splashing and shouting in the surf. A happy consummation—but one has seen this sort of thing before. The novelty lies, not in the pleasantly commonplace end—people enjoying themselves—but in the fantastically ingenious means whereby that end has been brought about.

Forty feet above the beach, in a seventy-five-acre oasis scooped out of the sand dunes, stands one of the marvels of modern technology, the Hyperion Activated Sludge Plant. But before we start to discuss the merits of activated sludge, let us take a little time to consider sludge in its unactivated state, as plain, old-fashioned dirt.

Dirt, with all its concomitant odors and insects, was once accepted as an unalterable element in the divinely established Order of Things. In his youth, before he went into power politics as Innocent III, Lotario de' Conti found time to write a book on the *Wretchedness of Man's Condition.* "How filthy the father," he mused, "how low the mother, how repulsive the sister!" And no wonder! For "dead human beings give birth to flies and worms; alive, they generate worms and lice." Moreover, "consider the plants, consider the trees. They bring forth flowers and leaves and fruits. But what do *you* bring forth? Nits, lice, vermin. Trees and plants exude oil, wine, balm—and *you,* spittle, snot, urine, ordure. *They* diffuse the sweetness of all fragrance—*you,* the most abominable stink." In the Age of Faith, Homo sapiens was also Homo pediculosus, also Homo immundus—a little lower than the angels, but dirty by definition, lousy, not *per accidens,* but in his very essence. And as for man's helpmate—*si nec extremis digitis flegma vel stercus tangere patimur, quomodo ipsum stercoris saccum amplecti desideramus?* "We who shrink from touching, even with the tips of our fingers, a gob of phlegm or a lump of dung, how is it that we crave for the embraces of this mere bag of night-soil?" But men's eyes are not, as Odo of Cluny wished they were, "like those of the lynxes of Boeotia"; they cannot see through the smooth and milky surfaces into the palpitating sewage within. That is why

There swims no goose so gray but soon or late
Some honest gander takes her for his mate.

That is why (to translate the notion into the language of medieval orthodoxy), every muck-bag ends by getting herself embraced—with the result that yet another stinker-with-a-soul finds himself embarked on a sea of misery, bound for a port which, since few indeed can hope for salvation, is practically certain to be Hell. The embryo of this future reprobate is composed of "foulest seed," combined with "blood made putrid by the heat of lust." And as though to make it quite clear what He thinks of the whole proceeding, God has decreed that "the mother shall conceive in stink and nastiness."

That there might be a remedy for stink and nastiness—namely soap and water—was a notion almost unthinkable in the thirteenth century. In the first place, there was hardly any soap. The substance was known to Pliny, as an import from Gaul and Germany. But more than a thousand years later, when Lotario de' Conti wrote his book, the burgesses of Marseilles were only just beginning to consider the possibility of manufacturing the stuff in bulk. In England no soap was made commercially until halfway through the fourteenth century. Moreover, even if soap had been abundant, its use for mitigating the "stink and nastiness," then inseparable from love, would have seemed, to every right-thinking theologian, an entirely illegitimate, because merely physical, solution to a problem in ontology and morals—an escape, by means of the most vulgarly materialistic trick, from a situation which God Himself had intended, from all eternity, to be as squalid as it was sinful. A conception without stink and nastiness would have the appearance—what a blasphemy!—of being Immaculate. And finally there was the virtue of modesty. Modesty, in that age of codes and pigeonholes, had its Queensberry Rules—no washing below the belt. Sinful in itself, such an offense against modesty in the present was fraught with all kinds of perils for modesty in the future. Havelock Ellis observed, when he was practicing obstetrics in the London slums, that modesty was due, in large measure, to a fear of being disgusting. When his patients realized that "I found nothing disgusting in whatever was proper and necessary to be done under the circumstances, it almost invariably happened that every sign of modesty at once disappeared." Abolish "stink and nastiness," and you abolish one of the most important sources of feminine modesty, along with one of the most richly rewarding themes of pulpit eloquence.

A contemporary poet has urged his readers not to make love to those who wash too much. There is, of course, no accounting for tastes; but there *is* an accounting for philosophical opinions. Among many other things, the greatly gifted Mr. Auden is a belated representative of the school which held that sex, being metaphysically tainted, ought also to be physically unclean.

Dirt, then, seemed natural and proper, and dirt in fact was everywhere. But, strangely enough, this all-pervading squalor never generated its own psychological antidote— the complete indifference of habit. Everybody stank, everybody was verminous; and yet, in each successive generation, there were many who never got used to these familiar facts. What has changed in the course of history is not the disgusted reaction to filth, but the moral to be drawn from that reaction. "Filth," say the men of the twentieth century, "is disgusting. Therefore let us quickly do something to get rid of filth." For many of our ancestors, filth was as abhorrent as it seems to almost all of us. But how different was the moral they chose to draw! "Filth is disgusting," they said. "Therefore the human beings who produce the filth are disgusting, and the world they inhabit is a vale, not merely of tears, but of excrement. This state of things has been divinely ordained, and all we can do is cheerfully to bear our vermin, loathe our nauseating carcasses and hope (without much reason, since we shall probably be damned) for an early translation to a better place. Meanwhile it is an observable fact that villeins are filthier even than lords. It follows, therefore, that they should be treated as badly as they smell." This loathing for the poor on account of the squalor in which they were condemned to live outlasted the Middle Ages and has persisted to the present day. The politics of Shakespeare's aristocratic heroes and heroines are the politics of disgust. "Footboys" and other members of the lower orders are contemptible because they are lousy—

not in the metaphorical sense in which that word is now used, but literally; for a louse, in Sir Hugh Evans' words, "is a familiar beast to man, and signifies love." And the lousy were also the smelly. Their clothes were old and unclean, their bodies sweaty, their mouths horrible with decay. It made no difference that, in the words of a great Victorian reformer, "by no prudence on their part can the poor avoid the dreadful evil of their surroundings." They were disgusting and that, for the aristocratic politician, was enough. To canvass the common people's suffrages was merely to "beg their stinking breath." Candidates for elective office were men who "stand upon the breath of garlic eaters." When the citizens of Rome voted against him, Coriolanus told them that they were creatures,

> whose breath I hate
> As reek o' th' rotten fens, whose loves I prize
> As the dead carcasses of unburied men
> That do corrupt my air.

And, addressing these same citizens, "You are they," says Menenius,

> You are they
> That made the air unwholesome when you cast
> Your stinking greasy caps in hooting at
> Coriolanus' exile.

Again, when Caesar was offered the crown, "the rabblement shouted and clapped their chopped hands, and threw up their sweaty night-caps, and uttered such a deal of stinking breath, because Caesar had refused the crown, that it had almost choked Caesar; for he swounded and fell down at it; and for mine own part," adds Casca, "I durst not laugh for fear of opening my lips and receiving the bad air." The same "mechanic slaves, with greasy aprons" haunted Cleopatra's imagination in her last hours.

> In their thick breaths,
> Rank of gross diet, shall we be enclouded,
> And forced to drink their vapours.

In the course of evolution man is supposed to have sacrificed the greater part of his olfactory center to his cortex, his sense of smell to his intelligence. Nevertheless, it remains a fact that in politics, no less than in love and social relations, smell judgments continue to play a major role. In the passages cited above, as in all the analogous passages penned or uttered since the days of Shakespeare, there is the implication of an argument, which can be formulated in some such terms as these. "Physical stink is a symbol, almost a symptom, of intellectual and moral inferiority. All the members of a certain group stink physically. Therefore, they are intellectually and morally vile, inferior and, as such, unfit to be treated as equals."

Tolstoy, who was sufficiently clear-sighted to recognize the undesirable political consequences of cleanliness in high places and dirt among the poor, was also sufficiently courageous to advocate, as a remedy, a general retreat from the bath. Bathing, he saw, was a badge of class distinction, a prime cause of aristocratic exclusiveness. For those who, in Mr. Auden's words, "wash too much," find it exceedingly distasteful to associate with those who wash too little. In a society where, let us say, only one in five can afford the luxury of being clean and sweet-smelling, Christian brotherhood will be all but impossible. Therefore, Tolstoy argued, the bathers should join the unwashed majority. Only where there is equality in dirt can there be a genuine and unforced fraternity.

Mahatma Gandhi, who was a good deal more realistic than his Russian mentor, chose a different solution to the problem of differential cleanliness. Instead of urging the bathers to stop washing, he worked indefatigably to help the non-bathers to keep clean. Brotherhood was to be achieved, not by universalizing dirt, vermin and bad smells, but by building privies and scrubbing floors.

Spengler, Sorokin, Toynbee—all the philosophical historians and sociologists of our time have insisted that a stable civilization cannot be built except on the foundations of religion. But if man cannot live by bread alone, neither can he live exclusively on metaphysics and worship. The gulf between theory and practice, between the ideal and the real, cannot be bridged by religion alone. In Christendom, for example, the doctrines of God's fatherhood and the brotherhood of man have never been self-implementing. Monotheism has proved to be powerless against the divisive forces first of feudalism and then of nationalistic idolatry. And within these mutually antagonistic groups, the injunction to love one's neighbor as oneself has proved to be as ineffective, century after century, as the commandment to worship one God.

A century ago the prophets who formulated the theories of the Manchester School were convinced that commerce, industrialization and improved communications were destined to be the means whereby the age-old doctrines of monotheism and human brotherhood would at last be implemented. Alas, they were mistaken. Instead of abolishing national rivalries, industrialization greatly intensified them. With the march of technological progress, wars became bloodier and incomparably more ruinous. Instead of uniting nation with nation, improved communications merely extended the range of collective hatreds and military operations. That human beings will, in the near future, voluntarily give up their nationalistic idolatry, seems, in these middle years of the twentieth century, exceedingly unlikely. Nor can one see, from this present vantage point, any technological development capable, by the mere fact of being in existence, of serving as an instrument for realizing those religious ideals, which hitherto mankind has only talked about. Our best consolation lies in Mr. Micawber's hope that, sooner or later, "Something will Turn Up."

In regard to brotherly love within the mutually antagonistic groups, something *has* turned up. That something is the development, in many different fields, of techniques for keeping clean at a cost so low that practically everybody can afford the luxury of not being disgusting.

For creatures which, like most of the carnivores, make their home in a den or burrow, there is a biological advantage in elementary cleanliness. To relieve nature in one's bed is apt, in the long run, to be unwholesome. Unlike the carnivores, the primates are under no evolutionary compulsion to practice the discipline of the sphincters. For these free-roaming nomads of the woods, one tree is as good as another and every moment is equally propitious. It is easy to house-train a cat or a dog, all but impossible to teach the same desirable habits to a monkey. By blood we are a good deal closer to poor Jocko than to Puss or Tray. Man's instincts were developed in the forest; but ever since the dawn of civilization, his life has been lived in the more elaborate equivalent of a rabbit warren. His notions of sanitation were not, like those of the cat, inborn, but had to be painfully acquired. In a sense the older theologians were quite right in regarding dirt as natural to man—an essential element in the divinely appointed order of his existence.

But in spite of its unnaturalness, the art of living together without turning the city into a dunghill has been repeatedly discovered. Mohenjo-daro, at the beginning of the third millennium B.C., had a water-borne sewage system; so, several centuries before the siege of Troy, did Cnossos; so did many of the cities of ancient Egypt, albeit only for the rich. The poor were left to demonstrate their intrinsic inferiority by stinking, in their slums, to high heaven. A thousand years later Rome drained her swamps and conveyed her filth to the contaminated Tiber by means of the Cloaca Maxima. But these solutions to the problem of what we may politely call "unactivated sludge" were exceptional. The Hindus preferred to condemn a tithe of their population to untouchability and the daily chore of carrying slops. In China the thrifty householder tanked the family sludge and sold it, when mature, to the highest bidder. There was a smell, but it paid, and the fields recovered some of the phosphorus and nitrogen of which the harvesters had robbed them. In medieval Europe every alley was a public lavatory, every window a sink and garbage chute. Droves of pigs were dedicated to St. Anthony and, with bells round their necks, roamed the streets, battening on the muck. (When operating at night, burglars and assassins often wore bells. Their victims heard the reassuring tinkle, turned over in their beds and went to sleep again—it was only the blessed pigs.) And meanwhile there were cesspools (like the black hole into which that patriotic Franciscan, Brother Salimbene, deliberately dropped his relic of St. Dominic), there was portable plumbing, there were members of the lower orders, whose duty it was to pick up the unactivated sludge and deposit it outside the city limits. But always the sludge accumulated faster than it could be removed. The filth was chronic and, in the slummier quarters, appalling. It remained appalling until well into the nineteenth century. As late as the early years of Queen Victoria's reign sanitation in the East End of London consisted in dumping everything into the stagnant pools that still stood between the jerry-built houses. From the peak of their superior (but still very imperfect) cleanliness the middle and upper classes looked down with unmitigated horror at the Great Unwashed. "The Poor" were written and spoken about as though they were creatures of an entirely different species. And no wonder! Nineteenth-century England was loud with Non-Conformist and Tractarian piety; but in a society most of whose members stank and were unclean the practice of brotherly love was out of the question.

The first modern sewage systems, like those of Egypt before them, were reserved for the rich and had the effect of widening still further the gulf between rulers and ruled. But endemic typhus and several dangerous outbreaks of Asiatic cholera lent weight to the warnings and denunciations of the sanitary reformers. In self-defense the rich had to do something about the filth in which their less fortunate neighbors were condemned to live. Sewage systems were extended to cover entire metropolitan areas. The result was merely to transfer the sludge problem from one place to another. "The Thames," reported a Select Committee in 1836, "receives the excrementitious matter from nearly a million and a half of human beings; the washing of their foul linen; the filth and refuse of many hundred manufactories; the offal and decomposing vegetable substances from the markets; the foul and gory liquid from the slaughter-houses; and the purulent abominations from hospitals and dissecting rooms, too disgusting to detail. Thus that most noble river, which has been given us by Providence for our health, recreation and beneficial use, is converted into the Common sewer of London, and the sickening mixture it contains is daily pumped up into the water for the inhabitants of the most civilized capital of Europe."

In England the heroes of the long campaign for sanitation were a strangely assorted band. There was a bishop, Blomfield of London; there was the radical Edwin Chadwick, a disciple of Jeremy Bentham; there was a physician,

Dr. Southwood Smith; there was a low-church man of letters, Charles Kingsley; and there was the seventh Earl of Shaftesbury, an aristocrat who had troubled to acquaint himself with the facts of working-class life. Against them were marshaled the confederate forces of superstition, vested interest and brute inertia. It was a hard fight; but the cholera was a staunch ally, and by the end of the century the worst of the mess had been cleared up, even in the slums. Writing in 1896, Lecky called it "the greatest achievement of our age." In the historian's estimation, the sanitary reformers had done more for general happiness and the alleviation of human misery than all the more spectacular figures of the long reign put together. Their labors, moreover, were destined to bear momentous fruit. When Lecky wrote, upper-class noses could still find plenty of occasions for passing olfactory judgments on the majority. But not nearly so many as in the past. The stage was already set for the drama which is being played today—the drama whose theme is the transformation of the English caste system into an equalitarian society. Without Chadwick and his sewers, there might have been violent revolution, never that leveling by democratic process, that gradual abolition of untouchability, which are in fact taking place.

Hyperion—what joy the place would have brought to those passionately prosaic lovers of humanity, Chadwick and Bentham! And the association of the hallowed name with sewage, of sludge with the great god of light and beauty—what romantic furies it would have evoked in Keats and Blake! And Lotario de' Conti—how thunderously, in the name of religion, he would have denounced this presumptuous demonstration that Homo immundus can effectively modify the abjection of his predestined condition! And Dean Swift, above all—how deeply the spectacle would have disturbed him! For, if Celia could relieve nature without turning her lover's bowels, if Yahoos, footmen and even ladies of quality did not *have* to stink, then, obviously, his occupation was gone and his neurosis would be compelled to express itself in some other, some less satisfactory, because less excruciating, way.

An underground river rushes into Hyperion. Its purity of 99.7 per cent exceeds that of Ivory Soap. But two hundred

million gallons are a lot of water; and the three thousandth part of that daily quota represents a formidable
quantity of muck. But happily the ratio between muck and
muckrakers remains constant. As the faecal tonnage rises,
so does the population of aerobic and anaerobic bacteria.
Busier than bees and infinitely more numerous, they work
unceasingly on our behalf. First to attack the problem
are the aerobes. The chemical revolution begins in a series
of huge shallow pools, whose surface is perpetually foamy
with the suds of Surf, Tide, Dreft and all the other monosyllables that have come to take the place of soap. For
the sanitary engineers, these new detergents are a major
problem. Soap turns very easily into something else; but
the monosyllables remain intractably themselves, frothing
so violently that it has become necessary to spray the
surface of the aerobes' pools with overhead sprinklers.
Only in this way can the suds be prevented from rising
like the foam on a mug of beer and being blown about
the countryside. And this is not the only price that must be
paid for easier dishwashing. The detergents are greedy for
oxygen. Mechanically and chemically, they prevent
the aerobes from getting all the air they require. Enormous
compressors must be kept working night and day to supply
the needs of the suffocating bacteria. A cubic foot of compressed air to every cubic foot of sludgy liquid. What will
happen when Zoom, Bang and Whiz come to replace the
relatively mild monosyllables of today, nobody, in the
sanitation business, cares to speculate.

When, with the assistance of the compressors, the aerobes
have done all they are capable of doing, the sludge, now
thickly concentrated, is pumped into the Digestion System.
To the superficial glance, the Digestion System looks remarkably like eighteen very large Etruscan mausoleums.
In fact it consists of a battery of cylindrical tanks, each
more than a hundred feet in diameter and sunk fifty feet
into the ground. Within these huge cylinders steam pipes
maintain a cherishing heat of ninety-five degrees—the
temperature at which the anaerobes are able to do their
work with maximum efficiency. From something hideous
and pestilential the sludge is gradually transformed by
these most faithful of allies into sweetness and light—light
in the form of methane, which fuels nine supercharged

Diesel engines, each of seventeen hundred horsepower, and sweetness in the form of an odorless solid which, when dried, pelleted and sacked, sells to farmers at ten dollars a ton. The exhaust of the Diesels raises the steam which heats the Digestion System, and their power is geared either to electric generators or centrifugal blowers. The electricity works the pumps and the machinery of the fertilizer plant, the blowers supply the aerobes with oxygen. Nothing is wasted. Even the emblems of modern love contribute their quota of hydrocarbons to the finished products, gaseous and solid. And meanwhile another torrent, this time about 99.95 per cent pure, rushes down through the submarine outfall and mingles, a mile offshore, with the Pacific. The problem of keeping a great city clean without polluting a river or fouling the beaches, and without robbing the soil of its fertility, has been triumphantly solved.

But untouchability depends on other things besides the bad sanitation of slums. We live not merely in our houses, but even more continuously in our garments. And we live not exclusively in health, but very often in sickness. Where sickness rages unchecked and where people cannot afford to buy new clothes or keep their old ones clean, the occasions for being disgusting are innumerable.

Thersites, in *Troilus and Cressida,* lists a few of the commoner ailments of Shakespeare's time: "the rotten diseases of the south, the guts-griping, ruptures, catarrhs, loads o'gravel i' the back, lethargies, cold palsies, raw eyes, dirt-rotten livers, wheezing lungs, bladders full of imposthume, sciaticas, lime-kilns i' the palm, incurable bone-ache, and the rivelled fee-simple of the tetter." And there were scores of others even more repulsive. Crawling, flying, hopping, the insect carriers of infection swarmed uncontrollably. Malaria was endemic, typhus never absent, bubonic plague a regular visitor, dysentery, without benefit of plumbing, a commonplace. And meanwhile, in an environment that was uniformly septic, everything that *could* suppurate *did* suppurate. The Cook, in Chaucer's "Prologue," had a "mormal," or gangrenous sore, on his shin. The Summoner's face was covered with the "whelkes" and "knobbes" of skin disease that would not yield to any known remedy. Every cancer was inoperable, and gnawed its way, through a hideous chaos of cellular proliferation and breakdown, to its foregone conclusion. The unmitigated horror surrounding illness explains the admiration felt, throughout the Middle Ages and early modern times, for those heroes and heroines of charity who voluntarily undertook the care of the sick. It explains, too, certain actions of the saints—actions which, in the context of modern life, seem utterly incomprehensible. In their filth and wretchedness, the sick were unspeakably repulsive. This dreadful fact was a challenge to which those who took their Christianity seriously responded by such exploits as the embracing of lepers, the kissing of sores, the swallowing of pus. The modern response to this challenge is soap and water, with complete asepsis as the ultimate ideal. The great gulf of disgust which used to separate the sick and the chronically ailing from their healthier fellows, has been, not indeed completely abolished, but narrowed everywhere and, in many places, effectively bridged. Thanks to hygiene, many who, because of their afflictions, used to be beyond the pale of love or even pity, have been re-admitted into the human fellowship. An ancient religious ideal has been implemented, at least in part, by the development of merely material techniques for dealing with problems previously soluble (and then how very inadequately, so far as the sick themselves were concerned!) only by saints.

"The essential act of thought is symbolization." Our minds transform experiences into signs. If these signs adequately represent the experiences to which they refer, and if we are careful to manipulate them according to the rules of a many-valued logic, we can deepen our understanding of experience and thereby achieve some control of the world and our own destiny. But these conditions are rarely fulfilled. In all too many of the affairs of life we combine ill-chosen signs in all kinds of irrational ways, and are thus led to unrealistic conclusions and inappropriate acts.

There is nothing in experience which cannot be transformed by the mind into a symbol—nothing which cannot be made to signify something else. We have seen, for example, that bad smells may be made to stand for social inferiority, dirt for a low IQ, vermin for immorality, sickness for a status beneath the human. No less important than these purely physiological symbols are the signs derived, not from the body itself, but from its coverings. A man's clothes are his most immediately perceptible attribute. Stinking rags or clean linen, liveries, uniforms, canonicals, the latest fashions—these are the symbols in terms of which men and women have thought about the relations of class with class, of person with person. In the *Institutions of Athens,* written by an anonymous author of the fifth century B.C., we read that it was illegal in Athens to assault a slave even when he refused to make way for you in the street. "The reason why this is the local custom shall be explained. If it were legal for the slave to be struck by the free citizen, your Athenian citizen himself would always be getting assaulted through being mistaken for a slave. Members of the free proletariat of Athens are no better dressed than slaves or aliens and no more respectable in appearance." But Athens—a democratic city state with a majority of "poor whites"—was exceptional. In almost every other society the wearing of cheap and dirty clothes has been regarded (such is the power of symbols) as the equivalent of a moral lapse—a lapse for which the wearers deserved to be ostracized by all decent people. In *Les Précieuses Ridicules* the high-flown heroines take two footmen, dressed up in their masters' clothes, for marquises. The comedy comes to its climax when the pretenders are stripped of their symbolic finery and the girls discover the ghastly truth. *Et eripitur persona, manet res—* or, to be more precise, *manet altera persona.* The mask is torn off and there remains—what? Another mask—the footman's.

In eighteenth-century England the producers of woolens were able to secure legislation prohibiting the import of cotton prints from the Orient and imposing an excise duty, not repealed until 1832, on the domestic product. But in spite of this systematic discouragement, the new industry prospered—inevitably; for it met a need, it supplied a vast and growing demand. Wool could not be cleaned, cotton was washable. For the first time in the history of Western Europe it began to be possible for all but the poorest women to look clean. The revolution then begun is still in progress. Garments of cotton and the new synthetic fibers have largely abolished the ragged and greasy symbols of earlier class distinctions. And meanwhile, for such fabrics as cannot be washed, the chemical industry has invented a host of new detergents and solvents. In the past, grease spots were a problem for which there was no solution. Proletarian garments were darkly shiny with accumulated fats and oils, and even the merchant's broadcloth, even the velvets and satins of lords and ladies displayed the ineradicable traces of last year's candle droppings, of yesterday's gravy. Dry cleaning is a modern art, a little younger than railway travel, a little older than the first Atlantic cable.

In recent years, and above all in America, the revolution in clothing has entered a new phase. As well as cleanliness, elegance is being placed within the reach of practically everyone. Cheap clothes are mass-produced from patterns created by the most expensive designers. Unfashionableness was once a stigma hardly less damning, as a symbol of inferiority, than dirt. Fifty years ago a girl who wore cheap clothes proclaimed herself, by their obvious dowdiness, to be a person whom it was all but out of the question, if one were well off, to marry. Misalliance is still deplored; but, thanks to Sears and Ohrbach, it seems appreciably less dreadful than it did to our fathers.

Sewage systems and dry cleaning, hygiene and washable fabrics, DDT and penicillin—the catalogue represents a series of technological victories over two great enemies: dirt and that system of untouchability, that unbrotherly contempt, to which, in the past, dirt has given rise.

It is, alas, hardly necessary to add that these victories are in no sense definitive or secure. All we can say is that, in certain highly industrialized countries, technological advances have led to the disappearance of some of the immemorial symbols of class distinction. But this does not guarantee us against the creation of new symbols no less compulsive in their anti-democratic tendencies than the old. A man may be clean; but if, in a dictatorial state, he lacks a party card, he figuratively stinks and must be treated as an inferior at the best and, at the worst, an untouchable.

In the nominally Christian past two irreconcilable sets of symbols bedeviled the Western mind—the symbols, inside the churches, of God's fatherhood and the brotherhood of man; and the symbols, outside, of class distinction, mammon worship and dynastic, provincial or national idolatry. In the totalitarian future—and if we go on fighting wars, the future of the West is bound to be totalitarian—the time-hallowed symbols of monotheism and brotherhood will doubtless be preserved. God will be One and men will all be His children, but in a strictly Pickwickian sense. Actually there will be slaves and masters, and the slaves will be taught to worship a parochial Trinity of Nation, Party and Political Boss. Samuel Butler's Musical Banks will be even more musical than they are today, and the currency in which they deal will have even less social and psychological purchasing power than the homilies of the Age of Faith.

Symbols are necessary—for we could not think without them. But they are also fatal—for the thinking they make possible is just as often unrealistic as it is to the point. In this consists the essentially tragic nature of the human situation. There is no way out, except for those who have learned how to go beyond all symbols to a direct experience of the basic fact of the divine immanence. *Tat tvam asi*—thou art That. When this is perceived, the rest will be added. In the meantime we must be content with such real but limited goods as Hyperion, and such essentially precarious and mutable sources of good as are provided by the more realistic of our religious symbols.

Mother

Heat and gravity, molecular motion and atomic disintegration—these are the physical prime moves of our economy. But there are also energies of thought, energies of feeling, instinct and desire—energies which, if canalized and directed, can be made to do useful work and ring up handsome profits. Some of these invisible energies were harnessed at the very dawn of civilization and have been turning the wheels of industry ever since. Personal vanity, for example, has powered half the looms and supported all the jewelers. The horror of death and the wish for some kind of survival have raised pyramids, have carved innumerable statues and inscriptions, have given employment to whole armies of painters, masons, embalmers and clergymen. And what of fear, what of aggressiveness and the lust for power, what of pride, envy and greed? These are the energies which, from the time of chipped flints to the time of split atoms, have powered the armament industry. In recent years manufacturers and retailers have been turning their attention to other, hitherto unexploited sources of psycho-industrial power. Directed by the advertisers into commercially profitable channels, snobbery and the urge to conformity have now been made to yield the equivalent of millions of horsepower of energy. The longing for sexual success and the dread of being repulsive have become the principal motive force in our ever growing cosmetics and deodorant industries. And how brilliantly our psychological engineers have tackled the problem of turning religious tradition, children's phantasies and family affection to commercial use! Read Dickens's account of an old-fashioned Christmas in *The Pickwick Papers* and compare what happened at Dingley Dell to what the victims of the modern American Christmas are expected to do now. In Dickens's time the Saviour's birthday was celebrated merely by overeating and drunkenness. Except for the servants, nobody received a present. Today Christmas is a major factor in our capitalist economy. A season of mere good cheer has been converted, by the steady application of propaganda, into a long-drawn buying spree, in the course of which everyone is under compulsion to exchange gifts with everyone else—to the immense enrichment of merchants and manufacturers.

And now compare the activities of the children described in *Little Women*, in *Puck of Pook's Hill*, in *Winnie the Pooh*, with the activities of children growing up in the age of electronics. Before the invention of television, the phantasies of childhood were private, random and gratuitous. Today they are public, highly organized and cannot be indulged in except at considerable expense to the parents, who must pay for a second TV set, buy the brands of reakfast food advertised by the purveyors of phantasy, nd supply the young viewers with revolvers and coonskin aps.

The same process of publicizing the private, standardzing the random and taxing the gratuitous may be oberved in the field of personal relationships. The family is n institution which permits and indeed encourages the generation of immense quantities of psychological energy. But until very recent times, this energy was allowed to run o waste without doing any good to industry or commerce. This was a situation which, in a civilization dependent or its very existence on mass production and mass conumption, could not be tolerated. The psychological engieers got to work and soon the private, random and gratutous sentiments of filial devotion were standardized and urned to economic advantage. Mother's Day and, despite he growing absurdity of poor Poppa, Father's Day were nstituted, and it began to be mandatory for children to celebrate these festivals by buying presents for their parents, or at least by sending them a greeting card. Not a etter, mind you; letters are private, random and bring money only to the Post Office. Besides, in these days of telephones and Progressive Methods of teaching orthography, few people are willing to write or able to spell. For the good of all concerned (except perhaps the recipients, who might have liked an occasional hand-written note), the greeting card was invented and marketed.

A few weeks ago I found myself, half an hour too early for an appointment, in the World's Largest Drug Store. How was the time to be passed? I had all the pills and toothpaste I needed, all the typing paper, electric light bulbs, alarm clocks, whisky, cameras, folding card tables. I had no use for toys or nylon hosiery, for skin food or chewing gum or fashion magazines. Nothing remained but the greeting cards. They were displayed, hundreds upon hundreds of them, in a many-tiered rack not less (for I made a rough measurement) than fifty-four feet long. There were cards for birthdays, cards for funerals, cards for weddings and for the consequences of weddings in all numbers from singles to quadruplets. There were cards for the sick, for the convalescent, for the bereaved. There were cards addressed to brothers, to sisters, to aunts, to nephews, to uncles, to cousins, to everyone up and down the family tree to the third and fourth generation. There were serious cards for Father, tender cards for Dad, humorous cards for Pop. And finally there was an immense assortment of cards for Mother. Each of these cards, I discovered, had its poem, printed in imitation handwriting, so that, if Mom were in her second childhood, she might be duped into believing that the sentiment was not a reach-me-down, but custom-made, a lyrical outpouring from the sender's overflowing heart.

> Mother dear, you're wonderful
>   In everything you do!
> The happiness of fam'ly life
>   Depends so much on YOU

Or, more subtly,

> You put the sweet in Home Sweet Home
>   By loving things you do.
> You make the days much happier
>   By being so sweet, too.

And so on, card after card. In the paradise of commercialized maternity no Freudian reptile, it is evident, has ever reared its ugly head. The Mother of the greeting cards inhabits a delicious Disneyland, where everything is syrup and Technicolor, cuteness and Schmalz. And this, I reflected, as I worked my way along the fifty-four-foot rack, is all that remains of the cult of the Great Mother, the oldest and, in many ways, the profoundest, of all religions.

For paleolithic man, every day was Mother's Day. Far more sincerely than any modern purchaser of a greeting card, he believed that "Mother dear, you're wonderful." Just how wonderful is attested by the carvings of Mother unearthed in the caves which, twenty thousand years ago, served our ancestors as cathedrals. In limestone, in soapstone, in mammoth ivory—there they stand, the Mother images of man's earliest worship. Their bowed heads are very small and their faces are perfectly featureless. They have next to no arms and their dwindling legs taper off, with no hint of feet, into nothing. Mother is all body, and that body, with its enormously heavy breasts, its prodigal wealth of belly, thigh and buttock is the portrait of no individual mother, but a tremendous symbol of fertility, an incarnation of the divine mystery of life in defiance of death, of perpetual renewal in the midst of perpetual perishing. Mother was felt to be analogous to the fruitful earth and, for centuries, her images were apt to exhibit all the massiveness of her cosmic counterpart. In Egypt, for example, Mother sometimes modulated imperceptibly into a hippopotamus. In Peru she often appeared as an enormous female Toby-jug, and everywhere she manifested herself as pot, jar, sacred vessel, grail.

The facts which we only think about (if we think about them at all) scientifically, in terms of biology and ecology, of embryology and genetics, our ancestors evidently thought about all the time. They did not understand them analytically, of course, but directly experienced them with their whole being, physiologically, emotionally and intellectually, whenever they were confronted by one of their Mother symbols.

How is it that we have permitted ourselves to become so unrealistic, so flippantly superficial in all our everyday thinking and feeling about man and the world he lives in? "The happiness of fam'ly life Depends so much on YOU." This, apparently, is as deep as the popular mind is now prepared to go into the subject of Mother. And the minority opinion of those who have graduated from greeting cards to Dr. Freud is hardly more adequate. They know that Mother dear can be wonderful in more ways than one— that there are wonderful, possessive mothers of only sons, whom they baby into chronic infantility, that there are wonderful, sweet old vampires who go on feeding, into their eighties, on the blood of an enslaved daughter. These are uncomfortable facts, which we must recognize in order to cope with. But this sort of thing is still a very long way from being the whole story of Mother. To those who would like to read something like the whole story I recommend a book which, as it happened, I had finished on the very morning of my encounter with the greeting cards at the World's Largest Drug Store. This book is *The Great Mother* by Erich Neumann, recently published as Number 47 of the Bollingen Series. It is not an easy book to read; for the author is a psychologist of the school of C. G. Jung and he writes, as most of Jung's followers write, with all of the old master's turgid copiousness. Jungian literature is like a vast quaking dog. At every painful step the reader sinks to the hip in jargon and generalizations, with never a patch of firm intellectual ground to rest on and only rarely, in that endless expanse of jelly, the blessed relief of a hard, concrete, particular fact. And yet, in spite of everything, the Jungian system is probably a better description of psychological reality than is the Freudian. It is not the best possible description—far from it; but it does at least lend itself to being incorporated into such a description. If you were to combine Jung with F. W. H. Myers, and if you were then to enrich the product with the theories of Tantrik Buddhism and the practices of Zen, you would have a working hypothesis capable of explaining most, perhaps indeed all, the unutterably odd facts of human experience and, along with the hypothesis, a set of operational procedures by means of which its unlikelier elements might be verified.

And now let us return to Mother. For our ancestors, as we have seen, Mother was not only the particular person who made or marred the happiness of fam'ly life; she was also the visible embodiment of a cosmic mystery. Mother manifested Life on all its levels—on the biological and physiological levels and also on the psychological level. Psychologically speaking, Mother was that oceanic Unconscious, out of which personal self-consciousness (the masculine element in subjective experience) is crystallized and in which, so to speak, it bathes. More obviously, Mother was the source of physical life, the principle of fecundity. But the principle of fecundity is also, in the very nature of things, the principle of mortality; for the giver of physical life is also, of necessity, the giver of death. Ours is a world in which death is the inevitable consequence of life, in which life requires death in order to renew itself. Wherever she has been worshiped—and there is no part of the world in which, at one time or another, she has not been worshiped—the Great Mother is simultaneously the Creator and the Destroyer. Mother gives and Mother takes away; she builds up and then tears down that she may build again—and yet again tear down, forever. For us, as self-conscious individuals, as social beings governed by law and trying to live up to ethical ideals, this divine impartiality can only seem appalling. Theologians have always found it exceedingly difficult to "justify the ways of God to man." They have, indeed, found it impossible; for the ways of God cannot be justified in merely human terms. In that profoundest and most splendid product of Hebrew thought, the Book of Job, God refuses to justify Himself; he is content to ask ironical questions and to point to the vast, incomprehensible fact of a world which, whatever else it may be, is most certainly not a world created according to human specifications.

The Book of Job was written in the fifth or perhaps even the fourth century B.C., when the ancient matriarchal system of thought and social organization had been replaced by the patriarchal, and the supreme God was worshiped, not as Mother, but as Father. The originality of the book consists in its demonstration that this masculine God had a great deal in common with the Great Mother of earlier religions. Jehovah is, by definition, the God of righteousness, of willed morality and self-conscious idealism; but He is also, insists the author of Job, the God of the fathomless Unconscious, the Lord of the irrational Datum, the First Principle of the incomprehensible Fact. A God of righteousness, Jehovah is at the same time the impartial creator, not only of all good things, but also of all that we regard as evil—the impartial destroyer, in His cosmic play, not only of evil, but of all that we regard as good. Long before the God of Job—the God who ironically makes nonsense of all the moralistic notions of Job's comforters—the Great Mother had her negative as well as her positive aspects. She was the terrible Mother as well as the Beneficent Mother, the Goddess of Destruction as well as the Creator and Preserver. Terrible Mothers are to be found in every religious tradition. In Mexico, for example, Mother often appears with a grinning skull for a head and a skirt of woven rattlesnakes. Among the ancient Greeks she is, in one of her numerous aspects, the snaky-haired Gorgon, whose glance has power to turn all living things to stone. In India, Kali, the Great Mother, is sometimes beneficent, sometimes terrible. She nourishes and she devours; she is serenely beautiful and she is a cannibalistic monster. In her positive aspect, she is simultaneously Nature and Intuition, the creator of spiritual no less than of physical life. She is the Eternal Feminine that leads us up and on, and she is the Eternal Feminine that leads us down and back. She puts the sweet in "Home Sweet Home," after which she drinks our blood.

Life giving birth to death, destruction preparing the way for new creation, self-consciousness emerging from the unconscious and finding itself torn between the urge to return to the impersonal darkness of nescience and the urge to go forward into the impersonal light of the total awareness— these are the cosmic and subjective mysteries, for which our ancestors found expression in their countless symbols of the Great Mother. Nothing of all this was made clear, nothing was analyzed or conceptualized. It was a non-logical system of potential science, of latent metaphysics. From their contemplation of these symbols men could derive no definite knowledge, only a kind of obscure understanding of the great scheme of things and their own place within it.

To cope with the mysteries of experience, modern man has no such cosmic symbol as the Great Mother; he has only science and technical philosophy. As a scientist, he observes the facts of generation, growth and death, he classifies his observations in terms of biological concepts, he tests his hypotheses by means of experiment. As a philosopher, he uses the methods of Logical Positivism to prove to his own satisfaction (or rather to his own deepest dissatisfaction) that all the theories of the metaphysicians, all the pregnant hints and suggestions of the symbol-makers have no assignable meaning—in a word, are sheer nonsense. And of course the Logical Positivists are perfectly right—provided always that we accept as self-evident the postulate that no proposition has meaning unless it can be verified by direct perception, or unless we can derive from it other "perceptive propositions," which can be so verified. But if we admit—and in practice we all behave as if we did admit it—that "the heart has its reasons" and that there are modes of understanding which do not depend upon perception or logical inferences from perception, then we shall have to take the metaphysicians and especially the metaphysical symbol-makers a little more seriously. I say "especially the symbol-makers"; for whenever we are dealing with a cosmic or subjective mystery, the verbalized concept is less satisfactory as a means of presentation than the pictorial or diagrammatic symbol. Symbols can express the given, experienced paradoxes of our life without analyzing them, as words (at any rate Indo-European words) must necessarily do, into their self-contradictory elements. Modern man still creates non-verbal symbols, still makes use of them, in many of the most important junctures of life, as a substitute for analytical thinking. Such symbols as flags, swastikas, hammers and sickles have had an enormous and, in the main, disastrous influence on the life of our time. All these, it should be noted, are social and political symbols. When it comes to symbolizing cosmic, rather than all too human, matters, we find ourselves very poorly equipped. Our religious symbols, such as the Cross, refer only to the realms of ethics and of what may be called pure spirituality. We have no religious symbols covering the other aspects of the cosmic mystery. The Hindu religion knows how to symbolize Nature and its processes of unceasing creation and unceasing destruction. The Christian, Jewish and Mohammedan religions do not. In the West, Nature has been completely isolated from the religious context, in which our ancestors used to view it. Our non-human environment and our own physical existence have now become domains exclusively reserved for science. Such exclusiveness is wholly to the bad. What we have to learn is some way of making the best of both worlds, of all the worlds—the world of clear conceptual knowledge and the world of obscure understanding, the world of verbal analysis and the world of comprehensive symbols, the world of science and the world of religion and metaphysics. Will it ever be possible to revive the Great Mother, or create some equivalent symbol of the cosmic mysteries of life and death? Or are we doomed to remain indefinitely, or until the masses lose their minds and run amuck, on the level of the greeting card? Triviality and make-believe are much more easily turned to economic advantage than realistic profundity. Much more than the schoolteachers and the professors, the philosophers and the theologians, our commercial propagandists are the real educators of the masses. If triviality and make-believe are to the advantage of their employers, triviality and make-believe are the attitudes these molders of modern thought will inculcate.

Adonis and the Alphabet

Twenty miles north of Beirut we crossed a river. Not much of a river, in terms of size and water; but what a volume of myth, what a length of history! The bridge on which we had halted spanned the River Adonis. We looked over the parapet and were a little disappointed to find the water pellucid, unstained, at this late season, by the red earth of the Lebanon, the blood, if you prefer, of the dying god. To the east, high up in a gorge among the mountains, at the very place where Adonis lost his life, had stood the temple to which uncounted thousands of his worshipers climbed every year on arduous pilgrimage. And at Byblos, a few miles beyond the river, was the sanctuary of Adonis's lover. For the Greeks she was Aphrodite; for Solomon, who built a high place for her at Jerusalem, Ashtaroth; she was Ishtar in Babylonia, Astarte in Phoenicia, Atargatis for the Syrians—and, for Shakespeare, the heroine of his earliest poem.

> "Fondling," she saith, "since I have hemm'd thee here
> Within the circuit of this ivory pale,
> I'll be a park, and thou shalt be my deer;
> Feed where thou wilt, on mountain or in dale:
>   Graze on my lips; and if those hills be dry,
>   Stray lower, where the pleasant fountains lie."

We have come a long way, in this rococo Venus and her reluctant boy, from the Dea Syria and the Corn Spirit, from the drama of death and resurrection acted out, symbolically, to the accompaniment of ritual couplings and sacred prostitution, of the wailings of half-naked women and the self-castrations of frenzied youths. "Graze on my lips, stray lower. . . ." The cosmic has become the comic; an enormous mystery has been transformed into a charming piece of near impropriety. This is the way a world ends, the old, dark world of chthonic deities and fertility cults—not (to parody Mr. Eliot) with a bang, but a simper. And a good thing, too, on the whole. Bang may be impressive; but what a bore in the long run, how crude and brutal! Those denunciatory rumblings of Hebrew prophets, those endless persecutions, those noisy revivals of what each revivalist regards as True Religion, those ham preachers with their thrilling voices and their all too noble gestures, those tragedians eloquently gloating over disaster, those Carlylean moralists, Christian or Stoic, bellowing away about the wickedness of being happy and the abominableness of nature—surely, surely we have had enough of them. Shakespeare's way of dealing with the fertility religions is humaner than the Inquisition's and at least as effective. Both as literature and as morals, *Venus and Adonis* is better than the *Malleus Maleficarum*. As for grazing on lips and straying lower—even at their most depraved these amusements are a thousand times less wicked than torturing people, and even burning them alive, because they prefer an older conception of God to the one that is currently fashionable among clergymen. But even so, Shakespeare's is not the final answer. We have had enough, and more than enough, of prophets, revivalists and tragedians. But we have also had enough of the satirists and debunkers, of the writers of farces and the tellers of bawdy stories, to whom long-suffering humanity has turned for an antidote to all those Jeremiahs and Savonarolas, and portentous Dantes, those preachers of crusades and heresy hunters, ancient and modern. *Heads* implies *tails;* simper is merely the obverse of bang, Félicia of Laura, *Bouvard et Pecuchet* of *Paradise Lost*. There is no escape except into the divine equanimity, which reconciles all the opposites and so transfigures the world.

We got into the car again and drove on between the sea and the mountains. A few minutes later the coastal highway had become the main street of a small town. We were in Jebeil, with the monuments of the Crusades towering ruinously overhead and the remains of Byblos—of half a dozen Bybloses, Roman, Greek, Phoenician, Colonial-Egyptian, Chalcolithic, Neolithic—emerging, under the spades of the archaeologists, from the earth beneath our feet.

There is no description of ancient Byblos. Lucian, in *The Syrian Goddess*, tells us that he visited the temple, but not what it looked like, nor what were the rites of Adonis in which he took part. And did he really think that the annual arrival of the Holy Head was a miracle? It is hard in the light of his later, total skepticism, to believe it. And yet the fact remains that, in *The Syrian Goddess*, he called it a miracle. The Holy Head belonged, presumably, to Osiris and came all the way from Egypt, floating on the waves and driven by mysteriously purposeful winds, which brought it punctually, after a seven-day crossing, to the land of Osiris's counterpart, Adonis. "I saw it," Lucian affirms; and there is no reason to doubt his word. After all, Chaucer and his contemporaries had all seen the *pigges bones* in the Pardoner's crystal reliquary.

Byblos, of course, was much more than a place of pilgrimage. It was a port, the oldest in Phoenicia, and a clearing house for trade between Egypt, Syria and the further East on the one hand and Europe and Asia Minor on the other. The proof of this lies embedded in two Greek words, *byblos* and *biblion*. Byblos was the common name for papyrus. We find it in Herodotus and, much earlier, in Homer, who has Odysseus make fast the doors of his house with "byblian tackle," in other words, ropes of papyrus fiber. To the Greeks of Ionia and, later, of Europe, string and paper were brought by Phoenician traders, whose home port gave its name to the finished article as well as to the Egyptian plant which supplied the raw material. A Greek would call for a sheet of byblos or a ball of byblian twine, just as, centuries later, an Englishman would ask for a yard of damask or a pound of damsons. And when the byblos came in rolls and had writing on it, the thing was a biblion, a bible or, as we should say (since we used to do our writing on tablets of beechwood), a book. And this Phoenician city, I reflected as we strolled through its narrow spaces and enormous times, had had another, more than merely etymological connection with literature. For it was here, about thirty-five centuries ago, that some nameless genius invented, or at least perfected, the ABC.

The discovery of this fact was due to a happy accident. In 1922 a landslide revealed an underground chamber and a huge sarcophagus. The archaeologists went to work and had soon unearthed a whole cemetery of royal tombs. One of these contained the sarcophagus of King Ahiram, who reigned in the thirteenth century before our era. On it had been carved an inscription in Phoenician characters. The alphabet, it was clear, had been in use hundreds of years earlier than had previously been supposed. King Ahiram's coffin is now in the Beirut Museum—that fascinating repository of perhaps the ugliest works of art ever created by man; for the Phoenicians (heaven knows why) seem to have been incapable of producing anything but monstrosities. No, I exaggerate; they were capable sometimes of producing cutenesses. Their figurines of hippopotami, for example, might have been modeled by Walt Disney. But if art was not their strong point, commerce undoubtedly was; and it might have been in the interests of commercial efficiency that one of them invented the new and enormously simpler system of writing which was destined to replace cuneiform and hieroglyphics throughout the Near East and Europe. As a man of letters, I felt I ought to lay a wreath on the tomb of the Unknown Letter-Maker of Byblos.

It was Sunday, and in the Crusader's elegant little church a Maronite service was in progress. The words of an incomprehensible liturgy reverberated under the vaults, and above the heads of the congregation a family of sparrows was going unconcernedly about its business. Nobody paid any attention to their noisy impudence. The little creatures were taken for granted. Along with the ancient stones, the altar, the intoning priest, they were an accepted feature of the Sunday landscape, an element in the sacred situation. In this part of the world, birds seem to be perfectly compatible with monotheism. These Maronite sparrows are matched by the Mohammedan pigeons in the Omayyad Mosque at Damascus. That splendid sanctuary is alive with wings and cooing, and when droppings fall on the head of some grave and bearded worshiper

—we actually saw it happen—there is no indignation, only a tolerant smile. Birds, after all, are God's creatures; and if Allah chooses not to provide them with a colon and a capacity for prolonged retention, who are we that we should dare to complain? Let us rather give thanks that dogs were not allowed to fly.

The dove was sacred in ancient Syria, and Atargatis was, among many other things, a Fish Goddess and the patroness of every animal except the pig. Within the precincts of her temple at Hierapolis, in northern Syria, there was a lake with an altar in it, and a congregation of carp; also a kind of holy zoo, where eagles, oxen, lions and bears wandered harmlessly and at liberty among the worshipers. Ancient traditions die hard, and perhaps the birds we had seen owed their immunity, in mosque and church, to the buried memories of a religion far older than either Islam or Christianity. Animals, say the theologians, have no souls. Having no souls, they have no rights, and may be treated by human beings as though they were mere things. In certain circumstances, indeed, they deserve a treatment even worse than that which we ordinarily accord to things. Blessed Cecilia, a thirteenth-century Roman nun, has told how St. Dominic came one evening to preach, from behind the grille, to the Sisters of her convent. His theme was devils; and hardly had he begun his sermon, when "the enemy of mankind came on the scene in the shape of a sparrow and began to fly through the air, hopping even on the Sisters' heads, so that they could have handled him had they been so minded, and all this to hinder the preaching. St. Dominic, observing this, called Sister Maximilla and said: 'Get up and catch him, and bring him here to me.' She got up and, putting out her hand, had no difficulty in seizing hold of him, and handed him out through the window to St. Dominic. St. Dominic held him fast in one hand, and commenced plucking off his feathers with the other, saying the while: 'You wretch, you rogue!' When he had plucked him clean of all his feathers, amidst much laughter from the Brothers and Sisters, and awful shrieks of the sparrow, he pitched him out, saying: 'Fly now if you can, enemy of mankind! You can cry out and trouble us, but you cannot hurt us.' "

What an ugly little picture it is! An intelligent and highly educated man wallowing in the voluntary ignorance of the lowest kind of superstition; a saint indulging his paranoid fancies to the point where they justified him in behaving like a sadist; a group of devout monks and nuns laughing full-throatedly at the shrieks and writhings of a tortured bird. Our own age is certainly bad; but in many respects the Age of Faith was even worse. Take, for example, this matter of torturing animals. There were a few humanitarians in the Middle Ages. Chaucer's Prioress, who could not bear to see a dog being beaten, was one of them. St. Hugh of Avalon was another. This older contemporary of St. Dominic had a pet swan and, instead of plucking birds alive, used to feed and tame them. And then, of course, there was St. Francis—though not St. Francis's followers. His rustic disciple, Brother Juniper, once heard a sick man express a desire for fried pig's trotters, and immediately rushed out of the house and hacked the feet off a living hog. When the saint rebuked him, it was not, as one might have expected, for an act of barbarous cruelty, but because he had damaged a valuable piece of private property. There were other early humanitarians—but not many. In Mme. de Rambure's anthology, *L'église et la Pitie envers les Animaux*, the exploits of medieval animal lovers fill no more than a hundred pages. English Common Law took no cognizance of acts of cruelty towards the brute creation; and to judge from Hogarth's gruesome picture of children tormenting, with every refinement of sadistic beastliness, their dogs, cats and birds, popular morality was as blind, in this respect, as the law. It was not until 1822 that the first piece of legislation on behalf of animals was enacted by Parliament. By 1876, the Royal Commission on Vivisection could state in its report that "the infliction upon animals of any unnecessary pain is justly abhorrent to the moral sense of Your Majesty's subjects generally." This was a far cry from Hogarth and St. Dominic, a change of heart and thought that marked perhaps the beginning of a religious revolution. The old, all too human bumptiousness which had been consecrated by verse twenty-six of the first chapter of Genesis, the doctrine that man is a being apart from the rest of creation and may do with it what he pleases, was giving place, under the influence of scientific knowledge, to a view of the

world at once more realistic and more charitable. That
which the theologians and the philosophers had been at
such pains to divide was coming together again in a system of thought and feeling that bore, at last, some resemblance to the system of facts in nature.

Spiritual progress is always in an ascending spiral.
Animal instinct gives place to human will and then to grace,
guidance, inspiration, which are simply instinct on a higher
level. Or consider the progress of consciousness. First there is
the infant's undifferentiated awareness, next comes discrimination and discursive reasoning, and finally (if the
individual wishes to transcend himself) there is a rise which
is also a return towards an obscure knowledge of the whole,
a realization of the timeless and the non-dual in time and
multiplicity. Similarly, in religion, there is the primitive worship of the god who is immanent in nature, next the worship
of divine transcendence, and then, on the intellectual level,
the philosophy of scientific monism and, on the existential
level, the mystical experience of the One, which corresponds,
two stories higher up, to the felt pantheism of the origins.
St. Dominic was the preacher and, at the same time,
the victim of a theological system which, in spite of the
doctrine of the Incarnation, stressed the transcendence of
God, the hatefulness of nature, the alienation of man
from the rest of the creation. This fact explains his behavior, but does not completely excuse it. Tradition is
strong, but not irresistible. Some measure of moral, intellectual and spiritual independence is always possible—
though it may, of course, be exceedingly dangerous, as
the Albigensians found in St. Dominic's day and as ideological heretics discover in ours, to assert one's right to such
independence. In this particular case, however, neither
life nor conscience was in danger. There was no dogma
equating sparrows with devils. The saint *could* have behaved, rationally and charitably; if he behaved as he
did, it was, I suppose, because he enjoyed being superstitious (*superstition* equals *concupiscence*, says Pascal), and
also, no doubt, because twelve years of medieval higher
education—twelve years, that is to say, of memorizing
dead men's words and playing logical games with them—
had left him with a notion of reality even more distorted,

in some respects, than that of the ignorant peasant or artisan.

And this brings us back to the Unknown Letter-Maker; for we live, each one of us, immersed in language, and our thoughts, feelings and behavior are, to a much greater extent than we care to admit, determined by the words and syntax of our native tongue and even by the signs through which those words and that syntax are made visible in writing. In the West it is only recently that, thanks to the logicians, the semanticists, the students of linguistics and metalinguistics, we have become fully aware of the part played by language as a virtual philosophy, a source of ontological postulates, a conditioner of thought and even perception, a molder of sentiments, a creater of behavior patterns. To the Indians, these ideas have been familiar for centuries. In every system of Hindu philosophy the phenomenal world is called *nama-rupa*, "name-and-form." This, at first glance, strikes us as odd. But after all (to quote the words of Heinrich Zimmer), "the possibilities for thought, practical or otherwise, at any given period are rigidly limited by the range and wealth of the available linguistic coinage. . . . The totality of this currency is called, in Indian philosophy, *naman* (Latin *nomen,* our word 'name'). The very substance, on and by which the mind operates when thinking, consists of this name-treasury of notions. *Naman* is the internal realm of concepts, which corresponds to the external realm of perceived 'forms,' the Sanskrit term for the latter being *rupa.* . . . *Rupa* is the outer counterpart of *naman; naman* the interior of *rupa.* *Nama-rupa* therefore denotes, on the one hand, man, the experiencing and thinking individual, man as endowed with mind and senses; and, on the other, all the means and objects of thought and perception. *Nama-rupa* is the whole world, subjective and objective, as observed and known."* But no language is perfect, no vocabulary is adequate to the wealth of the given universe, no pattern of words and sentences, however rich, however subtle, can do justice to the interconnected Gestalts with which

---

* Heinrich Zimmer, *Philosophies of India,* p. 23. New York, Pantheon Books, 1951.

experience presents us. Consequently the phenomenal forms of our name-conditioned universe are "by nature delusory and fallacious." Wisdom comes only to those who have learned how to talk and read and write without taking language more seriously than it deserves. As the only begetter of civilization and even of our humanity, language must be taken very seriously. Seriously, too, as an instrument (when used with due caution) for thinking about the relationships between phenomena. But it must never be taken seriously when it is used, as in the old credal religions and their modern political counterparts, as being in any way the equivalents of immediate experience or as being a source of true knowledge about the nature of things. In an unsystematic way, the great medieval mystics, such as Eckhart and Tauler and the author of *The Cloud of Unknowing*, were acutely aware of the danger of taking language as seriously as it was taken by most of their contemporaries. But their warnings were couched in general terms, and their ignorance of any language but Latin and their native dialect made it impossible for them to formulate any effective criticism. For example, they did not, and could not, see that Aristotle's logic was a systematization of Greek grammar, which makes a certain amount of sense for those who speak an Indo-European language, but not for those who speak Chinese or for those who have learned the artificial languages of mathematics and modern logic; and that, therefore, it cannot be regarded (as it was regarded for so many centuries) as Logic with a large L, the final and definitive formulation of the laws of thought. Similarly, they did not, and could not, know that the age-old preoccupation of Western philosophers with the notion of substance was the natural consequence of their speaking a language in which there were clearly distinguishable parts of speech, a verb "to be," and sentences containing subjects and predicates. " 'Substance,' " says Bertrand Russell in his *History of Western Philosophy*, "is a metaphysical mistake due to transference to the world-structure of the structure of sentences composed of a subject and a predicate." And what about "essence"? The question is relevant only in the domain of language. "A *word* may have an essence, a *thing* cannot." In Chinese there are no fixed parts of speech, sentences do not take the subject-predicate form, and there is no verb meaning "to be." Consequently, except under foreign influence, Chinese philosophers have never formulated the idea of "substance," and never projected the word into the universe.

Their concern has always been with the relationships between things, not with their "essences"; with the "how" of experience rather than the inferred "what." If the Arian controversy had reached China, one can imagine the native theologians speculating about the simultaneous threeness and oneness of the Persons, but never dividing, or not dividing, the Substance.

Western science began with the ideas of essence and substance, which were implicit in the Indo-European languages and had been made explicit in Greek philosophy and Latin theology; but it has been compelled, by the inner logic of the scientific process, to get rid of these notions and adopt instead an up-to-date, critical version of the Chinese view of things.

Language exists in two forms, the spoken and the written. As knowledge accumulated, and formal education was made more widely available, written language became progressively more and more important. *Littera scripta manet, volat irrevocabile verbum;* writing abides, the spoken word flies off and cannot be recalled. Socrates, who is remembered solely because Xenophon and Plato wrote about him, was himself an enemy of writing. Wisdom and a knowledge of metaphysical and moral truth cannot, he maintained, be conveyed in books, but only by means of rhetoric and dialectic. The Chinese sages, it may be remarked, were of a diametrically opposite opinion. For them, rhetoric and dialectic were beneath contempt. Serious philosophical ideas could be conveyed only in writing—and only, of course, in the kind of writing current in China, where language is rendered visible by means of a complicated system of signs, some of which (the pictograms) are actually representations of the things denoted, others (the ideograms) are compound symbols standing for ideas, and yet others (the phonograms) represent certain of the sounds which occur most commonly in the spoken language. Before the invention of the alphabet, the civilized peoples of the Near East employed one or other of two very ancient systems of writing—the hieroglyphic writing of Egypt and the cuneiform of Sumeria and, later, of Babylonia, Assyria and Persia. Both systems were fundamentally similar to the Chinese, inasmuch as both made use of hundreds of signs, some pictographic, some ideographic and some phonographic. The inventors of the alphabet performed the extraordinary feat of reducing these hundreds of signs to less than thirty. These twenty-odd consonants and vowels were so judiciously chosen that, by means of them, every word in every language could be rendered, not indeed perfectly, but well enough for most practical purposes—and rendered, what was more, in a form which indicated, more or less, how the word was to be pronounced. Efficiency in business and government; universal education; encyclopedias and dictionaries; the possibility of expressing one's meaning unequivocally and with the maximum of precision—these are a few of the benefits for which we have to thank the Unknown Letter-Maker. The ABC has been an enormous blessing, but like most blessings, not entirely unmixed. Rendered alphabetically, a word remains strictly itself. Rendered by means of pictograms, ideograms and phonograms, a word becomes something else, as well as itself. The Chinese interest in relations rather than substance is due in part, as we have seen, to the idiosyncrasies of a language in which there are no fixed parts of speech and no word for "to be"; in part to the nature of Chinese writing. "Chinese thought," says Professor Chang Tun-sun, "is not based upon the law of identity, but takes as its starting point relative orientation, or rather the relation of opposites." (For example, "non-resistance means strength," "fluency stutters," "*yin* entails *yang*." This last pair of correlated opposites is fundamental in Chinese thought, which regards the positive principle as dependent, for its existence, upon the negative, and the negative upon the positive. Brought up on Latin grammar and the ABC, St. Dominic could see only the differences between things, not their togetherness. God was one thing and Nature, since the Fall, something other and alien, something which willingly lent itself to the Enemy of Mankind, so that a sparrow was really the Devil in disguise and must be tortured, just as the Albigensians must be tortured for going one stage further and affirming that the Devil had actually created the material world.) The Chinese system of thought is "probably related to the nature of Chinese characters. Being ideographic, Chinese characters put emphasis on the signs and symbols of objects. The Chinese are interested in the interrelation between the different signs, without being bothered by the substance underlying them. . . . The characteristic of Chinese thought lies in its exclusive attention to the correlational implications between different signs."

When words are alphabetically rendered, they remain, as I have said, merely themselves. Spelled out, a name is still that particular name, and the corresponding form is still that particular form. The ABC confirms the phenomenal world of *nama-rupa*. In English, for example, the notion of "good" is rendered by the four letters, g-o-o-d. In Chinese, the same idea is represented by a combination of the sign for "woman" with the sign for "child." How touching! But now consider the Chinese word *fang*. *Fang* has many different meanings, but is represented by only one character, originally applied to *fang*, signifying "square"—a character which is a kind of picture or diagram of two boats tied together. When this sign stands for *fang* in any of its other meanings, it is used as a phonogram and has to be combined with another sign, so as to be distinguishable from "square." Thus, the sign for "woman" plus the phonogram for *fang* means "hinder." *Woman* plus *child* equals *good*. But this good has its price; for a man who has a wife and children has given hostages to fortune. The good of one context is the hindrance of another. What a wealth of ideas is implicit in the writing of these two common words! No wonder if the Chinese paid so much attention to "the correlational implications between different signs."

The universe is a many-dimensional pattern, infinite in extent, infinite in duration, infinite in significance and infinitely aware, we may surmise, of its own infinities. Within the cosmic order, every component pattern, every object and event, is related to every other; there is a co-varying togetherness of all things. But, by creatures like ourselves, most of the interconnections within the general Gestalt are, and will always be unrecognized. For us, "the world is full of a number of things," which we tend to see as so many independent entities. And we are confirmed in this tendency by alphabetic writing. For alphabetic writing creates an illusion of clarity and separateness. The words we read are written in such a way that they seem to be exclusively themselves, and this makes us believe that we know what's what, that a rose is a rose is a rose. But in fact a rose is a rose-plus is a rose-minus is a rose to the nth. The *what* we think we know is never only *what*. Besides, as an underlying substance, *what* is unknowable and non-existent. *What* exists only when it is known by the liberated and transfigured consciousness, which experiences the paradox of the absoluteness of relationships, the infinity and universality of particulars. This experience is what Eckhart calls the experience of "isness"—which is entirely different from the notion of being or the dogma of substance. For the unliberated, untransfigured mind, all that is knowable is the *how* of relationships. The characters employed in the older systems of writing helped men to remember this all-important fact. That "woman" plus a certain phonogram (which was originally a pictogram, representing two boats tied together, and stood for "square") should actually mean "hinder," is a most salutary reminder that the universe is bottomlessly odd. Lucian, Astarte, the alphabet, sparrows in church, St. Dominic, the Albigenses—what a rich mixed bag of disparate items! But, ultimately, nothing is irrelevant to anything else. There is a togetherness of all things in an endless hierarchy of living and interacting patterns.

Conditioned by their culture, their language, their position in time, their temperament, character and intelligence, men have paid attention now to one set of patterns, now to another. Today we have it in our power to perceive, infer and understand a far wider area of reality than was open to our ancestors. Nature, language, history, human behavior—our knowledge of these things is incomparably wider than that which was available in the past. But width, unfortunately, is all too often the enemy of depth. Clear knowledge of the Whole outside us requires to be supplemented by an obscure knowledge of the Whole within. Moreover, the clear external knowledge must be carried inwards, as far as analysis and introspection can take it, while the obscure knowledge within must be projected outwards, so that our theoretical conviction of the world's unity may be transformed into an intuition, a constant realization. How easy it is to say what ought to be done! And how difficult, alas, to do it and, therefore, how unlikely that, except by very few, it will ever be done!

Miracle in Lebanon

In one of the northern suburbs of Beirut there stands an ugly little Armenian church, to which, in the ordinary course of events, no tourist would ever dream of going. But in this month of May, 1954, the course of events had not been ordinary. The sight we had come to see was a miracle.

It had happened two or three days before. In the niche where, between services, the communion chalice was kept, a patch of light had appeared on the stone. There was no sunbeam to account for it, no indication, so we were assured, that the stone contained any phosphorescent or fluorescent substance. And yet the fact remained that, for the last few days, a soft glow had appeared every morning, persisted all day and faded out at night. For the Armenians, I suppose, the miracle clearly demonstrated how right their fathers had been to reject the competing orthodoxies of Rome and Byzantium in favor of the doctrine that, after his baptism (but not before), Christ's flesh consisted of ethereal fire and "was not subject to the ordinary phenomena of digestion, secretions and evacuations." For the rest of us, it was either a hoax, or an ordinary event in an unusual context, or else one of those delightful anomalies which distress the right-thinking scientist by actually turning up, every now and then, in all their mysterious pointlessness, and refusing to be explained away.

The church, when we arrived, was thronged, I was going to say, with pilgrims—but the word (at least in this present age of unfaith and, therefore, religious earnestness) calls up ideas of devotion; and of devotion, or even of decorum, there were no signs. But if these people were no pilgrims, in our non-Chaucerian sense of the term, neither were they mere sightseers. Curiosity was certainly one of their motives, but not, it was clear, the only or strongest one. What had brought most of them to church was a form of self-interest. They had come there, as the forty-niners came to California, in search of sudden profit—a horde of spiritual prospectors looking for nuggets of *mana*, veins of twenty-two-carat good luck, something, in a word, for nothing.

Something for nothing—but, concretely, what? When crowds close in on a movie star, they can beg autographs, steal handkerchiefs and fountain pens, tear off pieces of his or her garments as relics. Similarly, in the Middle Ages persons dying in the odor of sanctity ran the risk, when their bodies lay in state, of being stripped naked or even dismembered by the faithful. Clothing would be cut to ribbons, ears cropped, hair pulled out, toes and fingers amputated, nipples snipped off and carried home as amulets. But here, unfortunately, there was no corpse; there was only light, and light is intangible. You cannot slice off an inch of the spectrum and put it in your pocket. The people who had come to exploit this Comstock Lode of the miraculous found themselves painfully frustrated; there was nothing here that they could take away with them. For all practical purposes, the glow in the niche was immaterial. Then, happily for all concerned, a young woman noticed that, for some reason or other, one of the chandeliers, suspended from the ceiling of the church, was wet. Drops of rather dirty water were slowly forming and, at lengthening intervals, falling. Nobody supposed that there was anything supernatural about the phenomenon; but at least it was taking place in a supernatural context. Moreover the water on the chandelier possessed one immense advantage over the light in the niche: it was tangible as well as merely visible. A boy was hoisted onto the shoulders of a tall man. Handkerchiefs were passed up to him, moistened in the oozings of the lamp and then returned to their owners, made happy now by the possession of a charged fetish, capable, no doubt, of curing minor ailments, restoring lost potency and mediating prayers for success in love or business.

But "the search for the miraculous" (to use Ouspensky's phrase) is not invariably motived by self-interest. There are people who love truth for its own sake and are ready, like the founders of the Society for Psychical Research, to seek it at the bottom of even the muddiest, smelliest wells. Much more widespread than the love of truth is the appetite for marvels, the love of the Phony *an sich,* in itself and for its own sweet sake. There is also a curious psychological derangement, a kind of neurosis, sometimes mild, sometimes severe, which might be called "The Cryptogram-Secret Society Syndrome." What fun to be an initiate! How delicious to feel the paranoid glow which accompanies the consciousness of belonging to the innermost circle, of being one of the superior and privileged few who know, for example, that all history, past, present and future, is written into the stones of the Great Pyramid; that Jesus, like Madame Blavatsky, spent seven years in Tibet; that Bacon wrote all the works of Shakespeare and never died, merely vanished, to reappear a century later as the Comte de Saint-Germain, who is still living either (as Mrs. Annie Besant was convinced) in a Central European castle, or else, more probably, in a cave, with a large party of Lemurians, near the top of Mount Shasta; alternatively, that Bacon did die and was buried, not (needless to say) in what the vulgar regard as his tomb, but at Williamsburg, Virginia, or, better still, on an island off the coast of California, near Santa Barbara. To be privy to such secrets is a high, rare privilege, a distinction equivalent to that of being Mr. Rockefeller or a Knight of the Garter.

Esoteric phantasies about Fourth Dynasty monuments, sixteenth-century lawyers and eighteenth-century adventurers are harmless. But when practical politicians and power seekers go in for esotericism, the results are apt to be dangerous. Whether Fascist or revolutionary, every conspiratorial group has its quota of men and women afflicted by the Cryptogram-Secret Society Syndrome. Nor is this all. The intelligence services of every government are largely staffed by persons who (in happier circumstances or if their temperament were a little different), would be inoffensively engaged in hunting for Tibetan Masters, proving that the English are the Lost Ten Tribes, celebrating Black Masses or (the favorite occupation of Charles Williams's more eccentric characters) intoning the Tetragrammaton backwards. If these neurotics could be content to play the cloak-and-dagger game according to the rules of patriotism, all would be, relatively speaking, well. But the history of espionage demonstrates very clearly that many compulsive esotericists are not content to belong to only one Secret Society. To intensify their strange fun, they surreptitiously work for the enemy as well as their own gang, and end, in a delirium of duplicity, by doublecrossing everyone. The born secret agent, the man who positively enjoys spying, can never, because he is a neurotic, be relied upon. It may well be that a nation's actual security is in inverse ratio to the size of its security forces. The greater the number of its secret agents and hush-hush men, the more chances there are of betrayal.

But let us get back to our miracle. "What do you think of it?" I asked our Lebanese companion. He stroked his black beard, he smiled, he shrugged his shoulders in expressive silence. Being himself a professional thaumaturge—trained by the dervishes to lie on beds of nails, to go into catalepsy, to perform feats of telepathy, to send people into hypnotic trance by simply touching a point on the neck or back—he knew how hard a man must work if he would acquire even the most trifling of paranormal powers. His skepticism in regard to amateur wonder-workers and spontaneous miracles was complete and unshakable.

A queue had formed at the foot of the altar steps. We got into line and shuffled slowly forward to get our peep, in due course, into the niche. That I personally saw nothing was the fault, not of the chalice, but of my own poor eyesight. To my companions and everyone else the glow was manifest. It was an Armenian miracle; but even Maronites, even Uniats, even Moslems and Druses had to admit that something had happened.

We made our way towards the door. Perched on the tall man's shoulders, the boy was still busy at his task of turning handkerchiefs into relics. In the sacristy picture postcards of the chalice and the illuminated niche were already on sale.

In Edward Conze's admirable account of Buddhism* there is a striking passage on the historical, and perhaps psychologically inevitable relationship between spirituality and superstition, between the highest form of religion and the lowest. "Historically," Conze notes, "the display of supernatural powers and the working of miracles were among the most potent causes of the conversion of tribes and individuals to Buddhism." Even the most "refined and intellectual" of Buddhists "would be inclined to think that a belief in miracles is indispensable to the survival of any spiritual life. In Europe, from the eighteenth century onwards, the conviction that spiritual forces can act on material events has given way to a belief in the inexorable rule of natural law. The result is that the experience of the spiritual has become more and more inaccessible to modern society. No known religion has become mature without embracing both the spiritual and the magical. If it rejects the spiritual, religion becomes a mere weapon to dominate the world. . . . Such was the case in Nazism and in modern Japan. If, however, religion rejects the magical side of life, it cuts itself off from the living forces of the world to such an extent that it cannot bring even the spiritual side of man to maturity." Buddhism (like Christianity in its heyday) has combined "lofty metaphysics with adherence to the most commonly accepted superstitions of mankind. The Prajnaparamita text tells us that 'perfect wisdom can be attained only by the complete and total extinction of self-interest.' And yet, in the same texts, this supreme spiritual wisdom is 'recommended as a sort of magical talisman or lucky amulet.' . . . Among all the paradoxes with which the history of Buddhism presents us this combination of spiritual negation of self-interest with magical subservience to self-interest is perhaps one of the most striking."

The same paradox is to be found in Christianity. The

---

* See pp. 84 ff. of *Buddhism, Its Essence and Development* by Edward Conze, Preface by Arthur Waley. New York, Philosophical Library, 1951.

mystical spirituality of the fourteenth century had as its background and context the system of ideas which called into existence such men as Chaucer's Pardoner and the preacher who, in the Decameron, tours the country exhibiting a tail feather of the Holy Ghost. Or consider the flowering, three centuries later, of French spirituality in Charles de Condren and Olier, in Lallemant and Surin and Mme. de Chantal. These worshipers in spirit of a God who is Spirit were contemporary with and, in Surin's case, deeply involved in the most hideous manifestations of devil-centered superstition. White sand is clean, but sterile. If you want a herbaceous border, you must mulch your soil with dead leaves and, if possible, dig in a load of dung. Shall we ever see, in religion, the equivalent of hydroponics—spiritual flowers growing, without benefit of excrement or decay, in a solution of pure love and understanding? I devoutly hope so, but, alas, have my doubts. Like dirtless farming, dirtless spirituality is likely to remain, for a long time, an exception. The rule will be dirt and plenty of it. Occult dirt, bringing forth, as usual, a few mystical flowers and a whole crop of magicians, priests and fanatics. Anti-occult dirt—the dirt of ideological and technological superstition—in which personal frustrations grow like toadstools in the dark thickets of political tyranny. Or else (and this will be the ultimate horror) a mixture of both kinds of dirt, fertile in such monstrosities as mediumistic commissars, clairvoyant engineers, NKVD's and FBI's equipped with ESP as well as walky-talkies and concealed microphones.

This last possibility is not nearly so remote as it may sound. Hitler was an occultist as well as an ideologist, and, in their search for weapons with which to fight the Cold War, certain governmental agencies even in the democratic countries are showing a most unwholesome interest in parapsychology. We reproach the Victorian men of science with having been blind to the facts of psychology; we laugh at them for their absurd attempts to explain the universe in terms, exclusively, of miniature billiard balls in motion. Fifty years from now the human mind will have been thoroughly explored and the results of that research applied systematically. With what nostalgic regret our children's children will look back to those dear little Victorian billiard balls! Ignorance and inefficiency are among the strongest bulwarks of liberty. The Victorians knew very little about the brain and even less about the mind, and were therefore in no position to do anything to control them. Pure and applied psychology, neurology, bio-chemistry and pharmacology have made enormous advances during the last few years. By the beginning of the twenty-first century the theorists in these fields will possess enormous stores of knowledge, and the technicians will have developed innumerable ways of applying that knowledge in the interests of those who can command or buy their services. Every government, by then, will be employing as many psychologists and parapsychologists, as many neurologists and pharmacologists and sociologists and hatha-yogins, as it now employs chemists, physicists, metallurgists and engineers. There will be Psychic Energy Commissions operating huge secret laboratories dedicated, not to our hopelessly old-fashioned ideals of mass murder and collective suicide, but to the more constructive task of man's definitive domestication and total enslavement. Our present, ludicrously crude methods of propaganda and brain-washing will have given place to a number of really effective psycho-pharmaco-occult techniques for inculcating and maintaining conformity. Meanwhile new drugs for heightening psi faculties will have been developed. Pills will be used to reinforce the effects of intensive training, and the spies and informers of the future will operate with a degree of efficiency now scarcely imaginable. Under whatever name—CIA, CID, NKVD, FBI—the secret police will be virtually omniscient and therefore omnipotent. We have had religious revolutions, we have had political, industrial, economic and nationalistic revolutions. All of them, as our descendants will discover, were but ripples in an ocean of conservatism— trivial by comparison with the psychological revolution towards which we are now so rapidly moving. *That* will really be a revolution. When it is over, the human race will give no further trouble.

Usually Destroyed

Our guide through the labyrinthine streets of Jerusalem was a young Christian refugee from the other side of the wall which now divides the ancient city from the new, the non-viable state of Jordan from the non-viable state of Israel. He was a sad, embittered young man—and well he might be. His prospects had been blighted, his family reduced from comparative wealth to the most abject penury, their house and land taken away from them, their bank account frozen and devaluated. In the circumstances, the surprising thing was not his bitterness, but the melancholy resignation with which it was tempered.

He was a good guide—almost too good, indeed; for he was quite remorseless in his determination to make us visit all those deplorable churches which were built, during the nineteenth century, on the ruins of earlier places of pilgrimage. There are tourists whose greatest pleasure is a trip through historical associations and their own fancy. I am not one of them. When I travel, I like to move among intrinsically significant objects, not through an absence peopled only by literary references, Victorian monuments and the surmises of archaeologists. Jerusalem, of course, contains much more than ghosts and architectural monstrosities. Besides being one of the most profoundly depressing of the earth's cities, it is one of the strangest and, in its own way, one of the most beautiful. Unfortunately our guide was far too conscientious to spare us the horrors and the unembodied, or ill-embodied, historical associations. We had to see everything—not merely St. Anne's and St. James's and the Dome of the Rock, but the hypothetical site of Caiaphas's house and what the Anglicans had built in the seventies, what the Tsar and the German Emperor had countered with in the eighties, what had been considered beautiful in the early nineties by the

158

Copts or the French Franciscans. But, luckily, even at the dreariest moments of our pilgrimage there were compensations. Our sad young man spoke English well and fluently, but spoke it as eighteenth-century virtuosi played music—with the addition of *fioriture* and even whole cadenzas of their own invention. His most significant contribution to colloquial English (and, at the same time, to the science and art of history) was the insertion into almost every sentence of the word "usually." What he actually meant by it, I cannot imagine. It may be, of course, that he didn't mean anything at all, and that what sounded like an adverb was in fact no more than one of those vocalized tics to which nervous persons are sometimes subject. I used to know a professor whose lectures and conversation were punctuated, every few seconds, by the phrase, "With a thing with a thing." "With a thing with a thing" is manifestly gibberish. But our young friend's no less compulsive "usually" had a fascinating way of making a kind of sense—much more sense, very often, than the speaker had intended. "This area," he would say as he showed us one of the Victorian monstrosities, "this area" [it was one of his favorite words] "is very rich in antiquity. St. Helena built here a very vast church, but the area was usually destroyed by the Samaritans in the year 529 after Our Lord Jesus Christ. Then the Crusaders came to the area, and built a new church still more vast. Here were mosaics the most beautiful in the world. In the seventeenth century after Our Lord Jesus Christ the Turks usually removed the lead from the roof to make ammunition; consequently rain entered the area and the church was thrown down. The present area was erected by the Prussian Government in the year 1879 after Our Lord Jesus Christ and all these broken-down houses you see over there were usually destroyed during the war with the Jews in 1948."

Usually destroyed and then usually rebuilt, in order, of course, to be destroyed again and then rebuilt, *da capo ad infinitum*. That vocalized tic had compressed all history into a four-syllabled word. Listening to our young friend, as we wandered through the brown, dry squalor of the Holy City, I felt myself overwhelmed, not by the mere thought of man's enduring misery, but by an obscure, immediate sense of it, an organic realization. These pullulations among ruins and in the dark of what once were sepulchers; these hordes of sickly children; these galled asses and the human beasts of burden bent under enormous loads; these mortal enemies beyond the dividing wall; these priest-conducted groups of pilgrims befuddling themselves with the vain repetitions, against which the founder of their religion had gone out of his way to warn them—they were dateless, without an epoch. In this costume or that, under one master or another, praying to whichever God was temporarily in charge, they had been here from the beginning. Had been here with the Egyptians, been here with Joshua, been here when Solomon in all his glory ordered his slaves in all their misery to build the temple, which Nebuchadnezzar had usually demolished and Zedekiah, just as usually, had put together again. Had been here during the long pointless wars between the two kingdoms, and at the next destruction under Ptolemy, the next but one under Antiochus and the next rebuilding under Herod and the biggest, best destruction of all by Titus. Had been here when Hadrian abolished Jerusalem and built a brand-new Roman city, complete with baths and a theater, with a temple of Jupiter, and a temple of Venus, to take its place. Had been here when the insurrection of Bar Cocheba was drowned in blood. Had been here while the Roman Empire declined and turned Christian, when Chosroes the Second destroyed the churches and when the Caliph Omar brought Islam and, most unusually, destroyed nothing. Had been here to meet the Crusaders and then to wave them good-by, to welcome the Turks and then to watch them retreat before Allenby. Had been here under the Mandate and through the troubles of '48, and were here now and would be here, no doubt, in the same brown squalor, alternately building and destroying, killing and being killed, indefinitely.

"I do not think," Lord Russell has recently written, "that the sum of human misery has ever in the past been so great as it has been in the last twenty-five years." One is inclined to agree. Or are we, on second thoughts, merely flattering ourselves? At most periods of history moralists have liked to boast that theirs was the most iniquitous generation since the time of Cain—the most iniquitous and therefore, since God is just, the most grievously afflicted. Today, for example, we think of the thirteenth century as one of the supremely creative periods of human history. But the men who were actually contemporary with the cathedrals and Scholastic Philosophy regarded their age as hopelessly degenerate, uniquely bad and condignly punished. Were they right, or are we? The answer, I suspect is: Both. Too much evil and too much suffering can make it impossible for men to be creative; but within very wide limits greatness is perfectly compatible with organized insanity, sanctioned crime and intense, chronic unhappiness for the majority. Every one of the great religions preaches a mixture of profound pessimism and the most extravagant optimism. "I show you sorrow," says the Buddha, pointing to man in his ordinary unregenerate condition. And in the same context Christian theologians speak of the Fall, of Original Sin, of the Vale of Tears, while Hindus refer to the workings of man's home-made destiny, his evil karma. But over against the sorrow, the tears, the self-generated, self-inflicted disasters, what super-human prospects! If he so wishes, the Hindu affirms, a man can realize his identity with Brahman, the Ground of all being; if he so wishes, says the Christian, he can be filled with God; if he so wishes, says the Buddhist, he can live in a transfigured world where nirvana and samsara, the eternal and the temporal, are one. But, alas—and from optimism based on the experience of the few, the saints and sages return to the pessimism forced upon them by their observation of the many—the gate is narrow, the threshold high, few are chosen because few choose to be chosen. In practice man usually destroys himself—but has done so up till now a little less thoroughly than he has built himself up. In spite of everything, we are still here. The spirit of destruction has been willing enough, but for most of historical time its technological flesh has been weak. The Mongols had only horses as transport, only bows and spears and butchers' knives for weapons; if they had possessed our machinery, they could have depopulated the planet. As it was, they had to be content with small triumphs—the slaughter of only a few millions, the stamping out of civilization only in Western Asia.

In this universe of ours nobody has ever succeeded in getting anything for nothing. In certain fields, progress in the applied sciences and the arts of organization has certainly lessened human misery; but it has done so at the cost of increasing it in others. The worst enemy of life, freedom and the common decencies is total anarchy; their second worst enemy is total efficiency. Human interests are best served when society is tolerably well organized and industry moderately advanced. Chaos and ineptitude are anti-human; but so too is a superlatively efficient government, equipped with all the products of a highly developed technology. When such a government goes in for usually destroying, the whole race is in danger.

The Mongols were the aesthetes of militarism; they believed in gratuitous massacre, in destruction for destruction's sake. Our malice is less pure and spontaneous; but, to make up for this deficiency, we have ideals. The end proposed, on either side of the Iron Curtain, is nothing less than the Good of Humanity and its conversion to the Truth. Crusades can go on for centuries, and wars in the name of God or Humanity are generally diabolic in their ferocity. The unprecedented depth of human misery in our time is proportionate to the unprecedented height of the social ideals entertained by the totalitarians on the one side, the Christians and the secularist democrats on the other.

And then there is the question of simple arithmetic. There are far more people on the earth today than there were in any earlier century. The miseries which have been the usual consequence of the usual course of nature and the usual behavior of human beings are the lot today, not of the three hundred millions of men, women and children who were contemporary with Christ, but of more than two and a half billions. Obviously, then, the sum of our present misery cannot fail to be greater than the sum of misery in the past. Every individual is the center of a world, which it takes very little to transform into a world of unadulterated suffering. The catastrophes and crimes of the twentieth century can transform almost ten times as many human universes into private hells as did the catastrophes and crimes of two thousand years ago. Moreover, thanks to improvements in technology, it is possible for fewer people to do more harm to greater numbers than ever before.

After the capture of Jerusalem by Nebuchadnezzar, how many Jews were carried off to Babylon? Jeremiah

puts the figure at four thousand six hundred, the compiler
of the Second Book of Kings at ten thousand. Compared
with the forced migrations of our time, the Exile was the most
trivial affair. How many millions were uprooted by Hitler
and the Communists? How many more millions were driven
out of Pakistan into India, out of India into Pakistan?
How many hundreds of thousands had to flee, with our
young guide, from their homes in Israel? By the waters of
Babylon ten thousand at the most sat down and wept.
In the single refugee camp at Bethlehem there are more
exiles than that. And Bethlehem's is only one of dozens of
such camps scattered far and wide over the Near East.

So it looks, all things considered, as though Lord Russell
were right—that the sum of misery is indeed greater today
than at any time in the past. And what of the future?
Germ warfare and the H-bomb get all the headlines
and, for that very reason, may never be resorted to. Those
who talk a great deal about suicide rarely commit it. The
greatest threat to happiness is biological. There were
about twelve hundred million people on the planet when I
was born, six years before the turn of the century. Today
there are two thousand seven hundred millions; thirty years
from now there will probably be four thousand millions. At
present about sixteen hundred million people are underfed.
In the nineteen-eighties the total may well have risen to
twenty-five hundred millions, of whom a considerable number
may actually be starving. In many parts of the world
famine may come even sooner. In his Report on the Census
of 1951 the Registrar General of India has summed up
the biological problem as it confronts the second most
populous country of the world. There are now three hundred
and seventy-five million people living within the borders of
India, and their numbers increase by five millions annually.
The current production of basic foods is seventy million tons
a year, and the highest production that can be achieved
in the foreseeable future is ninety-four million tons. Ninety-
four million tons will support four hundred and fifty million
people at the present sub-standard level, and the population of India will pass the four hundred and fifty million
mark in 1969. After that, there will be a condition of what
the Registrar General calls "catastrophe."

In the index at the end of the sixth volume of Dr. Toynbee's *A Study of History*, Popilius Laenas gets five mentions and Porphyry of Batamaea, two; but the word you would expect to find between these names, Population, is conspicuous by its absence. In his second volume, Mr. Toynbee has written at length on "the stimulus of pressures"—but without ever mentioning the most important pressure of them all, the pressure of population on available resources. And here is a note in which the author describes his impressions of the Roman Campagna after twenty years of absence. "In 1911 the student who made the pilgrimage of the Via Appia Antica found himself walking through a wilderness almost from the moment when he passed beyond the City Walls. . . . When he repeated the pilgrimage in 1931, he found that, in the interval, Man had been busily reasserting his mastery over the whole stretch of country that lies between Rome and the Castelli Romani. . . . The tension of human energy on the Roman Campagna is now beginning to rise again for the first time since the end of the third century B.C." And there the matter is left, without any reference to the compelling reason for this "rise of tension." Between 1911 and 1931 the population of Italy had increased by the best part of eight millions. Some of these eight millions went to live in the Roman Campagna. And they did so, not because Man with a large M had in some mystical way increased the tension of human energy, but for the sufficiently obvious reason that there was nowhere else for them to go. In terms of a history that takes no cognizance of demographical facts, the past can never be fully understood, the present is quite incomprehensible and the future entirely beyond prediction.

Thinking, for a change, in demographic as well as in merely cultural, political and religious terms, what kind of reasonable guesses can we make about the sum of human misery in the years to come? First, it seems pretty certain that more people will be hungrier and that, in many parts of the world, malnutrition will modulate into periodical or chronic famine. (One would like to know something about the Famines of earlier ages, but the nearest one gets to them in Mr. Toynbee's index is a blank space between Muhammad Falak-al-Din and Gaius Fannius.) Second, it seems pretty certain that, though they may help in the long run, remedial measures aimed at reducing the birthrate will be powerless to avert the miseries lying in wait for the next generation. Third, it seems pretty certain that improvements in Agriculture (not referred to in Mr. Toynbee's index, though Agrigentum gets two mentions and Agis IV, King of Sparta, no less than forty-seven) will be unable to catch up with current and foreseeable increases in population. If the standard of living in industrially backward countries is to be improved, agricultural production will have to go up every single year by at least two and a half per cent, and preferably by three and a half per cent. Instead of which, according to the FAO, Far Eastern food production per head of population will be ten per cent less in 1956 (and this assumes that the current Five-Year Plans will be fully realized) than it was in 1938.

Fourth, it seems pretty certain that, as a larger and hungrier population "mines the soil" in a desperate search for food, the destructive processes of erosion and deforestation will be speeded up. Fertility will therefore tend to go down as human numbers go up. (One looks up Erosion in Mr. Toynbee's index but finds only Esarhaddon, Esotericism and Esperanto; one hunts for Forests, but has to be content, alas, with Formosus of Porto.)

Fifth, it seems pretty certain that the increasing pressure of population upon resources will result in increasing political and social unrest, and that this unrest will culminate in wars, revolutions and counter-revolutions.

Sixth, it seems pretty certain that, whatever the avowed political principles and whatever the professed religion of the societies concerned, increasing pressure of population upon resources will tend to increase the power of the central government and to diminish the liberties of individual citizens. For, obviously, where more people are competing for less food, each individual will have to work harder and longer for his ration, and the central government will find it necessary to intervene more and more frequently in order to save the rickety economic machine from total breakdown, and at the same time to repress the popular discontent begotten by deepening poverty.

If Lord Russell lives to a hundred and twenty (and, for all our sakes, I hope most fervently that he will), he may find himself remembering these middle decades of the twentieth century as an almost Golden Age. In 1954, it is true, he decided that the sum of human misery had never been so great as it had been in the preceding quarter century. On the other hand, "you ain't seen nuthin' yet." Compared with the sum of four billion people's misery in the eighties, the sum of two billion miseries just before, during and after the Second World War may look like the Earthly Paradise.

But meanwhile here we were in Jerusalem, looking at the usually destroyed antiquities and rubbing shoulders with the usually poverty-stricken inhabitants, the usually superstitious pilgrims. Here was the Wailing Wall, with nobody to wail at it; for Israel is on the other side of a barrier, across which there is no communication except by occasional bursts of rifle fire, occasional exchanges of hand grenades. Here, propped up with steel scaffolding, was the Church of the Holy Sepulchre—that empty tomb to which, for three centuries, the early Christians paid no attention whatsoever, but which came, after the time of Constantine, to be regarded, throughout Europe, as the most important thing in the entire universe. And here was Siloam, here St. Anne's, here the Dome of the Rock and the site of the Temple, here, more ominous than Pompeii, the Jewish quarter, leveled, usually, in 1948 and not yet usually reconstructed. Here, finally, was St. James's, of the Armenians, gay with innumerable rather bad but charming paintings, and a wealth of gaudily colored tiles. The great church glowed like a dim religious merry-go-round. In all Jerusalem it was the only oasis of cheerfulness. And not alone of cheerfulness. As we came out into the courtyard, through which the visitor must approach the church's main entrance, we heard a strange and wonderful sound. High up, in one of the houses surrounding the court, somebody was playing the opening Fantasia of Bach's Partita in A Minor—playing it, what was more, remarkably well. From out of the open window, up there on the third floor, the ordered torrent of bright pure notes went streaming out over the city's immemorial squalor. Art and religion, philosophy and science, morals and politics—these are the instruments by means of which men have tried to discover a coherence in the flux of events, to impose an order on the chaos of experience. The most intractable of our experiences is the experience of Time—the intuition of duration, combined with the thought of perpetual perishing. Music is a device for working directly upon the experience of Time. The composer takes a piece of raw, undifferentiated duration and extracts from it, as the sculptor extracts the statue from his marble, a complex pattern of tones and silences, of harmonic sequences and contrapuntal interweavings. For the number of minutes it takes to play or listen to his composition, duration is transformed into something intrinsically significant, something held together by the internal logics of style and temperament, of personal feelings interacting with an artistic tradition, of creative insights expressing themselves within and beyond some given technical convention. This Fantasia, for example—with what a tireless persistence it drills its way through time! How effectively—and yet with no fuss, no self-conscious heroics—it transfigures the mortal lapse through time into the symbol, into the very fact, of a more than human life! A tunnel of joy and understanding had been driven through chaos and was demonstrating, for all to hear, that perpetual perishing is also perpetual creation. Which was precisely what our young friend had been telling us, in his own inimitable way, all the time. Usually destroyed —but also, and just as often, usually rebuilt. Like the rain, like sunshine, like the grace of God and the devastations of Nature, his verbalized tic was perfectly impartial. We walked out of the courtyard and down the narrow street. Bach faded, a donkey brayed, there was a smell of undisposed sewage. "In the year of Our Lord 1916," our guide informed us, "the Turkish Government usually massacred approximately seven hundred and fifty thousand Armenians."

Famagusta or Paphos

Famagusta reminded me irresistibly of Metro-Goldwyn-Mayer's back lot at Culver City. There, under the high fog of the Pacific, one used to wander between the façades of Romeo and Juliet's Verona into Tarzan's jungle, and out again, through Bret Harte, into Harun al-Rashid and *Pride and Prejudice*. Here, in Cyprus, the mingling of styles and epochs is no less extravagant, and the sets are not merely realistic—they are real. At Salamis, in the suburbs of Famagusta, one can shoot *Quo Vadis* against a background of solid masonry and genuine marble. And downtown, overlooking the harbor, stands the Tower of Othello (screen play by William Shakespeare, additional dialogue by Louella Katz); and the Tower of Othello is not the cardboard gazebo to which the theater has accustomed us, but a huge High Renaissance gun emplacement that forms part of a defense system as massive, elaborate and scientific as the Maginot Line. Within the circuit of those prodigious Venetian walls lies the blank space that was once a flourishing city—a blank space with a few patches of modern Turkish squalor, a few Byzantine ruins and, outdoing all the rest in intrinsic improbability, the Mosque. Flanked by the domes and colonnades of a pair of pretty little Ottoman buildings, the Mosque is a magnificent piece of thirteenth-century French Gothic, with a factory chimney, the minaret, tacked onto the north end of its façade. Golden and warm under the Mediterranean blue, this lesser Chartres rises from the midst of palms and carob trees and Oriental coffee shops. The muezzin (reinforced—for this is the twentieth century—by loud-speakers) calls from his holy smoke stack, and in what was once the Cathedral of St. Nicholas, the Faithful—or, if you prefer, the Infidels—pray not to an image or an altar, but towards Mecca.

We climbed back into the car. "Paphos," I said to the chauffeur, as matter-of-factly as in more familiar surroundings one would say, "Selfridge's," or "the Waldorf-Astoria." But the birthplace of Venus, it turned out, was a long way off and the afternoon was already half spent. Besides, the driver assured us (and the books confirmed it) there was really nothing to see at Paphos. Better go home and read about the temple and its self-mutilated priests in Frazer. Better still, read nothing, but emulating Mallarmé, write a sonnet on the magical name. *Mes bouquins refermés sur le nom de Paphos.* "My folios closing on the name of Paphos, What fun, with nothing but genius, to elect A ruin blest by a thousand foams beneath The hyacinth of its triumphal days! Let the cold come, with silence like a scythe! I'll wail no dirge if, level with the ground, This white, bright frolic should deny to all Earth's sites the honour of the fancied scene. My hunger, feasting on no mortal fruits, finds in their studied lack an equal savor. Suppose one bright with flesh, human and fragrant! My foot upon some snake where our love stirs the fire, I dream much longer, passionately perhaps, Of the other fruit, the Amazon's burnt breast."

Mes bouquins refermés sur le nom de Paphos,
Il m'amuse d'élire avec le seul génie
Une ruine, par mille écumes bénie
Sous l'hyacinthe, au loin, de ses jours triomphaux.

Coure le froid avec ses silences de faux,
Je n'y hululerai pas de vide nénie
Si ce trés blanc ébat au ras du sol dénie
A tout site l'honneur du paysage faux.

Ma faim qui d'aucuns fruits ici ne se régale
Trouve en leur docte manque une saveur égale:
Qu'un éclate de chair humain et parfumant!

Le pied sur quelque guivre où notre amour tisonne,
Je pense plus longtemps, peut-être éperdument
A l'autre, au sein brûlé d'une antique amazone.

How close this is to Keats's:

> Heard melodies are sweet, but those unheard
> Are sweeter; therefore, ye soft pipes, play on;
> Not to the sensual ear, but, more endeared,
> Pipe to the spirit ditties of no tone.

Parodying the Grecian Urn in terms of Mallarmé's Amazonian metaphor, we have: "Felt breasts are round, but those unfelt are rounder; therefore, absent paps, swell on." And the Keatsian formula can be applied just as well to Paphos. "Seen archaeological remains are interesting; but those unseen are more impressively like what the ruins of Aphrodite's birthplace *ought* to be." All of which, in a judicial summing up, may be said to be, on the one hand, profoundly true and, on the other, completely false. Unvisited ruins, ditties of no tone, solipsistic love of non-existent bosoms—these are all chemically pure, uncontaminated by those grotesque or horrible irrelevances which Mallarmé called "blasphemies" and which are the very stuff and substance of real life in a body. But this kind of chemical purity (the purity, in Mallarmean phraseology, of dream and Azure) is not the same as the saving purity of the Pure in Heart; this renunciation of irrelevant actuality is not the poverty in which the Poor in Spirit find the Kingdom of Heaven. Liberation is for those who react . correctly to given reality, not to their own, or other people's notions and fancies. Enlightenment is not for the Quietists and Puritans who, in their different ways, deny the world, but for those who have learned to accept and transfigure it. Our own private silences are better, no doubt, than the heard melodies inflicted upon us by the juke box. But are they better than *Adieu m'Amour* or the slow movement of the second Razumovsky Quartet? Unless we happen to be greater musicians than Dufay or Beethoven, the answer is, emphatically, No. And what about a love so chemically pure that it finds in the studied lack of fruits a savor equal or superior to that of human flesh? Love is a cognitive process, and in this case nuptial knowledge will be only a knowledge of the lover's imagination in its relations to his physiology. And it is the same with the

stay-at-home knowledge of distant ruins. In certain cases—
and the case of Paphos, perhaps, is one of them—fancy
may do a more obviously pleasing job than archaeological research or a sightseer's visit. But, in general, imagination falls immeasurably short of the inventions of Nature
and History. By no possibility could I, or even a great poet
like Mallarmé, have fabricated Salamis-Famagusta. To
which, of course, Mallarmé would have answered that
he had no more wish to fabricate Salamis-Famagusta
than to reproduce the real, historical Paphos. The picturesque detail, the unique and concrete datum—these held
no interest for the poet whose advice to himself and others
was: "Exclude the real, because vile; exclude the too precise meaning and *rature ta vague littérature*, correct
your literature until it becomes (from the realist's point of
view) completely vague." Mallarmé defined literature as
the antithesis of journalism. Literature, for him, is never a
piece of reporting, never an account of a *chose vue*—a
thing seen in the external world or even a thing seen, with
any degree of precision, by the inner eye. Both classes of
seen things are too concretely real for poetry and must be
avoided. Heredity and a visual environment conspired to
make of Mallarmé a Manichean Platonist, for whom
the world of appearances was nothing or worse than
nothing, and the Ideal World everything. Writing in 1867
from Besançon where, a martyr to Secondary Education,
he was teaching English to a pack of savage boys who
found him boring and ridiculous, he described to his friend
Henri Cazalis the consummation of a kind of philosophical conversion. "I have passed through an appalling
year. Thought has come to think itself, and I have reached
a Pure Conception. . . . I am now perfectly dead and the
impurest region in which my spirit can venture is Eternity . . .
I am now impersonal and no longer the Stéphane you have
known—but the Spiritual Universe's capacity to see and
develop itself through that which once was I." In another
historical context Mallarmé would have devoted himself
to Quietism, to the attainment of a Nirvana apart
from and antithetical to the world of appearances. But
he lived under the Second Empire and the Third Republic;
such a course was out of the question. Besides, he was a

poet and, as such, dedicated to the task of "giving a purer meaning to the words of the tribe"—*un sens plus pur aux mots de la tribu*.

"Words," he wrote, "are already sufficiently themselves not to receive any further impression from outside." This "outside," this world of appearances, was to be reduced to nothing, and a world of autonomous and, in some sort, absolute words substituted for it. In other, Mallarméan words, "the pure cup of no liquor but inexhaustible widow-hood announces a rose in the darkness"—a mystic rose of purged, immaculate language that is, in some sort, independent of the given realities for which it is supposed to stand, that exists in its own right, according to the laws of its own being. These laws are simultaneously syntacti-cal, musical, etymological and philosophical. To create a poem capable of living autonomously according to these laws is an undertaking to which only the literary equiva-lent of a great contemplative saint is equal. Such a saint-surrogate was Mallarmé—the most devout and dedicated man of letters who ever lived. But "patriotism is not enough." Nor are letters. The poet's cup can be filled with something more substantial than words and inex-haustible widowhood, and still remain undefiled. It would be possible, if one were sufficiently gifted, to write a sonnet about Salamis-Famagusta as it really is, in all the wild incongruous confusion left by three thousand years of history—a sonnet that should be as perfect a work of art, as immaculate and, though referring to the world of ap-pearances, as self-sufficient and absolute as that which Mallarmé wrote on the name of Paphos and the fact of absence. All *I* can do, alas, is to describe and reflect upon this most improbable reality in words a little less impure, perhaps, than those of the tribe, and in passing to pay my homage to that dedicated denier of reality, that self-mortified saint of letters, whose art enchants me as much today as it did forty years ago when, as an undergrad-uate, I first discovered it. Dream, azure, blasphemy, studied lack, inexhaustible widowhood—fiddlesticks! But how incredibly beautiful are the verbal objects created in order to express this absurd philosophy!

Tel qu'en Lui-même enfin l'éternité le change . . .

Cet unanime blanc conflit
D'une guirlande avec la même . . .

Le pur vase d'aucun breuvage
Que l'inexhaustible veuvage . . .

O si chère de loin et proche et blanche, si
Délicieusement toi, Mary, que je songe

A quelque baume rare émané par mensonge
Sur aucun bouquetier de cristal obscurci . . .

Treasures of sound and syntax, such lines are endowed with some of the intense *thereness* of natural objects seen by the transfiguring eye of the lover or the mystic. Utterly dissimilar from the given marvels of the world, they are yet, in some obscure way, the equivalents of the first leaves in springtime, of a spray of plum blossom seen against the sky, of moss growing thick and velvety on the sunless side of oaks, of a seagull riding the wind. The very lines in which Mallarmé exhorts the poet to shut his eyes to given reality partake, in some measure at least, of that reality's divine and apocalyptic nature.

Ainsi le choeur des romances
A la levre vole-t-il
Exclus-en si tu commences
Le réel parce que vil
Le sens trop précis rature
Ta vague littérature.

Reading, one smiles with pleasure—smiles with the same smile as is evoked by the sudden sight of a woodpecker on a tree trunk, of a hummingbird poised on the vibration of its wings before a hibiscus flower.

Faith,
Taste and History

Among tall stories, surely one of the tallest is the history of Mormonism. A founder whose obviously homemade revelations were accepted as more-than-gospel truth by thousands of followers; a lieutenant and successor who was "for daring a Cromwell, for intrigue a Machiavelli, for executive force a Moses, and for utter lack of conscience a Bonaparte"; a body of doctrine combining the most penetrating psychological insights with preposterous history and absurd metaphysics; a society of puritanical but theatergoing and music-loving polygamists; a church once condemned by the Supreme Court as an organized rebellion, but now a monolith of respectability; a passionately loyal membership distinguished, even in these middle years of the twentieth century, by the old-fashioned Protestant and pioneering virtues of self-reliance and mutual aid—together, these make up a tale which no self-respecting reader even of Spillane, even of science fiction, should be asked to swallow. And yet, in spite of its total lack of plausibility, the tale happens to be true.

My book knowledge of its truth had been acquired long since and intermittently kept up to date. It was not, however, until the spring of 1953 that I had occasion actually to see and touch the concrete evidences of that strange history.

We had driven all day in torrential rain, sometimes even in untimely snow, across Nevada. Hour after hour in the vast blankness of desert plains, past black bald mountains that suddenly closed in through the driving rain, to recede again, after a score of wintry miles, into the gray distance.

At the state line the weather had cleared for a little, and there below us, unearthly in a momentary gleam of sunshine, lay the Great Salt Desert of Utah, snow-white between the nearer crags, with the line of blue or inky peaks rising, far off, from the opposite shore of that dry ghost of an inland sea.

There was another storm as we entered Salt Lake City, and it was through sheets of falling water that we caught our first glimpse, above the chestnut trees, of a flood-lit object quite as difficult to believe in, despite the evidence of our senses, as the strange history it commemorates.

The improbability of this greatest of the Mormon Temples does not consist in its astounding ugliness. Most Victorian churches are astoundingly ugly. It consists in a certain combination of oddity, dullness and monumentality unique, so far as I know, in the annals of architecture.

For the most part Victorian buildings are more or less learned pastiches of something else—something Gothic, something Greek or nobly Roman, something Elizabethan or Flamboyant Flemish or even vaguely Oriental. But this Temple looks like nothing on earth—looks like nothing on earth and yet contrives to be completely unoriginal, utterly and uniformly prosaic.

But whereas most of the churches built during the past century are gimcrack affairs of brick veneered with imitation stone, of lattice work plastered to look like masonry, this vast essay in eccentric dreariness was realized, from crypt to capstone, in the solidest of granite. Its foundations are cyclopean, its walls are three yards thick. Like the Escorial, like the Great Pyramid, it was built to last indefinitely. Long after the rest of Victorian and twentieth-century architecture shall have crumbled back to dust, this thing will be standing in the Western desert, an object, to the neo-neolithic savages of post-atomic times, of uncomprehending reverence and superstitious alarm.

To what extent are the arts conditioned by, or indebted to, religion? And is there, at any given moment of history, a common socio-psychological source that gives to the various arts—music and painting, architecture and sculpture—some kind of common tendency? What I saw that night in Temple Square and what I heard next day during an organ recital in the Tabernacle, brought up the old problem in a new and, in many ways, enlightening context.

Here, in the floodlights, was the most grandiose by far of

all Western cathedrals. This Chartres of the desert was begun and largely built under economic and social conditions hardly distinguishable from those prevailing in France or England in the tenth century. In 1853, when the Temple's foundation stone was laid, London could boast its Crystal Palace, could look back complacently on its Exhibition of the marvels of Early Victorian technology. But here in Utah men were still living in the Dark Ages—without roads, without towns, with no means of communication faster than the ox wagon or mule train, without industry, without machines, without tools more elaborate than saws and scythes and hammers—and with precious few even of those. The granite blocks of which the Temple is built were quarried by man power, dressed by man power, hauled over twenty miles of trackless desert by man power and ox power, hoisted into position by man power. Like the cathedrals of medieval Europe the Temple is a monument, among other things, to the strength and heroic endurance of striped muscle.

In the Spanish colonies, as in the American South, striped muscle was activated by the whip. But here in the West there were no African slaves and no local supply of domesticable aborigines. Whatever the settlers wanted to do had to be done by their own hands. The ordinary run of settlers wanted only houses and mills and mines and (if the nuggets were large enough) Paris fashions imported at immense expense around the Horn. But these Mormons wanted something more—a granite Temple of indestructible solidity. Within a few years of their arrival in Utah they set to work. There were no whips to stimulate their muscles, only faith—but in what abundance! It was the kind of mountain-moving faith that gives men power to achieve the impossible and bear the intolerable, the kind of faith for which men die and kill and work themselves beyond the limits of human capacity, the kind of faith that had launched the Crusades and raised the towers of Angkor-Vat. Once again it performed its historic miracle. Against enormous odds, a great cathedral was built in the wilderness. Alas, instead of Bourges or Canterbury, it was *This*.

Faith, it is evident, may be relied on to produce sustained action and, more rarely, sustained contemplation. There is, however, no guarantee that it will produce good art. Religion is always a patron of the arts, but its taste is by no means impeccable. Religious art is sometimes excellent, sometimes atrocious; and the excellence is not necessarily associated with fervor nor the atrocity with lukewarmness. Thus, at the turn of our era, Buddhism flourished in Northwestern India. Piety, to judge by the large number of surviving monuments, ran high; but artistic merit ran pretty low. Or consider Hindu art. For the last three centuries it has been astonishingly feeble. Have the many varities of Hinduism been taken less seriously than in the times when Indian art was in its glory? There is not the slightest reason to believe it. Similarly there is not the slightest reason to believe that Catholic fervor was less intense in the age of the Mannerists than it had been three generations earlier. On the contrary, there is good reason to believe that, during the Counter-Reformation, Catholicism was taken more seriously by more people than at any time since the fourteenth century. But the bad Catholicism of the High Renaissance produced superb religious art; the good Catholicism of the later sixteenth and seventeenth centuries produced a great deal of rather bad religious art. Turning now to the individual artist—and after all, there is no such thing as "Art," there are only men at work— we find that the creators of religious masterpieces are sometimes, like Fra Angelico, extremely devout, sometimes no more than conventionally orthodox, sometimes (like Perugino, the supreme exponent of pietism in art) active and open disbelievers.

For the artist in his professional capacity, religion is important because it offers him a wealth of interesting subject matter and many opportunities to exercise his skill. Upon the quality of his production it has little or no influence. The excellence of a work of religious art depends on two factors, neither of which has anything to do with religion. It depends primarily on the presence in the artist of certain tendencies, sensibilities and talents; and, secondarily, it depends on the earlier history of his chosen art, and on what may be called the logic of its formal relations. At any given moment that internal logic points towards conclusions beyond those which have been reached by the majority of contemporary artists. A recognition of this fact may impel certain artists—especially young artists—to try to realize those possible conclusions in concrete actuality. Sometimes these attempts are fully successful; sometimes, in spite of their author's talents, they fail. In either case, the outcome does not depend on the nature of the artist's metaphysical beliefs, nor on the warmth with which he entertains them.

The Mormons had faith, and their faith enabled them to realize a prodigious ideal—the building of a Temple in the wilderness. But though faith can move mountains, it cannot of itself shape those mountains into cathedrals. It will activate muscle, but has no power to create architectural talent where none exists. Still less can it alter the facts of artistic history and the internal logic of forms.

For a great variety of reasons, some sociological and some intrinsically aesthetic, some easily discernible and others obscure, the traditions of the European arts and crafts had disintegrated, by the middle years of the nineteenth century, into a chaos of fertile bad taste and ubiquitous vulgarity. In their fervor, in the intensity of their concern wtih metaphysical problems, in their readiness to embrace the most eccentric beliefs and practices, the Mormons, like their contemporaries in a hundred Christian, Socialist or Spiritualist communities, belonged to the Age of the Gnostics. In everything else they were typical products of rustic nineteenth-century America. And in the field of the plastic arts nineteenth-century America, especially rustic America, was worse off even than nineteenth-century Europe. Barry's Houses of Parliament were as much beyond these Temple-builders as Bourges or Canterbury.

Next morning, in the enormous wooden tabernacle, we listened to the daily organ recital. There was some Bach and a piece by César Franck and finally some improvised variations on a hymn tune. These last reminded one irresistibly of the good old days of the silent screen—the days when, in a solemn hush and under spotlights, the tailcoated organist at the console of his Wurlitzer would rise majestically from the cellarage, would turn and bend his swanlike loins in acknowledgement of the applause, would resume his seat and slowly extend his white hands. Silence, and then boom! the picture palace was filled with the enormous snoring of thirty-two-foot contratrombones and bombardes. And after the snoring would come the "Londonderry Air" on the *vox humana,* "A Little Grey Home in the West" on the *vox angelica,* and perhaps (what bliss!) "The End of a Perfect Day" on the *vox treacliana,* the *vox bedroomica,* the *vox unementionabilis.*

How strange, I found myself reflecting, as the glutinous tide washed over me, how strange that people should listen with apparently equal enjoyment to this kind of thing and the Prelude and Fugue in E-flat Major. Or had I got hold of the wrong end of the stick? Perhaps mine was the strange, the essentially abnormal attitude. Perhaps there was something wrong with a listener who found it difficult to adore both these warblings around a hymn tune *and* the Prelude and Fugue.

From these unanswerable questions my mind wandered to others, hardly less puzzling, in the domain of history. Here was this huge instrument. In its original and already monumental state, it was a product of pioneering faith. An Australian musician and early Mormon convert, Joseph Ridges, had furnished the design and supervised the work. The timber used for making the pipes was hauled by oxen from forests three hundred miles to the south. The intricate machinery of a great organ was home-made by local craftsmen. When the work was finished, what kind of music, one wonders, was played to the Latter-day Saints assembled in the tabernacle? Hymns, of course, in profusion. But also Handel, also Haydn and Mozart, also Mendelssohn and perhaps even a few pieces by that queer old fellow whom Mendelssohn had resurrected, John Sebastian Bach.

It is one of the paradoxes of history that the people who built the monstrosities of the Victorian epoch should have been the same as the people who applauded, in their hideous halls and churches, such masterpieces of orderliness and unaffected grandeur as *The Messiah,* and who preferred to all his contemporaries that most elegantly classical of the moderns, Felix Mendelssohn. Popular taste in one field may be more or less completely at variance with popular taste outside that field. Still more suprisingly, the fundamental tendencies of professionals in one of the arts may be at variance with the fundamental tendencies of professionals in other arts.

Until very recently the music of the fifteenth, sixteenth and early seventeenth centuries was, to all but learned specialists, almost completely unknown. Now, thanks to long-playing phonograph records, more and more of this buried treasure is coming to the surface. The interested amateur is at last in a position to hear for himself what, before, he could only read about. He knows, for example, what people were singing when Botticelli was painting "Venus and Mars"; what Van Eyck might have heard in the way of love songs and polyphonic masses; what kind of music was being sung or played in St. Mark's while Tintoretto and Veronese were at work, next door, in the Doge's Palace; what developments were taking place in the sister art during the more than sixty years of Bernini's career as sculptor and architect.

Dunstable and Dufay, Ockeghem and Josquin, Lassus, Palestrina, Victoria—their overlapping lives cover the whole of the fifteenth and sixteenth centuries. Music, in those two centuries, underwent momentous changes. The dissonances of the earlier, Gothic polyphony were reduced to universal consonance; the various artifices—imitation, diminution, augmentation and the rest—were perfected and, by the greater masters, used to create rhythmical patterns of incredible subtlety and richness. But through the whole period virtually all serious music retained those open-ended, free-floating forms which it had inherited from the Gregorian Chant and, more remotely, from some Oriental ancestor. European folk music was symmetrical, four-square, with regular returns to the same starting point and balanced phrases, as in metrical poetry, of pre-established and foreseeable length. Based upon plain chant and written, for the part, as a setting to the liturgical texts, learned music was analogous, not to scanned verse, but to prose. It was a music without bars—that is to say, with no regularity of emphasis. Its component elements were of different lengths, there were no returns to recognizable starting points, and its geometrical analogue was not some closed figure like the square or circle, but an open curve undulating away to infinity. That such a music ever reached a close was due, not to the internal logic of its forms, but solely to the fact that even the longest liturgical texts come at last to their Amen. Some attempt to supply a purely musical reason for not going on forever was made by those composers who wrote their masses around a *cantus firmus*—a melody borrowed, almost invariably, from the closed, symmetrical music of popular songs. Sung or played in very slow time, and hidden in the tenor, sometimes even in the bass, the *cantus firmus* was, for all practical purposes, inaudible. It existed for the benefit, not of listeners, but of the composer; not to remind bored churchgoers of what they had heard last night in the tavern, but to serve a strictly artistic purpose. Even when the *cantus firmus* was present, the general effect of unconditioned, free-floating continuousness persisted. But, for the composer, the task of organization had been made easier; for, buried within the fluid heart of the music, was the unbending armature of a fully metrical song.

While Dufay was still a choir boy at Cambrai, Ghiberti was at work on the bronze doors of Santa Maria del Fiore, the young Donatello had been given his first commissions. And when Victoria, the last and greatest of the Roman masters, died in 1613, Lorenzo Bernini was already a full-blown infant prodigy. From Early Renaissance to Baroque, the fundamental tendency of the plastic arts was through symmetry and beyond it, away from closed forms towards unbalanced openness and the implication of infinity. In music, during this same period, the fundamental tendency was through openness and beyond it, away from floating continuousness towards meter, towards four-square symmetry, towards regular and foreseeable recurrence. It was in Venice that the two opposite tendencies, of painting and of music, first became conspicuous. While Tintoretto and Veronese moved towards openness and the asymmetrical, the two Gabrielis moved, in their motets and their instrumental music, towards harmony, towards regular scansion and the closed form. In Rome, Palestrina and Victoria continued to work in the old free-floating style. At St. Mark's, the music of the future—the music which in due course was to develop into the music of Purcell and Couperin, of Bach and Handel—was in process of being born. By the sixteen-thirties, when even sculpture had taken wing for the infinite, Bernini's older contemporary, Heinrich Schuetz, the pupil of Giovanni Gabrieli, was writing (not always, but every now and then) symmetrical music that sounds almost like Bach.

For some odd reason this kind of music has recently been labeled "baroque." The choice of this nickname is surely unfortunate. If Bernini and his Italian, German and Austrian followers are baroque artists (and they have been so designated for many years), then there is no justification, except in the fact that they happened to be living at the same time, for applying the same epithet to composers, whose fundamental tendencies in regard to form were radically different from theirs.

About the only seventeenth-century composer to whom the term "baroque" can be applied in the same sense as we apply it to Bernini, is Claudino Monteverdi. In his operas and his religious music, there are passages in which Monteverdi combines the openness and boundlessness of the older polyphony with a new expressiveness. The feat is achieved by setting an unconditionally soaring melody to an accompaniment, not of other voices, but of variously colored chords. The so-called baroque composers are baroque (in the established sense of the word) only in their desire for a more direct and dramatic expression of feeling. To realize this desire, they developed modulation within a fully tonal system, they exchanged polyphony for harmony, they varied the tempo of their music and the volume of its sound, and they invented modern orchestration. In this concern with expressiveness they were akin to their contemporaries in the fields of painting and sculpture. But in their desire for squareness, closedness and symmetry they were poles apart from men whose first wish was to overthrow the tyranny of centrality, to break out of the cramping frame or niche, to transcend the merely finite and the all too human.

Between 1598 and 1680—the years of Bernini's birth and death—baroque painting and sculpture moved in one direction, baroque music, as it is miscalled, moved in another, almost opposite direction. The only conclusion we can draw is that the internal logic and the recent history of the art in which a man is working exercise a more powerful influence upon him than do the social, religious and political events of the time in which he lives. Fifteenth-century sculptors and painters inherited a tradition of symmetry and closedness. Fifteenth-century composers inherited a tradition of openness and asymmetry. On either side the intrinsic logic of the forms was worked out to its ultimate conclusion. By the end of the sixteenth century neither the musical nor the plastic artists could go any further along the roads they had been following. Going beyond themselves, the painters and sculptors pursued the path of open-ended asymmetry, the free-floating musicians turned to the exploration of regular recurrence and the closed form. Meanwhile the usual wars and persecutions and sectarian throat-cuttings were in full swing; there were economic revolutions, political and social revolutions, revolutions in science and technology. But these merely historical events seem to have affected artists only materially—by ruining them or making their fortunes, by giving or withholding the opportunity to display their skill, by changing the social or religious status of potential patrons. Their thought and feeling, their fundamental artistic tendencies were reactions to events of a totally different order—events not in the social world, but in the special universe of each man's chosen art.

Take Schuetz, for example. Most of his adult life was spent in running away from the recurrent horrors of the Thirty Years' War. But the changes and chances of a discontinuous existence left no corresponding traces upon his work. Whether at Dresden or in Italy, in Denmark or at Dresden again, he went on drawing the artistically logical conclusions from the premises formulated under Gabrieli at Venice and gradually modified, through the years, by his own successive achievements and the achievements of his contemporaries and juniors.

Man is a whole, but a whole with an astounding capacity for living, simultaneously or successively, in water-tight compartments. What happens here has little or no effect on what happens there. The seventeenth-century taste for closed forms in music was inconsistent with the seventeenth-century taste for asymmetry and openness in the plastic arts. The Victorian taste for Mendelssohn and Handel was inconsistent with the Victorian taste for Mormon Temples, Albert Halls and St. Pancras Railway Stations. But in fact these mutually exclusive tastes coexisted and had no perceptible effect on one another. Consistency is a verbal criterion, which cannot be applied to the phenomena of life. Taken together, the various activities of a single individual may "make no sense," and yet be perfectly compatible with biological survival, social success and personal happiness.

Objective time is the same for every member of a human group and, within each individual, for each inhabitant of a watertight compartment. But the self in one compartment does not necessarily have the same *Zeitgeist* as the selves in other compartments or as the selves in whom other individuals do their equally inconsistent living. When the stresses of history are at a maximum, men and women tend to react to them in the same way. For example, if their country is involved in war, most individuals become heroic and self-sacrificing. And if the war produces famine and pestilence, most of them die. But where the historical pressures are more moderate, individuals are at liberty, within rather wide limits, to react to them in different ways. We are always synchronous with ourselves and others; but it often happens that we are not contemporary with either.

At Logan, for example, in the shadow of another Temple, whose battlemented turrets gave it the air of an Early Victorian "folly," of a backdrop to Edmund Kean in *Richard III*, we got into conversation with a charming contemporary, not of Harry Emerson Fosdick or Bishop Barnes, but of Brother Juniper—a Mormon whose faith had all the fervor, all the unqualified literalness, of peasant faith in the thirteenth century. He talked to us at length about the weekly baptisms of the dead. Fifteen hundred of them baptized by proxy every Saturday evening and thus, at long last, admitted to that heaven where all the family ties persist throughout the aeons. To a member of a generation brought up on Freud, these posthumous prospects seemed a bit forbidding. Not so to Brother Juniper. He spoke of them with a kind of quiet rapture. And how celestially beautiful, in his eyes, was this cyclopean gazebo! How inestimable the privilege, which he had earned, of being allowed to pass through its doors! Doors forever closed to all Gentiles and even to a moiety of the Latter-day Saints. Around that heavenly Temple the lilac trees were in full scent and the mountains that ringed the fertile valley were white with the snowy symbol of divine purity. But time pressed. We left Brother Juniper to his paradise and drove on.

That evening, in the tiny Natural History Museum at Idaho Falls, we found ourselves talking to two people from a far remoter past—a fascinating couple straight out of a cave. Not one of your fancy Magdalenian caves with all that modernistic art work on the walls. No, no— a good old-fashioned, down-to-earth cave belonging to nice ordinary people three thousand generations before the invention of painting. These were Australopiths, whose reaction to the stuffed grizzly was a remark about sizzling steaks or bear meat; these were early Neanderthalers who could not see a fish or bird or four-footed beast without immediately dreaming of slaughter and a guzzle.

"Boy!" said the cave lady, as we stood with them before the solemn, clergyman-like head of an enormous moose. "Would *he* be good with onions!"

It was fortunate, I reflected, that we were so very thin, they so remarkably well fed and therefore, for the moment, so amiable.

Doodles in a Dictionary

In only one respect do I resemble Shakespeare: I know little Latin and less Greek. Once, long ago, I knew quite a lot of both. I had to; for I was brought up in what it is now fashionable to call the Western Tradition, the educational system which equated wisdom with a knowledge of the classical authors in the original and defined culture as an ability to write grammatically correct Greek and Latin prose. And not merely prose; for at Eton, in my day, we strictly meditated the thankless Muse. The whole of every Tuesday, from seven in the morning until ten at night, was devoted to the exhausting and preposterous task of translating thirty or forty lines of English poetry into Latin or, on great occasions, Greek verses. For those who were most successful in producing pastiches of Ovid or Horace or Euripides, there were handsome prizes. I still have a Matthew Arnold in crimson morocco, a Shelley in half-calf, to testify to my onetime prowess in these odd fields of endeavor. Today I could no more write a copy of Greek iambics, or even of Latin hexameters, than I could fly. All I can remember of these once indispensable arts is the intense boredom by which the practice of them was accompanied. Even today the sight of Dr. Smith's *Shorter Latin Dictionary,* or of Liddell's and Scott's *Greek Lexicon,* has power to recall that ancient ennui. What dreary hours I have spent frantically turning those pages in search of a word for "cow" that could be scanned as a dactyl, or to make sure that my memory of the irregular verbs and the Greek accents was not at fault! I hate to think of all that wasted time. And yet, in view of the fact that most human beings are destined to pass most of their lives at jobs in which it is impossible for them to take the slightest interest, this old-fashioned training with the dictionary may have

186

been extremely salutary. At least it taught one to know and expect the worst of life. Whereas the pupil in a progressive school, where everything is made to seem entertaining and significant, lives in a fool's paradise. As a preparation for life, not as it ought to be, but as it actually is, the horrors of Greek grammar and the systematic idiocy of Latin verses were perfectly appropriate. On the other hand, it must be admitted that they tended to leave their victims with a quite irrational distaste for poor dear Dr. Smith.

Not long ago, for example, I had an urgent call from my friend Jake Zeitlin, the bookseller. "I have something to show you," he said, "something very exciting." I walked over to his shop without delay. But when, triumphantly, he held up a small Latin dictionary, my heart sank and I found myself feeling—such is the force of the conditioned reflex—some of the weariness of spirit which such objects had evoked during my school days, nearly half a century ago. True, this particular dictionary was the work of an Agrégé des Classes de Grammaire des Lycées, and the equivalents of the Latin words were in French. But the resemblance to Dr. Smith was sufficiently close to trigger my customary reaction. Looking at it, I felt all of a sudden like one who has just inhaled a lungful of stale air at the entrance to a subway station. But then the book was opened and reverently laid before me. On the almost blank flyleaf was an exquisite pen-and-ink drawing of three horses in tandem straining on the traces of a heavy two-wheeled cart. It was a marvel of expressiveness, of truth to nature, of economy of means. How had this lovely thing found its way into the dismal counterpart of Shorter Smith? The answer, when it came, was as simple as it was surprising. This dictionary had belonged, in the late seventies and earliest eighties of the last century, to a boy called Henri de Toulouse-Lautrec.

In 1880, when most of these drawings were made, Toulouse-Lautrec was sixteen. The first of the two accidents which were to transform a merely delicate child into a grotesquely deformed cripple had taken place in the spring of 1878; the second, fifteen months later, in the late summer of 1879. By 1880 the broken thighbones had mended, more or less; and he still believed—to judge from the pictures he drew of himself at this time—that his legs would start growing again. He was mistaken. His trunk developed normally and became in due course the torso of an adult man; the legs remained what they had been at the time of his first fall, the short, spindly shanks of a boy of fourteen. Meanwhile life had to be lived; and in spite of pain, in spite of enforced inactivity, in spite of the suspicion and then the certainty that henceforward he had to face the world as a dwarfish monster, Lautrec lived it with unfailing courage and irrepressible high spirits. His education, interrupted after less than three years at the *lycée,* was carried on under private tutors, and in 1880 he sat for his baccalaureate examination, failed, took the test again in 1881 and came through with flying colors. It was in the interval between the two examinations that he decorated the margins of his dictionary with the drawings at which I was now looking, entranced, in Jake Zeitlin's shop.

Up to the age of ten (provided of course that his teachers don't interfere) practically every child paints like a genius. Fifteen years later the chances of his still painting like a genius are about four hundred thousand to one. Why this infinitesimal minority should fulfill the promise of childhood, while all the rest either dwindle into mediocrity or forget the very existence of the art they once practiced (within the limits of childish capacity) with such amazing skill and originality, is an unsolved riddle. When we have learned its answer, we may be able to transform education from the sadly disappointing affair it now is into the instrument of social and individual reconstruction which it ought to be. Meanwhile we can only record the facts without understanding them. For some as yet entirely mysterious reason, Lautrec was one of the infinitesimal minority. His interest in painting began very early and along with it, presumably, went the ordinary childish genius. At three, it is recorded, he asked to be allowed to sign the parish register on the occasion of his baby brother's christening. It was objected, not unreasonably, that he didn't know how to write. "Very well," he answered, "I will draw an ox." Throughout his childhood oxen remained a favorite subject; and along with oxen, dogs, poultry, falcons (his father,

Count Alphonse de Toulouse-Lautrec, was a passionate falconer), and above all horses. He would spend long hours in the barnyard of one or other of the family châteaux, gazing intently at the birds and animals. And what he saw he remembered, not vaguely and imprecisely as the rest of us remember things, but in all its detail. And later, when the imaginative and symbolic art of childhood gave place to his first adolescent essays in representation, he was able to reproduce these memories with amazing precision. Later, as a mature artist, he seldom used models; he preferred to rely on a memory which could supply him with everything he needed. Is this kind of memory inborn, or can it be acquired by suitable training? Are we all capable of accurate recall, and do we fail to realize our innate potentialities because of some improper use of our minds and bodies? Here is another riddle which educators might profitably investigate.

Lautrec was good at Latin and in the course of his three years at school carried off several prizes for composition and translation. But proficiency did not exclude boredom, and when the learned foolery of grammar and versification became unbearable, he would open the equivalent of Shorter Smith, dip his pen in the ink and draw a tiny masterpiece. *Dictionnaire Latin-Français*. Above the words is a cavalryman galloping to the left, a jockey walking his horse towards the right. We open the book at random and find *Prophetice, Propheticus*, with a falcon alighting on them. *Coetus* and *Cohaerentia* are topped by a pair of horse's hoofs, glimpsed from the back as the animal canters past. Two pages of the preface are made beautiful, the first by an unusually large drawing of a tired old nag, the second by a no less powerful version of the three horses in tandem which adorned the flyleaf.

The draftsman was only sixteen; but these furtive doodlings, while his tutor's back was turned, are the works of an already mature artist, and exhibit an easy mastery of the medium and an understanding of the subject matter which, in the case even of men of outstanding talent, are ordinarily the fruit of long experience and constant practice. Lautrec's master, the academician and fashionable portrait painter, Bonnat, was of another opinion. "Perhaps you are curious to know," the boy wrote in a letter to his Uncle Charles, "what sort of encouragement I am getting from Bonnat. He tells me: 'Your painting isn't bad; it's clever, but still it isn't bad. But your drawing is simply atrocious.' " This to a pupil who could scribble from memory little things of which even the greatest master would not feel ashamed! The reason for Bonnat's disapproval becomes clear when we read what a fellow student wrote of Lautrec in the life class. "He made a great effort to copy the model exactly; but in spite of himself he exaggerated certain typical details, sometimes the general character, so that he distorted without trying to or even wanting to. I have seen him forcing himself to 'prettify' his study of a model—in my opinion, without success. The expression *'se forcer à faire joli'* is his own."

The word "fact" is derived from *"factum,"* something made. And in fact, a fact is never as we like to suppose, a wholly independent, given thing, but always what we choose to make of that given thing. A fact is that particular version of the given which, in any particular context, we find useful. The same event, say the explosion of an H-bomb, is simultaneously a fact in the sphere of physics and chemistry, a fact in physiology, medicine and genetics, a psychological fact, a political fact, an economic fact, an ethical fact, even an aesthetic fact—for the atomic cloud is wonderfully beautiful. A great representational artist, such as Lautrec or Goya, as Degas or Rembrandt, is interested in several aspects of experience—the aesthetic, the biological, the psychological and, sometimes, the ethical —and the facts which he sets down on paper or canvas are forms which he extracts from given reality, which he *makes,* for the purpose of expressing and communicating his own special preoccupations. For this reason he finds no incompatibility between truth to nature and distortion. Indeed, if there is to be truth to the particular aspects of nature in which he is interested, there must be a certain amount of distortion. Sometimes the distortion is mainly a matter of omission. (Few even of the most realistic painters portray *every* eyelash.) Sometimes it is due to an exaggeration of that which, in the given, reveals most clearly the side of Nature to which the artist aspires to

be true. Hsieh Ho, the fifth-century Chinese artist who formulated the famous Six Principles of Chinese painting, expresses the same truth in another way. "The first principle
is that, through a vitalizing spirit, a painting should possess
the movement of life." A number of other renderings of the
First Principle have been suggested, such as "a painting
should possess rhythmic vitality"; "a painting should express
the life movement of the spirit through the rhythm of things";
"a painting should manifest the fusion of the rhythm of
the spirit with the movement of living things." But, however
the renderings may vary, "it is quite evident," in the words
of the great Sinologist, Osvald Sirén, "that the First Principle refers to something beyond the material form, call it
character, soul, or expression. It depends on the operation
of the spirit, or the mysterious breath of life, by which the
figures may become as though they were moving or breathing." It is to this rhythm of the spirit manifested by the
movement of given events that the artist pays attention;
and in order to render this spiritual essence of things, he
may be compelled to distort appearances, to refrain both
from exactly copying or conventionally prettifying. In his
own way Lautrec was a faithful exponent of Hsieh Ho's
First Principle. Even as a boy, as yet completely ignorant
of the masters under whose influence his mature style was
to be formed, Hokusai, Degas, Goya, even in the margins
of his Latin dictionary he was making manifest the vitalizing spirit in the movements of life.

The horse is now an almost extinct animal and in a few
years, I suppose, will be seen only in zoos and, perhaps,
on race tracks and in the parks of Texas oil millionaires.
For the man in the street—a street now blessedly undefiled
by the mountains of dung which, in my childhood used to
make of every metropolis an Augean stable—the disappearance of the horse is a blessing. For the budding artist,
it is a disaster. The Percheron, the thoroughbred hunter,
the sleek cob, the splendid creatures that drew the rich
man's carriage, even the miserable hacks in the shafts
of cabs and omnibuses—each in its own way manifestly
embodied the rhythm of the spirit in the movement of its
equine life. Today, in the great cities of Europe and America, the movement of life is confined to human beings, most

of whom are incredibly graceless, and to a few dogs, cats and starlings. Communications are assured (and at the same time obstructed) by automobiles. But automobiles completely lack the movement of life. They are static objects fitted with a motor. To make them look as though they had the movement of life, their manufacturers give them inconvenient shapes and decorate them with arrowy strips of chromium. But it is all in vain. The most rakish sports car remains, even at a hundred miles an hour, essentially undynamic. Whereas even at five miles an hour, even a cab horse is a manifestation of life movement, an embodiment of the rhythm of the spirit. In the past, the horse was ubiquitous. Wherever he turned the young artist saw life movement. Walking or trotting, cantering or galloping, it challenged his powers of representation and expression, it spurred him to explore the underlying mystery of the spirit which lives and moves in forms. What amazing works of art have owed their existence to the horse! In ancient Mesopotamia, in Greece, in China and Japan, among the Etruscans and at Rome, in the battle pictures of the Renaissance, in scores of paintings by Rubens, by Velázquez, by Géricault, by Delacroix—what a cavalcade! The invention of the internal-combustion engine has deprived the painters and sculptors of the twentieth century of one of the richest sources of artistic inspiration. Along with Degas, Lautrec was almost the last of the great portrayers of horses. Indeed, if Count Alphonse had had his way, Henri would never have painted anything else. "This little book," wrote the count on the fly-leaf of a manual of falconry presented to his son when he was eleven, "will teach you to enjoy the life of the great outdoors, and if one day you should experience the bitterness of life, dogs and falcons and, above all, horses will be your faithful companions and will help you to forget a little." And it is not only the bitterness of human life, it is also its appalling vulgarity that dogs and falcons and horses will help us forget. This, surely, is why Disney's nature films have achieved so wide a popularity. After an overdose of all too human hams, what an enormous relief to see even a tarantula, even a pair of scorpions! But, alas, life in the great outdoors was not the life which fate had prepared for Henri de Toulouse-Lautrec. His accident debarred him from participation in any form of sport or country exercise. And although he still loved horses and was never tired of studying their life movements at the circus and on the race track, he loved Montmartre and alcohol, cabaret singers and prostitutes with an even intenser passion. "Any curiosity," wrote one of his friends, "delighted him, stirred him to joyful enthusiasm. He would fish out such odds and ends as a Japanese wig, a ballet slipper, a peculiar hat, a shoe with an exaggeratedly high heel and show them to you with the most amusing remarks; or else he would unexpectedly turn up, in the pile of debris, a fine Hokusai print, a letter written by a pimp to his mistress, a set of photographs of such splendid masterpieces of painting as Uccello's 'Battle' in the National Gallery or Carpaccio's 'Courtesans Playing with Animals' in the Correr Museum, all of which he accompanied by enthusiastic exclamations and sensitive or explosive comments." The drunks and tarts, the lecherous gentlemen in top hats, the sensation-hunting ladies in feather boas, the stable boys, the Lesbians, the bearded surgeons performing operations with a horrifying disregard of the first principles of asepsis—these also were curiosities, more remarkable even than Japanese wigs, and these became the subject matter of most of Lautrec's pictures, the environment in which he liked to live. He portrayed them simply as curiosities, passing no moral judgment, merely rendering the intrinsic oddity of what he saw around him. It was in this spirit of the curiosity hunter, the collector of odds and ends, that he visited the theater. Plays as such did not interest him. Good or bad, they were merely strings of words. What he liked in a theater was not the literature, but the actors—the way they grimaced and gesticulated, the curious effects produced by the lights from above and beneath, the garish costumes moving against preposterously romantic backgrounds of painted canvas. The first beginnings of this interest in the theater are visible in Lautrec's dictionary. Above *pugillus*, there is a diminutive jester in cap and bells—a memory, presumably, of some figure seen during the carnival at Nice. And encroaching upon *Quamprimum, Quamquam, Quamvis* and *Quanam* is a personage whose attitude and vaguely medieval costume would seem to be those of an actor in one of the touring companies which Henri may have seen on the Riviera. And finally, opposite *Naenia* (the word for "funeral chant") there is a beautiful sketch of a young actress dressed as a page in tights (for legs were not bared until well after the First World War), the briefest of trunk hose and a doublet. There is no effort in this or any other drawing by the youthful Lautrec to stress the femininity of his model. Our current obsession with the bosom is conspicuously absent. Generally speaking, hope springs eternal in the male breast in regard to the female breast. Here there is no undue optimism. In Lautrec, the clear-sighted artist is stronger than the yearning adolescent, as it was to be stronger, later on, than the frequenter of brothels. There is never anything sexy about Lautrec's art; but there also is never anything deliberately, sarcastically antifeminist in it. Degas, it is evident, took pleasure in posing his models in the most unalluring postures. A lady who had visited an exhibition of his works once asked him why he chose to make all his women look so ugly. "Madame," the painter replied, "because women generally *are* ugly." Unlike Degas, Lautrec never set out to prove that they were either ugly or attractive. He just looked at them, as he had looked from his earliest childhood at oxen, horses, falcons, dogs; then, from memory and with appropriate distortions, rendered their life movement, now graceful, now grotesque, and the underlying rhythm of the mysterious spirit that manifests itself in every aspect of our beautiful, frightful, unutterably odd and adorable universe.

Gesualdo:
Variations on a Musical Theme

Space has been explored, systematically and scientifically, for more than five centuries; time, for less than five generations. Modern geography began in the fourteen-hundreds with the voyages of Prince Henry the Navigator. Modern history and modern archaeology came in with Queen Victoria. Except in the Antarctic there is today no such thing as a *terra incognita*; all the corners of all the other continents have now been visited. In contrast, how vast are the reaches of history which still remain obscure! And how recently acquired is most of our knowledge of the past! Almost everything we know about palaeolithic and neolithic man, about the Sumerian, Hittite and Minoan civilizations, about pre-Buddhist India and pre-Columbian America, about the origins of such fundamental human arts as agriculture, metallurgy and writing, was discovered within the last sixty or seventy years. And there are still new worlds of history to conquer. Even in such well-dug regions as the Near and Middle East literally thousands of sites await the burrowing archaeologist, and thousands more are scattered far and wide over Asia, Africa and the Americas. Moreover, there is work for the explorer in times and cultures much nearer home. For, strange as it may seem, it is only within the last generation that certain aspects of quite recent European history have come to be critically investigated. A very striking example of this failure to explore our own back yard is supplied by the history of music. Practically everybody likes music; but practically nobody has heard any music composed before 1680. Renaissance poetry, painting and sculpture have been studied in minutest detail, and the labors of five generations of scholars have been made available to the public in hundreds of monographs, general histories, critical appreciations and guidebooks. But Renaissance music—an art which was fully the equal of Renaissance poetry, painting and sculpture—has received relatively little attention from scholars and is almost unknown to the concert-going public. Donatello and Piero della Francesca, Titian and Michelangelo—their names are household words and, in the original or in reproduction, their works are familiar to everyone. But how few people have heard, or even heard of, the music of Dufay and Josquin, of Okeghem and Obrecht, of Ysaac and Wert and Marenzio, of Dunstable, Byrd and Victoria! All that can be said is that, twenty years ago, the number was still smaller than it is today. And a couple of generations earlier the ignorance was almost total. Even so great a historian as Burckhardt—the man who wrote with such insight, such a wealth of erudition, about every other aspect of the Renaissance in Italy—knew next to nothing about the music of his chosen period. It was not his fault; there were no modern editions of the music and nobody ever played or sang it. Consider, by way of example, the *Vespers*, composed in 1610 by one of the most famous, one of the most historically important of Italian musicians, Claudio Monteverdi. After the middle of the seventeenth century this extraordinary masterpiece was never again performed until the year 1935. One can say without any exaggeration that, until very recent times, more was known about the Fourth Dynasty Egyptians, who built the pyramids, than about the Flemish and Italian contemporaries of Shakespeare who wrote the madrigals.

This sort of thing, let us remember, has happened before. From the time of the composer's death in 1750 to the performance under Mendelssohn, in 1829, of the *Passion According to St. Matthew,* no European audience had ever heard a choral work by John Sebastian Bach. What Mendelssohn and the nineteenth-century musicologists, critics and virtuosi did for Bach another generation of scholars and performers has begun to do for Bach's predecessors, whose works have been rediscovered, published in critical editions, performed here and there and even occasionally recorded. It is gradually dawning upon us that the three centuries before Bach are just as interesting musically speaking, as the two centuries after Bach.

There exists in Los Angeles a laudable institution called the Southern California Chamber Music Society. This society sponsors a series of Monday evening concerts, at which, besides much fine and seldom-heard classical and contemporary music, many pre-Bach compositions are performed. Among these earlier compositions one group stands out in my memory as uniquely interesting—a group of madrigals and motets by an almost exact contemporary of Shakespeare, Carlo Gesualdo. Another English poet, John Milton, was an admirer of Gesualdo and, while in Italy, bought a volume of his madrigals which, with a number of other books, he sent home by ship from Venice. Milton's admiration is understandable; for Gesualdo's music is so strange and, in its strangeness, so beautiful that it haunts the memory and fires the imagination. Listening to it, one is filled with questioning wonder. What sort of a man was it who wrote such music? Where does it fit into the general musical scheme, and what is its relevance for us? In the paragraphs that follow I shall try, in the light of my sadly limited knowledge of Gesualdo's time and of Gesualdo's art, to answer, or at least to speculate about, these questions.

Let us begin, then, with the biographical facts. Carlo Gesualdo was born in or about 1560, either at Naples or in one of his father's numerous castles in the neighborhood of Naples. The Gesualdi were of ancient and noble lineage, had been barons for fifteen generations, counts for eight, dukes for four or five, and, for the past three generations, hereditary Princes of Venosa. Carlo's mother hailed from northern Italy and was a sister of the great Cardinal Carlo Borromeo, who died in 1584 and was canonized in 1610. In his later years Gesualdo could speak not only of my father, the Prince, but even (going one better) of my uncle, the Saint. Of the boy's education we know nothing and can only infer, from his later achievements, that he must have had a very thorough grounding in music.

Every age has its own characteristic horrors. In ours there are the Communists and nuclear weapons, there are nationalism and the threat of overpopulation. The violence in which we indulge is truly monstrous; but it is, so to say, official violence, ordered by the proper authorities, sanctioned by law, ideologically justified and confined to periodical world wars, between which we enjoy the blessings of law, order and internal peace. In the Naples of Gesualdo's day, violence was ruggedly individualistic, unorganized and chronic. There was little nationalism and world wars were unknown; but dynastic squabbles were frequent and the Barbary Corsairs were incessantly active, raiding the coasts of Italy in search of slaves and booty. But the citizen's worst enemies were not the pirates and the foreign princes; they were his own neighbors. Between the wars and the forays of the infidels there were no lucid intervals, such as we enjoy between our wholesale massacres, of civic decency, but an almost lawless and policeless free-for-all in a society composed of a class of nobles, utterly corrupted by Spanish ideas of honor (Naples was then a Spanish colony), a small and insignificant middle class and a vast mob of plebeians living in bestial squalor and savagery, and sunk, head over ears, in the most degrading superstition. It was in this monstrous environment that Carlo grew up, an immensely talented and profoundly neurotic member of the overprivileged minority.

In 1586 he married Maria d'Avalos, a girl of twenty, but already a widow. (Her previous husband, it was whispered, had died of too much connubial bliss.) Gesualdo had two children by this lady, one of his own begetting, the other almost certainly not; for after two years of marriage, the lovely and lively Donna Maria had taken a lover, Don Fabrizio Carafa, Duke of Andria. On the night of October 16, 1590, accompanied by three of his retainers, armed with swords, halberds and arquebuses, Gesualdo broke into his wife's room, found the lovers in bed and had them killed. After which he took horse and galloped off to one of his castles where, after liquidating his second child (the one of doubtful paternity), he remained for several months—not to escape the law (for he was never prosecuted and, if he had been, would certainly have been acquitted as having done only what any injured husband had the right and even the duty to do), but to avoid the private vengence of the Avalos and Carafa families.

These last were outraged, not so much by the murder (which was entirely in order) as by the fact that the killing had been done by lackeys and not by Gesualdo himself. According to the code of honor, blue blood might be spilled only by the possessor of blue blood, never by a member of the lower classes.

Time passed and the storm, as all storms finally do, blew over. From his feudal keep in the hills Gesualdo was able to return to Naples and the cultivated society of madrigal-singing amateurs and professional musicians. He began composing, he even published. Second and third editions of his madrigals were called for. He was almost a best seller.

The Prince of Venosa, the *Serenissimo* as he was called by his respectful contemporaries, was now an eligible widower, and sometime in 1592 or 1593 his paternal uncle, the Archbishop of Naples, entered into negotiations with Alfonso II, Duke of Ferrara, with a view to securing for his nephew a princess of the great house of Este. Suitable financial arrangements were made, and in February, 1594, the nuptials of Carlo Gesualdo and Donna Leonora d'Este were celebrated at Ferrara with all the usual pomp. After a short stay in the south, Gesualdo returned to Ferrara with his bride, now pregnant, rented a palace and settled down for a long stay.

Ferrara in 1594 was a setting sun, still dazzling, but on the brink of darkness. Three years later, on the death of Duke Alfonso without a male heir, the city, which was a papal fief, reverted to its overlord, the Pope, and was incorporated into the States of the Church. The glory that was Ferrara vanished overnight, forever.

That Ferrara should ever have become a glory is one of the unlikeliest facts in that long succession of actualized improbabilities which make up human history. The ducal territory was small and, in those malarious days, unhealthy. Its material resources were scanty, and the most important local industry was the smoking of eels, caught in the winding channels of the delta of the Po. Militarily, the state was feeble in the extreme. Powerful and not always friendly neighbors surrounded it and, to make matters worse, it lay on the invasion route from Germany and Austria. In spite of which Ferrara became and for a hundred and fifty years—from the middle of the fifteenth to the end of the sixteenth century—remained not only a sovereign state of considerable political importance, but also one of the most brilliant intellectual centers of Western Europe. This position the city owed entirely to the extraordinary ability and good taste of its rulers, the dukes of the house of Este. In the game of international and interdynastic politics, the Estensi were consummately skillful players. At home they were not too tyrannical, and had a happy knack, when discontent ran high, of blaming their ministers for everything and so maintaining their own popularity.

Their domestic life was relatively harmonious. Unlike many of the ruling families of Italy, the Estensi seldom murdered one another. True, a few years before Carlo's marriage to Leonora, the Duke had had his sister's lover strangled. But this was an exceptional act—and anyhow he refrained from strangling the lady; the integrity of the clan was preserved. But from our present point of view the most remarkable thing about the Dukes of Ferrara was their steady patronage of talent, especially in the fields of literature and music. The greatest Italian poets of the sixteenth century—from Ariosto at the beginning to Guarini and Tasso at the end—were summoned to Ferrara, where the dukes either gave them jobs in the administration of the state, or else paid them a pension, so that they might devote the whole of their time to literature. Musicians were no less welcome than poets. From 1450 to 1600 most of the greatest composers of the time visited Ferrara, and many of them stayed at the court for long periods. They came from Burgundy and Flanders, the most productive centers of early Renaissance music; they came from France, they came even from faraway England. And later, when the Italians had learned their lesson from the North and had become, in their turn, the undisputed leaders in the field, they came from all over the peninsula. The huge square *castello* at the heart of the city, the ducal hunting lodges, the summer palaces by the sea, the mansions of the nobles and the foreign ambassadors—all of them resounded with music: Learned polyphonic music and popular songs and dances. Music for lutes (there was a functionary at the ducal court whose sole duty it was to keep the lutes perpetually in tune) and music for the organ, for viols, for wind instruments, for the earliest forms of harpsichord and clavichord. Music performed by amateurs sitting around the fire or at a table, and music rendered by professional virtuosi. Music in church, music at home and (this was a novelty) music in the concert hall. For there were daily concerts in the various ducal palaces, concerts in which as many as sixty players and singers would take part. On grand occasions—and at Ferrara there seems to have been a grand occasion at least twice a week—there were masques with choral interludes, there were plays with overtures and incidental music, there were performances, in those sunset years of decline, of the first rudimentary operas. And what wonderful voices could be heard at Alfonso's court! Ferrara's Three Singing Ladies were world famous. There was Lucrezia Bendidio, there was Laura Peperara and, most remarkable of the trio, there was the beautiful, learned and many-talented Tarquinia Molza. But every Eden, alas, has its serpent, and, in Tarquinia's musical paradise, there was not merely a reptile to rear its ugly head; there were several Adams as well.

Tarquinia married and was widowed; then, in her middle thirties she fell under the spell of that most charming and romantic of men, Torquato Tasso. The poet, who wrote a great deal about love, but very seldom made it, was alarmed, and, putting up a barrage of platonic verse, beat a hasty retreat. Tarquinia had to be content, for several years, with lovers of less exalted intellectual rank. Then, in her forties, she found another man of genius, the great Flemish composer, Giaches Wert, who was in the employ of the Duke of Mantua. Their passion was reciprocal and so violent that it created a scandal. The unhappy Tarquinia was exiled to Modena and Wert returned, alone, to the court of the Gonzagas.

For a man of Gesualdo's gifts and sensibilities, Ferrara combined the advantages of a seat of higher education with those of a heaven on earth. It was a place where he could simultaneously enjoy himself and learn. And learn he certainly did. The madrigals he composed before 1594 are admirable in their workmanship; but their style, though his own, is still within the bounds of sixteenth-century music. The madrigals and motets written after his stay at Ferrara are beyond those bounds—far out in a kind of no-man's land.

Gesualdo left no memoirs and, in spite of his high contemporary reputation and his exalted position in the world, very little is known of his later life, except that he was unhappy and dogged by misfortune. His son by his second wife died in childhood. His son by the murdered Donna Maria, the heir to all the family titles and estates, grew up to loathe his father and long for his death; but it was he who died first. One of Gesualdo's daughters went to the bad and presented him with several illegitimate grandchildren. Meanwhile he was constantly tormented, says a contemporary gossip writer, by a host of demons. His lifelong neurosis had deepened, evidently into something like insanity. Apart from music, which he went on composing with undiminished powers, his only pleasure seems to have been physical pain. He would, we are told, submit ecstatically to frequent whippings. These at last became a physiological necessity. According to that much persecuted philosopher, Tommaso Campanella, the Prince of Venosa could never go to the bathroom (*cacare non poterat*) unless he had first been flogged by a servant specially trained to perform this duty. Remorse for the crimes of his youth weighed heavily on Gesualdo's conscience. The law might excuse, public opinion might even approve; but Holy Writ was explicit: *Thou shalt not kill*. A few years before his death in 1613 he endowed a Capuchin friary in his native town of Gesualdo and built a handsome church. Over the altar hung a huge penitential picture, painted to the prince's order and under his personal direction. This picture, which still survives, represents Christ the Judge seated on high and flanked by the Blessed Virgin and the Archangel Michael. Below Him, arranged symmetrically, in descending tiers, to right and left, are Saint Francis and Saint Mary Magdalen, Saint Dominic and Saint Catherine of Siena, all of them, to judge by their gestures, emphatically interceding with the Savior on behalf of Carlo Gesualdo, who kneels in the lower left-hand corner, dressed in black velvet and an enormous ruff, while, splendid in the scarlet robes of a Prince of the Church, his uncle, the Saint, stands beside him, with one hand resting protectively on the sinner's shoulder. Opposite them kneels Carlo's aunt, Isabella Borromeo, in the costume of a nun, and at the center of this family group is the murdered child, as a heavenly cherub. Below, at the very bottom of the composition, Donna Maria and the Duke of Andria are seen roasting everlastingly in those flames from which the man who had them butchered still hopes against hope to be delivered.

So much for the facts of our composer's life—facts which confirm an old and slightly disquieting truth: namely, that between an artist's work and his personal behavior there is no very obvious correspondence. The work may be sublime, the behavior anything from silly to insane and criminal. Conversely the behavior may be blameless and the work uninteresting or downright bad. Artistic merit has nothing to do with any other kind of merit. In the language of theology, talent is a gratuitous grace, completely unconnected with saving grace or even with ordinary virtue or sanity.

From the man we now pass to his strange music. Like most of the great composers of his day, Gesualdo wrote exclusively for the human voice—to be more precise, for groups of five or six soloists singing contrapuntally. All his five- or six-part compositions belong to one or other of two closely related musical forms, the madrigal and the motet. The motet is the older of the two forms and consists of a setting, for any number of voices from three to twelve, of a short passage, in Latin, from the Bible or some other sacred text. Madrigals may be defined as nonreligious motets. They are settings, not of sacred Latin texts, but of short poems in the vernacular. In most cases, these settings were for five voices; but the composer was free to write for any number of parts from three to eight or more.

The madrigal came into existence in the thirties of the sixteenth century and, for seventy or eighty years, remained the favorite art form of all composers of secular music. Contrapuntal writing in five parts is never likely to be popular, and the madrigal made its appeal, not to the general public, but to a select audience of professional musicians and highly educated amateurs, largely aristocratic and connected for the most part with one or other of the princely or ecclesiastical courts of the day. (One is amazed, when one reads the history of renaissance music, by the good taste of Europe's earlier rulers. Popes and emperors, kings, princes and cardinals—they never make a mistake. Invariably, one might almost say infallibly, they choose for their chapel masters and court composers the men whose reputation has stood the test of time and whom we now recognize as the most gifted musicians of their day. Left to themselves, what sort of musicians would our twentieth-century monarchs and presidents choose to patronize? One shudders to think.)

Gesualdo wrote madrigals, and a madrigal, as we have seen, is a non-religious motet. But what else is it? Let us begin by saying what it is not. First and foremost, the madrigal, though sung, is not a song. It does not, that is to say, consist of a tune, repeated stanza after stanza. Nor has it anything to do with the art form known to later musicians as the aria. An aria is a piece of music for a solo voice, accompanied by instruments or by other voices. It begins, in most cases, with an introduction, states a melodic theme in one key, states a second theme in another key, goes into a series of modulations and ends with a recapitulation of one or both themes in the original key. Nothing of all this is to be found in the madrigal. In the madrigal there is no solo singing. All the five or more voices are of equal importance, and they move, so to speak, straight ahead, whereas the aria and the song move in the equivalent of circles or spirals. In other words, there are, in the madrigal, no returns to a starting point, no systematic recapitulations. Its form bears no resemblance to the sonata form or even to the suite form. It might be described as a choral tone poem, written in counterpoint. When counterpoint is written within a structural pattern, such as the fugue or canon, the listener can follow the intricacies of the music almost indefinitely. But where the counterpoint has no structural pattern imposed upon it, where it moves forward freely, without any returns to a starting point, the ear finds it very hard to follow it, attentively and understandingly, for more than a few minutes at a stretch. Hence the brevity of the typical madrigal, the extraordinary succinctness of its style.

During the three quarters of a century of its existence, the madrigal underwent a steady development in the direction of completer, ever intenser expressiveness. At the beginning of the period it is a piece of emotionally neutral polyphony, whose whole beauty consists in the richness and complexity of its many-voiced texture. At the end, in the work of such masters as Marenzio, Monteverdi and, above all, Gesualdo, it has become a kind of musical miracle, in which seemingly incompatible elements are reconciled in a higher synthesis. The intricacies of polyphony are made to yield the most powerfully expressive effects, and this polyphony has become so flexible that it can, at any moment, transmute itself into blocks of chords or a passage of dramatic declamation.

During his stay at Ferrara, Gesualdo was in contact with the most "advanced" musicians of his day. A few miles away, at Mantua, the great Giaches Wert, sick and prematurely old, was still composing; and at the same court lived a much younger musician, Claudio Monteverdi, who was to carry to completion the revolution in music begun by Wert. That revolution was the supersession of polyphony by monody, the substitution of the solo voice, with instrumental or vocal accompaniment, for the madrigalist's five or six voices of equal importance. Gesualdo did not follow the Mantuans into monody; but he was certainly influenced by Wert's essays in musical expressionism. Those strange cries of grief, pain and despair, which occur so frequently in his later madrigals, were echoes of the cries introduced by Wert into his dramatic cantatas.

At Ferrara itself Gesualdo's closest musical friends were Count Fontanelli and a professional composer and virtuoso, Luzzasco Luzzaschi. Like Gesualdo, Fontanelli was an aristocrat and had murdered an unfaithful wife; unlike Gesualdo, he was not a man of genius, merely a good musician passionately interested in the latest developments of the art. Luzzaschi was a writer of madrigals, and had invented a number of expressive devices, which Gesualdo employed in his own later productions. More important, he was the only man who knew how to play on, and even compose for, an extraordinary machine, which was the greatest curiosity in Duke Alfonso's collection of musical instruments. This was the archicembalo, a large keyboard instrument belonging to the harpsichord family, but so designed that a player could distinguish, for example, between B flat and A sharp, could descend chromatically from E, through E flat, D sharp, D, D flat, C sharp to a final C major chord. The archicembalo required thirty-one keys to cover each octave and must have been fantastically difficult to play and still harder, one would imagine, to compose for. The followers of Schoenberg are far behind Luzzaschi; *their* scale has only twelve tones, *his*, thirty-one. Luzzaschi's thirty-one-tone compositions (none of which, unfortunately, survive) and his own experiments on the archicembalo profoundly influenced the style of Gesualdo's later madrigals. Forty years ago, the Oxford musicologist, Ernest Walker, remarked that Gesualdo's most famous madrigal, *Moro lasso,* sounded like "Wagner gone wrong." Hardly an adequate criticism of Gesualdo, but not without significance.

The mention of Wagner is fully justified; for the incessant chromaticisms of Gesualdo's later writing found no parallel in music until the time of *Tristan.* As for the "gonewrongness"—this is due to Gesualdo's unprecedented and, until recent times, almost unimitated treatment of harmonic progression. In his madrigals successive chords are related in ways which conform neither to the rules of sixteenth-century polyphony, nor to the rules of harmony which hold good from the middle of the seventeenth century to the beginning of the twentieth. An infallible ear is all that, in most cases, preserves these strange and beautiful progressions from seeming altogether arbitrary and chaotic. Thanks to that infallible ear of his, Gesualdo's harmonies move, always astonishingly, but always with a logic of their own, from one impossible, but perfectly satisfying, beauty to another. And the harmonic strangeness is never allowed to continue for too long at a stretch. With consummate art, Gesualdo alternates these extraordinary passages of Wagner-gone-wrong with passages of pure traditional polyphony. To be fully effective, every elaboration must be shown in a setting of simplicity, every revolutionary novelty should emerge from a background of the familiar. For the composers of arias, the simple and familiar background for their floridly expressive melodies was a steady, rhythmically constant accompaniment. For Gesualdo, simplicity and familiarity meant the rich, many-voiced texture of contrapuntal writing. The setting for Wagner-gone-wrong is Palestrina.

Every madrigal is the setting of a short poem in the vernacular, just as every motet is the setting of a short passage from the Vulgate or some other piece of sacred Latin literature. The texts of the motets were generally in prose, and the early polyphonists saw no obvious reason for imposing upon this essentially rectilinear material a circular musical form. After the invention of the aria, the composers of music for prose texts habitually distorted the sense and rhythm of their words in order to force them into the circular, verselike patterns of their new art form. From Alessandro Scarlatti, through Bach and Handel, Mozart, Haydn and Mendelssohn—all the great composers from 1650 to 1850 provide examples, in their musical settings, of what may be called the versification of prose. To do this, they were compelled to repeat phrases and individual words again and again, to prolong single syllables to inordinate length, to recapitulate, note for note, or with variations, entire paragraphs. How different was the procedure of the madrigalists! Instead of versifying prose, they found it necessary, because of the nature of their art form, to prosify verse. The regular recurrences of lines and stanzas—these have no place in the madrigal, just as they have no place in the motet. Like good prose, the madrigal is rectilinear, not circular. Its movement is straight ahead, irreversible, asymmetrical. When they set a piece of poetry to music, the madrigalists set it phrase by phrase, giving to each phrase, even each word, its suitable expression and linking the successive moods by a constant adaptation of the polyphonic writing, not by the imposition from outside of a structural pattern. Every madrigal, as I have said, is a choral tone poem. But instead of lasting for a whole hour, like the huge, spectacular machines of Liszt and Richard Strauss, it concentrates its changing moods into three or four minutes of elaborate and yet intensely expressive counterpoint.

The Italian madrigalists chose their texts, for the most part, from the best poets. Dante was considered too harsh and old-fashioned; but his great fourteenth-century successor, Petrarch, remained a perennial favorite. Among more recent poets, Ariosto, though set fairly frequently, was much less popular than Guarini and Tasso, whose emotional tone was more emphatic and who took pleasure in just those violent contrasts of feeling which lent themselves most perfectly to the purposes of the madrigalist. In their shorter pieces (pieces written expressly to be set to music) Tasso and his contemporaries made use of a kind of epigrammatic style, in which antithesis, paradox and oxymoron played a major part and were turned into a literary convention, so that every versifier now talked of dolorous joy, sweet agony, loathing love and living death —to the immense delight of the musicians, for whom these emotional ambiguities, these abrupt changes of feeling offered golden opportunities.

Gesualdo was a personal friend of Torquato Tasso and, during the last, mad, wandering years of the poet's life, helped him with money and letters of introduction. As we should expect, he set a number of Tasso's poems to music. For the rest he made use of anything that came to hand. Many of his finest madrigals are based on snatches of verse having no literary merit whatsoever. That they served his purpose was due to the fact that they were written in the current idiom and contained plenty of emphatically contrasting words, which he could set to appropriately expressive music. Gesualdo's indifference to the poetical quality of his texts, and his methods of setting words to music, are very clearly illustrated in one of the most astonishing of his madrigals, *Ardita zanzaretta*—a work, incidentally, whose performance at Los Angeles in the Autumn of 1955 was probably the first in more than three hundred years. This extraordinary little masterpiece compresses into less than three minutes every mood from the cheerfully indifferent to the perversely voluptuous, from the gay to the tragic, and in the process employs every musical resource, from traditional polyphony to Wagner-gone-wrong chromaticism and the strangest harmonic progressions, from galloping rhythms to passages of long, suspended notes. Then we look at the text and discover that this amazing music is the setting of half-a-dozen lines of doggerel. The theme of *Ardita zanzaretta* is the same as the theme of a tiny poem by Tasso, tasteless enough in all conscience, but written with a certain elegance of style. A little mosquito *(zanzaretta)* settles on the bosom of the beloved, bites and gets swatted by the exasperated lady. What a delicious fate, muses Tasso, to die in a place where it is such bliss to swoon away!

> *Felice te felice,*
> *piú che nel rogo oriental Fenice!*

(Oh happy, happy bug—more happy than the Phoenix on its oriental pyre!)

Gesualdo's nameless librettist takes the same subject, robs it of whatever charm Tasso was able to lend it, and emphasizes the bloodiness of the mosquito's fate by introducing—twice over in the space of only six lines—the word *stringere,* meaning to squeeze, squash, squelch. Another improvement on Tasso is the addition of a playful sally by the lover. Since he longs to share the mosquito's fate, he too will take a bite in the hope of being squashed to death on the lady's bosom. What follows is a literal translation of this nonsense, accompanied by a description of the music accompanying each phrase. "A bold little mosquito bites the fair breast of her who consumes my heart." This is set to a piece of pure neutral polyphony, very rapid and, despite its textural richness, very light. But the lady is not content with consuming the lover's heart; she also "keeps it in cruel pain." Here the dancing polyphony of the first bars gives place to a series of chords moving slowly from dissonance to unprepared dissonance. The pain, however unreal in the text, becomes in the music genuinely excruciating. Now the mosquito "makes its escape, but rashly flies back to that fair breast which steals my heart away. Whereupon she catches it." All this is rendered in the same kind of rapid, emotionally neutral polyphony as was heard in the opening bars. But now comes another change. The lady not only catches the insect, "she squeezes it and gives it death." The word *morte,* death, occurs in almost all Gesualdo's madrigals. Sometimes it carries its literal meaning; more often, however, it is used figuratively, to signify sensual ecstasy, the swoon of love. But this makes no difference to Gesualdo. Whatever its real significance, and whoever it is that may be dying (the lover metaphorically or, in a literal sense, a friend, a mosquito, the crucified Savior), he gives to the word, *morte,* a musical expression of the most tragic and excruciating kind. For the remorseful assassin, death was evidently the most terrifying of prospects.

From the insect's long-drawn musical martyrdom, we return to cheerfulness and pure polyphony. "To share its happy fate, I too will bite you." Gesualdo was a pain-loving masochist and this playful suggestion of sadism left him unmoved. The counterpoint glides along in a state of emotional neutrality. Then comes a passage of chromatic yearning on the words "my beloved, my precious one." Then polyphony again. "And if you catch and squeeze me. . . ." After this, the music becomes unadulterated Gesualdo. There is a cry of pain—*ahi!*—and then "I will swoon away and, upon that fair breast, taste delicious poison." The musical setting of these final words is a concentrated version of the love-potion scene in *Tristan*—the chief difference being that Gesualdo's harmonic progressions are far bolder than any attempted, two and a half centuries later, by Richard Wagner.

Should pictures tell stories? Should music have a connection with literature? In the past the answer would have been, unanimously, yes. Every great painter was a raconteur of Biblical or mythological anecdotes; every great composer was a setter-to-music of sacred or profane texts. Today the intrusion of literature into the plastic arts is regarded almost as a crime. In the field of music, this anti-literary reign of terror has been less savage. Program music is deplored (not without reason, considering the horrors bequeathed to us by the Victorian era); but in spite of much talk about "pure music," good composers still write songs, masses, operas and cantatas. Good painters would do well to follow their example and permit themselves to be inspired to still better painting by the promptings of a literary theme. In the hands of a bad painter, pictorial storytelling, however sublime the subject matter, is merely comicstrip art on a large scale. But when a good painter tells the same story, the case is entirely different. The exigencies of illustration—the fact that he has to show such-and-such personages, in such-and-such an environment, performing such-and-such actions—stimulates his imagination on every level, including the purely pictorial level, with the result that he produces a work which, though literary, is of the highest quality as a formal composition. Take any famous painting of the past—Botticelli's "Calumny of Apelles," for example, or Titian's "Bacchus and Ariadne." Both of these are admirable illustrations; but both are much more than illustrations—they are very complex and yet perfectly harmonious and unified arrangements of forms and colors. Moreover the richness of their formal material is a direct consequence of their literary subject matter. Left to itself, the pictorial imagination even of a painter of genius could never conjure up such a subtle and complicated pattern of shapes and hues as we find in these illustrations of texts by Lucian and Ovid. To achieve their purely plastic triumphs, Botticelli and Titian required to be stimulated by a literary theme. It is a highly significant fact that, in no abstract or non-representational painting of today, do we find a purely formal composition having anything like the richness, the harmonious complexity, created in the process of telling a story, by the masters of earlier periods. The traditional distinction between the crafts and the fine arts is based, among other things, on degrees of complexity. A good picture is a greater work of art than a good bowl or a good vase. Why? Because it unifies in one harmonious whole more, and more diverse, elements of human experience than are or can be unified and harmonized in the pot. Some of the non-representational pictures painted in the course of the last fifty years are very beautiful; but even the best of them are minor works, inasmuch as the number of elements of human experience which they combine and harmonize is pitifully small. In them we look in vain for that ordered profusion, that lavish and yet perfectly controlled display of intellectual wealth, which we discover in the best works of the "literary" painters of the past.

In this respect the composer is more fortunate than the painter. It is psychologically possible to write "pure music" that shall be just as harmoniously complex, just as rich in unified diversities, as music inspired by a literary text. But even in music the intrusion of literature has often been beneficent. But for the challenge presented by a rather absurd anecdote couched in very feeble language, Beethoven would never have produced the astonishing "pure music" of the second act of *Fidelio*. And it was Da Ponte, with his rhymed versions of the stories of Figaro and Don Giovanni, who stimulated Mozart to reveal himself in the fullness of his genius. Where music is a matter of monody and harmony, with a structural pattern (the sonata form or the suite form) imposed, so to speak, from the outside, it is easy to write "pure music," in which the successive moods shall be expressed, at some length, in successive movements. But where there is no structural pattern, where the style is polyphonic and the movement of the music is not circular, but straight ahead, irreversible and rectilinear, the case is different. Such a style demands extreme brevity and the utmost succinctness of expression. To meet these demands for brevity and succinctness, the musical imagination requires a text—and a text, moreover, of the kind favored by the madrigalists, paradoxical, antithetical, full of

> All things counter, original, spare, strange
> Whatever is fickle, freckled (who know how?)
> With swift, slow; sweet, sour; adazzle, dim.

Contemporary musicians, who aspire to write "pure music" in forms as rich, subtle and compact as those devised by Gesualdo and his contemporaries, would do well to turn once more to the poets.

Appendix

Every civilization is, among other things, an arrangement for domesticating the passions and setting them to do useful work. The domestication of sex presents a problem whose solution must be attempted on two distinct levels of human experience, the psycho-physiological and the social. On the social level the relations of the sexes have everywhere been regulated by law, by uncodified custom, by taboo and religious ritual. Hundreds of volumes have been filled with accounts of these regulations, and it is unnecessary to do more than mention them in passing. Our present concern is with the problem of domesticating sex at the source, of civilizing its manifestations in the individual lover. This is a subject to which, in our Western tradition, we have paid much too little attention. Indeed, it is only in very recent years that, thanks to the declining influence of the Judaeo-Christian ethic, we have been able to discuss it realistically. In the past the problem used to be dealt with in one or other of three equally unsatisfactory ways. Either it was not mentioned at all, with the result that adolescents coming to maturity were left to work out their sexual salvation, unassisted, within the framework of the prevailing, and generally barbarous socio-legal system. Or else it was mentioned—but mentioned on the one hand with obscene delight or obscene disapproval (the tone of the pornographers and the Puritan moralists), or with a vague and all too "spiritual" sentimentality (the tone of the troubadours, Petrarchians and romantic lyrists). Today we are condemned neither to silence, nor obscenity, nor sentimentality; we are at liberty, at last, to look at the facts and to ask ourselves what, if anything, can be done about them. One of the best ways of discovering what can be done is to look at what has been done. What experiments have been made in this field, and how successful have they been?

I shall begin not at the faraway beginning of everything, among the Trobrianders, for example, or the Tahitians, but rather at the beginning of our own current phase of civilization—in the middle years, that is to say, of the nineteenth century.

Victoria had been on the throne for seven years when, in 1844, John Humphrey Noyes published his book, *Bible Communism*. (It is worth remarking that, for the American public of a hundred years ago, Communism was essentially biblical. It was preached and practiced by men and women who wanted to emulate the earliest Christians. The appeal was not to Marx's *Manifesto*—still unpublished when Noyes wrote his book—but to the Acts of the Apostles.) In the fourth chapter of *Bible Communism* and again, at greater length, in his *Male Continence*, written more than twenty years later, Noyes set forth his theories of sex and described the methods employed by himself and his followers of transforming a wild, God-eclipsing passion into a civilized act of worship, a prime cause of crime and misery into a source of individual happiness, social solidarity and good behavior.

"It is held in the world!," Noyes writes in *Bible Communism*, "that the sexual organs have two distinct functions—viz: the urinary and the propagative. We affirm that they have three—the urinary, the propagative and the amative., i.e. they are conductors first of the urine, secondly of the semen and thirdly of the social magnetism. . . ." After Mrs. Noyes had come dangerously near to death as the result of repeated miscarriages, Noyes and his wife decided that, henceforth, their sexual relationships should be exclusively amative, not propagative. But how were the specifically human aspects of sex to be detached from the merely biological? Confronted by this question, Robert Dale Owen had advocated *coitus interruptus;* but Noyes had read his Bible and had no wish to emulate Onan. Nor did he approve of contraceptives—"those tricks," as he called them, "of the French voluptuaries." Instead he advocated Male Continence and what Dr. Stockham was later to call *Karezza*. With the most exemplary scientific detachment

he began by "analyzing the act of sexual intercourse. It
has a beginning, a middle and an end. Its beginning
and most elementary form is the simple presence of the male
organ in the female." Presence is followed by motion, motion
by crisis. But now "suppose the man chooses to enjoy not
only the simple presence, but also the reciprocal motion,
and yet to stop short of the crisis. . . . If you say that this is
impossible, I answer that I *know* it is possible—nay, that
it is easy." He knew because he himself had done it. "Beginning in 1844, I experimented on the idea" (the idea that
the amative function of the sexual organs could be separated from the propagative) "and found that the self-
control it required is not difficult; also that my enjoyment
was increased; also that my wife's experience was very
satisfactory, which it had never been before; also that
we had escaped the horrors and the fear of involuntary
propagation." Noyes was a born prophet, a missionary
in the bone. Having made a great discovery, he felt im-
pelled to bring the good news to others—and to bring it,
what was more, in the same package with what he believed
to be true Christianity. He preached, he made disciples,
he brought them together in a community, first in Vermont
and later at Oneida, in upstate New York. "Religion," he
declared, "is the first interest, and sexual morality the
second in the great enterprise of establishing the Kingdom
of God on earth." At Oneida the religion was Perfectionist
Christianity and the sexual morality was based upon the
psycho-physiological practices of Male Continence and
social law of Complex Marriage. Like all earlier founders
of religious communities, Noyes disapproved of exclusive
attachments between the members of his group. All were to
love all, unpossessively, with a kind of impersonal charity
which, at Oneida, included sexual relationships. Hence the
establishment, within the community, of Complex Marriage.
Noyes did not condemn monogamy; he merely believed
that group love was better than exclusive love. "I would
not," he wrote, "set up a distinction of right and wrong
between general and special love, except that special
love, when false, makes more mischief. I insist that all
love, whether general or special, must have its authority
in the sanction and the inspiration of the ascending fellow-

ship. All love that is at work in a private corner, away from the general circulation, where there are no series of links connecting it with God, is false love; it rends and devours, instead of making unity, peace and harmony." At Oneida there was to be no love in a private corner, no idolatrous and God-eclipsing attachment of one for one, outside the general circulation. Each was married to all; and when any given pair decided (with advice and permission of the Elders) to consummate their latent nuptials, Male Continence guaranteed that their union should be fruitful only of "social magnetism." Love was for love's sake and for God's, not for offspring.

The Oneida Community endured for thirty years and its members, from all acounts, were excellent citizens, singularly happy and measurably less neurotic than most of their Victorian contemporaries. The women of Oneida had been spared what one of Noyes's lady correspondents described as "the miseries of Married Life as it is in the World." The men found their self-denial rewarded by an experience, at once physical and spiritual, that was deeper and richer than that of unrestrained sexuality. Here is the comment of a young man who had lived in the community and learned the new Art of Love. "This Yankee nation," he wrote to Noyes, "claims to be a nation of inventors, but this discovery of Male Continence puts you, in my mind, at the head of all inventors." And here are Noyes's own reflections on the psychological, social and religious significance of his discovery. "The practice which we propose will advance civilization and refinement at railroad speed. The self-control, retention of life and advance out of sensualism, which must result from making freedom of love a bounty on the chastening of sensual indulgence, will at once raise the race to new vigour and beauty, moral and physical. And the refining efforts of sexual love (which are recognized more or less in the world) will be increased a hundredfold when sexual intercourse becomes a method of ordinary conversation and each becomes married to all." Furthermore, "in a society trained in these principles, amative intercourse will have its place among the 'fine arts.' Indeed, it will take rank above music, painting, sculpture, etc.; for it combines the charms and benefits of them all. There is as much room for cultivation of taste and skill in this department as in any." And this is not all. Sexual love is a cognitive act. We speak—or at least we used to speak—of carnal knowledge. This knowledge is of a kind that can be deepened indefinitely. "To a true heart, one that appreciates God, the same woman is an endless mystery. And this necessarily flows from the first admission that God is unfathomable in depths of knowledge and wisdom." Male Continence transforms the sexual act into a prolonged exchange of "social magnetism"; and this prolonged exchange makes possible an ever deepening knowledge of the mystery of human nature—that mystery which merges ultimately, and becomes one with the mystery of Life itself.

Noyes's conception of the sexual act (when properly performed) as at once a religious sacrament, a mode of mystical knowledge and a civilizing social discipline has its counterpart in Tantra. In the twenty-seventh chapter of Sir John Woodroffe's *Shakti and Shakta* the interested reader will find a brief account of the Tantrik's sexual ritual, together with a discussion of the philosophy which underlies the practice. "Nothing in natural function is low or impure to the mind which recognizes it as Shakti and the working of Shakti. It is the ignorant and, in a true sense, vulgar mind which regards any natural function as low or coarse. The action in this case is seen in the light of the inner vulgarity of mind. . . . Once the reality of the world as grounded in the Absolute is established, the body seems to be less an obstacle to freedom; for it is a form of that self-same Absolute." In Tantra the sexual sacrament borrows the method of Yoga, "not to frustrate, but to regulate enjoyment. Conversely enjoyment produces Yoga by the union of body and spirit. . . . Here are made one Yoga which liberates and Bhoga which enchains." In Hindu philosophy (which is not philosophy in the modern Western sense of the word, but rather the description and tentative explanation of a praxis aimed at the transformation of human consciousness), the relations between body, psyche, spirit and Divine Ground are described in terms of a kind of occult physiology, whose language comes nearer to expressing the unbroken continuity of experience, from the "lowest" to the "highest," than any hitherto devised in the West. "Coition," in terms of this occult physiology, "is the union of the Shakti Kundalini, the 'Inner Woman' in the lowest centre of the Sadhaka's body with the Supreme Shiva in the highest centre in the upper Brain. This, the Yogini Tantra says, is the best of all unions for those who are Yati, that is, who have controlled their passions."*

In the West the theory and practice of Tantra were never orthodox, except perhaps during the first centuries of Christianity. At this time it was common for ecclesiastics and pious laymen to have "spiritual wives," who were called Agapetae, Syneisaktoi or Virgines Subintroductae. Of the precise relationships between these spiritual wives and husbands we know very little; but it seems that, in some cases at least, a kind of Karezza, or bodily union without orgasm, was practiced as a religious exercise, leading to valuable spiritual experiences.

For the most part, Noyes's predecessors and the Christian equivalents of Tantra must be sought among the heretics— the Gnostics in the first centuries of our era, the Cathars in the early Middle Ages and the Adamites or Brethren and Sisters of the Free Spirit from the later thirteenth century onwards. In his monograph on *The Millennium of Hieronymus Bosch* Wilhelm Franger has brought together much interesting material on the Adamites. They practiced, we learn, a *modum specialem coeundi*, a special form of intercourse, which was identical with Noyes's Male Continence or the *coitus reservatus* permitted by Roman Catholic casuists. This kind of sexual intercourse, they declared, was known to Adam before the Fall and was one of the constituents of Paradise. It was a sacramental act of charity and, at the same time, of mystical cognition, and, as such, was called by the Brethren *acclivitas*— the upward path. According to Aegidius Cantor, the leader

---

* Male Continence, sex as a sacrament and coitus as a long-drawn, cognitive exchange of "social magnetism" have been discussed in contemporary medical terms by Dr. Rudolf von Urban whose book *Sexual Perfection and Marital Happiness* is one of the most significant modern contributions to the solution of an age-old problem.

of the Flemish Adamites in the first years of the fifteenth century, "the natural sexual act can take place in such a manner that it is equal in value to a prayer in the sight of God." A Spanish follower of the Adamite heresy declared, at his trial that "after I had first had intercourse with her [the prophetess, Francisca Hernandez] for some twenty days, I could say that I had learned more wisdom in Valladolid than if I had studied for twenty years in Paris. For not Paris, but only Paradise could teach such wisdom." Like Noyes and his followers, the Adamites practiced a form of sexual communism, and practiced it not, as their enemies declared, out of a low taste for orgiastic promiscuity, but because Complex Marriage was a method by which every member of the group could love all the rest with an impartial and almost impersonal charity; could see and nuptially know in each beloved partner the embodiment of the original, unfallen Adam—a godlike son or daughter of God.

Among literary testimonials to Male Continence, perhaps the most elegant is a little poem by Petronius. Long and inevitably disgusting experience had taught this arbiter of the elegancies that there must be something better than debauchery. He found it in physical tenderness and the peace of soul which such tenderness begets.

> Foeda est in coitu et brevis voluptas,
> et taedet Veneris statim peractae.
> Non ergo ut pecudes libidinosae
> caeci protinus irruamus illuc;
> nam languescit amor peritque flamma;
> sed sic sic sine fine feriati
> et tecum jaceamus osculantes.
> Hic nullus labor est ruborque nullus;
> hoc juvit, juvat et diu juvabit;
> hoc non deficit, incipitque semper.

Which was Englished by Ben Jonson, as follows:

> Doing, a filthy pleasure is, and short;
> And done, we straight repent us of the sport;
> Let us not then rush blindly on unto it,

Like lustful beasts that only know to do it;
For lust will languish, and that heat decay.
But thus, thus, keeping endless holiday,
Let us together closely lie and kiss;
There is no labour, nor no shame in this;
This hath pleased, doth please and long will please; never
Can this decay, but is beginning ever.

And here, from a novelist and poet of a very different kind is a passage that hints at what is revealed by physical tenderness, when it is prolonged by Male Continence into a quasi-mystical experience. "She had sunk to a final rest," Lawrence writes, near the end of *The Plumed Serpent*,* "within a great opened-out cosmos. The universe had opened out to her, new and vast, and she had sunk to the deep bed of pure rest. . . . She realized, almost with wonder, the death in her of the Aphrodite of the foam: the seething, frictional, ecstatic Aphrodite. By a swift dark instinct, Cipriano drew away from this in her. When, in their love, it came back on her, the seething electric female ecstasy, which shows such spasms of delirium, he recoiled from her. It was what she used to call her 'satisfaction.' She had loved Joachim for this, that again, and again, and again he could give her this orgiastic 'satisfaction,' in spasms that made her cry aloud.

"But Cipriano would not. By a dark and powerful instinct he drew away from her as soon as this desire rose again in her, for the white ecstasy of frictional satisfaction, the throes of Aphrodite of the foam. She could see that, to him, it was repulsive. He just removed himself, dark and unchangeable, away from her.

"And she, as she lay, would realize the worthlessness of this foam-effervescence, its strangely externality to her. It seemed to come from without, not from within. And succeeding the first moment of disappointment, when this sort of 'satisfaction' was denied her, came the knowledge that she did not really want it, that it was really nauseous to her.

"And he in his dark, hot silence would bring her back to

* By D. H. Lawrence. New York, Knopf, 1926.

the new, soft, heavy, hot flow, when she was like a fountain gushing noiseless and with urgent softness from the deeps. There she was open to him soft and hot, yet gushing with a noiseless soft power. And there was no such thing as conscious 'satisfaction.' What happened was dark and untellable. So different from the beak-like friction of Aphrodite of the foam, the friction which flares out in circles of phosphorescent ecstasy, to the last wild spasm which utters the involuntary cry, like a death-cry, the final love-cry."

Male Continence is not merely a device for domesticating sexuality and heightening its psychological significance; it is also, as the history of the Oneida Community abundantly proves, a remarkably effective method of birth control. Indeed, under the name of *coitus reservatus,* it is one of the two methods of birth control approved by the authorities of the Roman Church—the other and more widely publicized method being the restriction of intercourse to the so-called safe periods. Unfortunately large-scale field experiments in India have shown that, in the kind of society which has the most urgent need of birth control, the safe period method is almost useless. And whereas Noyes, the practical Yankee, devoted much time and thought to the problem of training his followers in Male Continence, the Roman Church has done little or nothing to instruct its youth in the art of *coitus reservatus.* (How odd it is that while primitive peoples, like the Trobrianders, are careful to teach their children the best ways of domesticating sex, we, the Civilized, stupidly leave ours at the mercy of their wild and dangerous passions!)

Meanwhile, over most of the earth, population is rising faster than available resources. There are more people with less to eat. But when the standard of living goes down, social unrest goes up, and the revolutionary agitator, who has no scruples about making promises which he knows very well he cannot keep, finds golden opportunities. Confronted by the appalling dangers inherent in population increase at present rates, most governments have permitted and one or two have actually encouraged their subjects to make use of contraceptives. But they have done so in the teeth of protests from the Roman Church. By outlawing contraceptives and by advocating instead two methods of birth control, one of which doesn't work, while the other, effective method is never systematically taught, the prelates of that Church seem to be doing their best to ensure, first, a massive increase in the sum of human misery and, second, the triumph, within a generation or two, of World Communism.